HELSINKI HOMICIDE: NOTHING BUT THE TRUTH

JARKKO SIPILA

Translated by
Peter Ylitalo Leppa

Ice Cold Crime LLC

Originally published in Finnish as *Mitään Salaamatta* by Gummerus, Helsinki, Finland. 2006.

Translated by Peter Ylitalo Leppa

Published by
Ice Cold Crime LLC
5780 Providence Curve
Independence, MN 55359

Printed in the United States of America

Cover by Ella Tontti

Library of Congress Control Number: 2011910291

ISBN-13: 978-0-9824449-3-1
ISBN-10: 0-9824449-3-1

Also by Jarkko Sipila

In English:

Helsinki Homicide: Against the Wall (Ice Cold
 Crime, 2009)
Helsinki Homicide: Vengeance (Ice Cold
 Crime, 2010)

In Finnish:

Koukku (Book Studio, 1996)
Kulmapubin koktaili (Book Studio, 1998)
Kosketuslaukaus (Book Studio, 2001)
Tappokäsky (Book Studio, 2002)
Karu keikka (Book Studio, 2003)
Todennäköisin syin (Gummerus, 2004)
Likainen kaupunki (Gummerus, 2005)
Mitään salaamatta (Gummerus, 2006)
Kylmä jälki (Gummerus, 2007)
Seinää vasten (Gummerus, 2008)
Prikaatin kosto (Gummerus, 2009)
Katumurha (Gummerus, 2010)
Paha puha tyttö, with Harri Nykänen (Crime Time, 2010)
Muru (Crime Time, 2011)

In German:

Die weiße Nacht des Todes (Rohowolt Verlag, 2007)
Im Dämmer des Zweifels (Rohowolt Verlag, 2007)

HELSINKI HOMICIDE:
NOTHING BUT
THE TRUTH

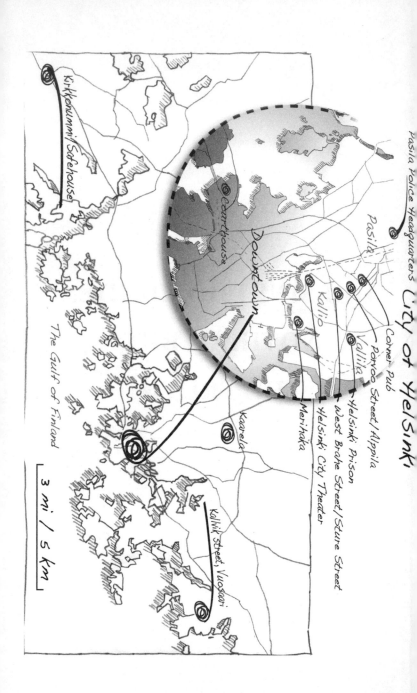

City of Helsinki

Pasila Police Headquarters

Kirkkonummi Safehouse

Courthouse

Downtown

Pasila

Kallio

Vallila

Corner Pub

Porvoo Street/Alppila

Helsinki Prison

West Brahe Street/Sture Street

Helsinki City Theater

Merihaka

Kaarela

The Gulf of Finland

Kallvik Street, Vuosaari

3 mi / 5 km

CAST OF CHARACTERS

Kari Takamäki....................Detective Lieutenant, Helsinki PD Violent Crimes Unit

Suhonen....................Undercover Detective, VCU

Anna Joutsamo.............................VCU Sergeant

Mikko Kulta..............................VCU Detective

Jaakko Nykänen.........Head of Intelligence, National Bureau of Investigation

Eero Salmela.........Suhonen's old friend and ex-con

Tomi Salmela....................................Eero's son

Mari Lehtonen ....Eyewitness

Laura Lehtonen ....Mari's daughter

Risto Korpi.......................................Gang boss

Jere "Guerilla" Siikala...........................Gangster

Esa Nyberg...Gunman

Matti Ahola...Gangster

Mats Martin............................Defense Attorney

Helena Muuri ....District Prosecutor

Anton Teittinen...........Mari Lehtonen's ex-husband

Rauli Salo............................Corrections Officer

Sanna Römpötti..........................Crime Reporter

I swear by Almighty God that the testimony I shall give shall be the truth, the whole truth, and nothing but the truth.

SUNDAY, SEPTEMBER 17

CHAPTER 1
SUNDAY, 7:45 P.M.
PASILA POLICE HEADQUARTERS

She'd heard that answer dozens of times before: No comment.

What a clown, thought Sergeant Anna Joutsamo. No comment, my ass. Not that it mattered. The police had already amassed enough evidence for a life sentence, with more on the way once Forensics finished up at the murder scene.

Esa Nyberg was sitting behind the table of a dreary interrogation room, dressed in police-issue green coveralls, his arms folded over his chest, his long hair in a tangled mess. His eyes seemed to stare into space. Not that there was much to see but pale gray walls. In addition to Nyberg and Sergeant Joutsamo, Mikko Kulta, a Helsinki VCU detective, sat at the table.

"Enough with the games," said Joutsamo, in a tone that revealed her waning patience. She smoothed her jeans and straightened her dark hair with a flourish. "I understand you don't want to talk about the case without a lawyer present, but I'm sure you can handle a few basic questions."

"No comment," said Nyberg tersely.

"I didn't ask anything," said Joutsamo.

"No comment."

Mikko Kulta sat beside Joutsamo with a barely suppressed smile tugging at the corners of his mouth.

Joutsamo rose from her chair and circled behind Nyberg. "Listen Esa... Right now, you're making decisions that will impact the rest of your life. We already know you pulled the trigger, we just don't know why. My advice to you is to think this through very carefully. Manslaughter will get you between four and six; murder—at least twelve, more like sixteen. You're twenty-three now. If you choose not to cooperate and are convicted of murder, you'll be thirty-nine when you get out. That's a lot of life you'll miss out on during those extra ten years," said Joutsamo, and she paused strategically to let her words sink in.

Nyberg didn't reply. Joutsamo wasn't sure if that was a good sign or not. At least his canned response had faltered for the moment. As long as he was thinking, that was enough.

Joutsamo studied the tattoos bursting from beneath the collar of his coveralls, some kind of Japanese or Chinese characters. The VCU had files on various tattoo symbols and their meanings, but they'd do the research later. Right now all Joutsamo wanted was a reaction from Nyberg. Something to move the case along.

The police needed a motive for the murder—they already had the shooter. Nyberg was clearly that, but somebody else was pulling the strings. That's why they needed him to talk.

But the young man just sat motionless. Nobody had said anything for thirty seconds. The ventilation system hummed softly. Detective Kulta looked up at Joutsamo, who was still standing behind Nyberg. She shrugged her shoulders.

"Which would you rather do? Five or fifteen?" she asked.

"No comment."

Joutsamo cursed silently.

"Here's a suggestion," said Kulta. "I'll be visiting the Helsinki prison tomorrow to see a guy doing time for a deadly arson a few years back. When I put him away, I promised to bring him a bag of coffee every year for his birthday. With this shooting all over the front pages, I bet he'll ask about it. Suppose I started a rumor that we know who ordered the hit because the shooter talked."

From behind, Joutsamo could see Nyberg tense his neck muscles.

"Filthy fucking pig."

"How much you wanna bet that within six hours every last Jack will know about it, including everyone at Protective Custody, and start wondering whether the new snitch is headed there or somewhere else. The PC unit over there is so crammed they'll need to send someone packing to make space for the newbie. Trust me, you'll need the protection."

"You do that and you're dead."

"Whatcha gonna do?" said Kulta with outright contempt. "Run me over with your wheelchair after your buddies bust your kneecaps first chance they get?"

Nyberg seemed ready to pounce, but Joutsamo wasn't worried. The man was no match for the thickset Kulta, and against the two of them, there would be no problem. But he just sat quietly.

"Whaddya think? Maybe you have some ideas on what we should do."

Nyberg thought for about ten seconds before responding, "No comment."

Kulta looked over Nyberg's shoulder at Joutsamo and nodded. "Guess that's it. Figured I'd head out for a beer and think about what to tell the birthday boy." He turned his gaze on Nyberg. "You can think about your own plans in your piss-stained cell… Anna, care to join me?"

"I suppose I could. For a cider anyhow."

"My treat."

Kulta pressed the buzzer next to the door of the interrogation room and a stern-looking guard with a crew cut came to the door. They handed over Nyberg, but to be sure, they followed the two of them to the entrance of the jail area where a second guard was waiting.

The door clanged shut behind the two detectives and Kulta glanced hopefully at Joutsamo. "You really coming to the bar with me?"

"Nope," she said, already headed toward the VCU's conference room.

"Well, I wouldn't have paid for your cider anyway."

"No?"

"Course I would've," he grinned. "Anyhow, I bet you a ten-spot Nyberg doesn't crack in the morning either."

Joutsamo's expression was serious. "No deal. We're both in agreement on that one… Unfortunately."

* * *

Detective Lieutenant Kari Takamäki was on the phone speaking in a lowered voice when Joutsamo stepped into the conference room. Kulta followed. Takamäki, a little over forty, had short brown hair, sharp features and taut cheeks highlighted by a muscular jaw. His piercing blue eyes straddled a handsome nose. He shot Joutsamo a questioning look and she shook her head.

The conference room had been converted into a sort of command center. A couple of computers were arranged around the table where Kirsi Kohonen, a red-haired detective, sat sifting through various databases. For now, the flip chart was blank, and the magnetic white board where they posted pictures of the corpse and crime scene was empty, though somebody had written the time and place of the murder with a marker: Porvoo Street 21, Sunday, 4:32 P.M.

The investigation had started without regard for the Sabbath. Even before the victim had been identified, the police had a picture of the suspect. Joutsamo, on duty at the time, had obtained the photo from a nearby convenience store security camera, which had been trained on the street.

The same camera had played a role in solving a 2005 robbery of the same convenience store, which is how Joutsamo had known about it. A couple of crackpots had waved a knife and made off with a few hundred euros, which they promptly drank. The men were identified from the video footage, just as Nyberg was in this case. Joutsamo herself had recognized him. Despite his young age, the gangster was well known to VCU from plenty of shady connections and a violent past, but the clincher was that Joutsamo had once arrested him for aggravated assault. Nyberg had pulverized a junkie's elbow over a debt.

Takamäki hung up the phone. "Didn't talk, huh?"

"No comment," said Joutsamo. "Like talking to a brick wall."

"Not surprised."

Kulta had already managed to grab a cup of coffee. "The guy says 'no comment' almost as often as a certain lieutenant Takamäki at a press conference."

"You try to strong-arm him?" asked Takamäki.

"With no result," said Kulta. "He's not talking."

"And you've run all the tests?"

"Of course," said Joutsamo.

Nyberg's clothing had been brought to Forensics immediately upon arrival at the station. They had tested his hands and beneath his nose for gunpowder residue, and taken blood samples for drugs and alcohol. The samples provided them with his DNA. His prints were already in the database, but they took them anyway. The police didn't get his cell phone, since he wasn't carrying one at the time of his arrest.

"Should probably run a lie-detector test," said Kulta, sipping his coffee.

"Doubt that would help," said Takamäki. "He can't lie if he doesn't comment."

"At least we'd see what questions rile him."

Takamäki glanced at the clock: just past eight in the evening. In the windowless conference room, they hadn't the slightest idea about the weather. When Takamäki was summoned to the station more than three hours earlier, the sky had been bright and sunny. The day's temperature had been closer to what you might expect for late August rather than September, but the days were getting shorter. By now it would be nearly dark out.

Damn. It just had to happen now, this murder. Only a week earlier, security measures for a massive

6

international meeting involving a number of heads of state and the resulting obligatory anarchist demonstration had stretched the entire department's resources and overtime quotas to the breaking point.

Takamäki's thoughts strayed back to his family for a moment: had Kalle finished his math homework? Takamäki had been helping his younger son with it and promised to play some street hockey with him afterward. Then the phone call had come.

"So how do we proceed?" asked Joutsamo. Takamäki tried to clear his head, but the promise he had made to his son lingered in his mind.

"Why don't you boil some water for your tea. I need to make one last call."

"Uh...sure," muttered Joutsamo, and she ambled over to the conference room's kitchenette. Coffee was never in short supply at the station, but Joutsamo only drank it under exceptional circumstances. And though Joutsamo had been on the team for four years already, nobody ever remembered to boil water for her tea.

Takamäki slipped out into the hallway and took his cell phone out of its holster. The lieutenant had on jeans and an army green sweater. Daily jogging had kept his cheeks tight and his stomach firm. "Hey," said Takamäki into the phone.

"Hey," said Kalle.

"You get it done?"

"Yeah."

"Good. Difficult?"

"Nah. Joonas helped me out with a couple."

"Good." Takamäki paused briefly. "I'm not gonna make it home tonight, but you can sure watch the game if you want."

"So what happened?" asked the boy, with a shade too much enthusiasm in his voice as far as Takamäki was concerned. A little disappointment would have seemed more appropriate, since Takamäki had promised to watch a pay-per-view soccer match between Arsenal and Chelsea with him after street hockey. Maybe the kid would make a fine cop someday.

Takamäki paused for a few seconds. "A shooting. Might have been a contract hit."

"You gonna be on TV tonight?"

Takamäki smiled. "No, not this time. We haven't informed the press, yet. You keep quiet about it too."

"So who was shot? Some kinda gang war?"

"No comment," Takamäki laughed. "Listen, you watch the game and then go to bed. I'll be working late. Mom home yet?"

"Not yet. Have you set up any phone taps?"

Takamäki was quiet for a while. Clearly classified information. "What do *you* think?"

"Yes."

"Well, you might be right. Straight to bed after the game, alright?"

"Yeah, yeah. But you're gonna tell me about this case."

"At some point, maybe. G'night. Tell Mom too."

"Okay... Oh yeah. Our bet... The score?"

Right, thought Takamäki. Between math problems, they'd speculated on the score of the game and settled on a one-euro wager. Kalle put his money on Chelsea. "Well, I'll go with a scoreless game. Both teams will be playing strong defense."

"Alright. One euro, then. Chelsea wins, the money's mine. Tie and it's yours, but if Arsenal wins, it's a draw."

"Got it. G'night."

"Night Dad."

Takamäki hung up the phone with a momentary feeling of satisfaction over not having forgotten to call. But soon enough, the feeling was gone.

This shooting case was at a critical phase, and still in disarray. He'd need to stay focused. It looked like a hired hit: somebody had wanted Tomi Salmela dead, but who, and why? He had no answers. In less than half a minute, he had already forgotten the details of their friendly wager.

CHAPTER 2
SUNDAY, 8:15 P.M.
THE JAIL AT PASILA POLICE
HEADQUARTERS

Fucking pigs, thought Esa Nyberg, balling his hand into a fist. He lay on the bunk of a spartan cell at the police station, the cot thin and flattened from use. The assholes had to be bluffing. They wouldn't go spreading a nark rumor like that. And even if they did, he'd just drag the pricks to court. If that wasn't slander, what was?

Nyberg closed his eyes and tried to calm himself, but it wasn't so easy. Not quite five hours ago he had shot a man dead. The thought made his heart flutter. Numerous times he had beaten people to within an inch of death, but he had never killed anyone. None of it seemed real. There was a hell of a lot of power in the act, and he had enjoyed it. Might have been a bit jittery with the trigger. Could have pulled a little smoother, but he had heard the first kill was always like that. Ease came with experience, or so he had read in his war books.

Shit. He'd have been a first-class soldier. As always, the thought soothed him. He pictured himself in the trenches during the Winter War, fighting the Soviets, the softly falling snow punctuated by exploding grenades. Someone next to him caught a bullet in the head and keeled over. His rifle sight panned from Russkie to Russkie, felling each one with a single shot.

Why couldn't he be in a war right now? He'd briefly considered the Foreign Legion, and maybe it still wasn't too late. He was only twenty-three years old. Might get shipped off to some African country to mow down spooks. Fuck. Boot camp would be rough, but he'd manage. He had no problem with the push-ups. Then he'd march down Paris's Avenue des Champs-Élysées with a Foreign Legion *kepi* perched on his head. The old man would have been proud, if he hadn't gone and croaked.

Nyberg opened his eyes to the toxic green of the cell walls glaring back. He rose nimbly to a seated position on the bunk. Goddamn. That fucker Salmela had to learn his lesson—one he wouldn't forget. One he'd remember in the fires of hell.

They'd caught up with him. Fucking cops had appeared outta nowhere and slammed him to the pavement. Name, rank and serial number. They were supposed to get nothing more, and they hadn't. That's what they had all agreed.

The Viet Cong used shock therapy in the Rambo flicks, but the cops hadn't resorted to that yet. They could wire his nuts and he still wouldn't talk. What a shitty attempt at sweating a suspect, he thought. Trying to spread rumors that he was a nark—nobody in the pen would believe that. Rambo hadn't cracked either, and went on to take his vengeance. He would too…just had to bide his time and keep his trap shut. Don't comment, don't even speak, don't listen to their promises. Police suspect or prisoner of war, the two were one and the same.

As Nyberg lay back down and closed his eyes the murder crept back into his mind. For an instant he felt the fear of his deed, but a rush of power washed away his uncertainty. He wouldn't talk.

* * *

Takamäki, Joutsamo, Kohonen, Kulta and a couple of other cops from Takamäki's team had gathered in the conference room. Takamäki had phoned his undercover man Suhonen, but got no answer. He had left a message.

"Let's run through this quickly," said Takamäki. He had a reputation for running efficient meetings to bring everyone up to date. "At 4:33 P.M, someone called 911 to report a gunshot. That likely pegs the time of the murder at around 4:32."

"Nice that someone called," said Kulta.

Takamäki shot a glare from beneath his brow. "Mikko, if you got something important to say, then say it. But if it's just your everyday bullshit, then keep it to yourself. Alright?"

"Alright."

Kulta had a habit of blurting out thoughtless remarks, but now was obviously not the time.

Takamäki went on, "The caller was a man by the name of Konsta Sten, from the second floor of the building. Within four minutes, the first officers arrived on the scene to find a corpse lying just inside the apartment door. The victim was later identified as Tomi Salmela."

Since Salmela's background was not necessarily known to everybody, Takamäki reeled off a list of facts that Kirsi Kohonen had mined from the database. "Salmela was eighteen years old with

12

plenty of drug, theft and assault convictions, but nothing particularly serious. A two-bit junkie," he summed up. "Based on his rap sheet, he'd seem a hell of a strange target for a contract hit, but clearly we don't know enough. What we do know is that the trigger man was this Esa Nyberg. With his street enforcer background, it would seem logical he'd promote himself to a contract killer sooner or later."

"The guy's some kinda military freak," said Joutsamo.

"Have we searched his place?" asked Takamäki.

"We don't know where he lives yet," said Joutsamo. "No permanent address on record, though we have a few leads. We'll figure it out when we get a minute."

"Okay," said Takamäki as he glanced toward the door. Suhonen was stepping into the conference room.

"Hey," he droned. "Sorry to bust in on your meeting."

Suhonen's specialty was the surveillance of violent criminals and organized crime rings.

"Right," said Takamäki. "I left you a message…"

"Yeah, I heard about the case already. I was with a buddy of mine putting away my bike for the winter. No reception. Back on the grid now, though."

"You got something?"

"Yeah, but go ahead. I'd rather listen first."

Takamäki nodded. He was glad Suhonen had arrived. With as much time as he spent undercover, Suhonen had access to just the kind of street intelligence that was so desperately needed when the motive was still unclear.

"So. Things started to come together pretty quickly once Joutsamo recognized Nyberg on the security footage. The SWAT team took him down in Töölö at the entrance of an apartment building. He's not talking. They found a pistol in his jacket pocket, but we don't know yet if it's the murder weapon."

"So why kill Salmela?" Suhonen asked, knowing he'd get no answer.

Takamäki grinned. "That's what I wanted to ask you."

"Well, I did meet him once."

The others looked dumbfounded for a moment. "Huh?" Joutsamo finally managed.

"Sure. We had coffee together at the Ruskeasuo Teboil station about a year back."

"And?" said Joutsamo.

"Well…he didn't mention having a target on his back."

Joutsamo glanced at Takamäki, who shrugged. He trusted Suhonen to volunteer details if they were relevant to the case. If for one reason or another, Suhonen didn't care to comment, then he had good reason. The man had so much intel that even the lieutenant didn't know all of his sources.

"But let's get back on track," said Takamäki in an attempt to avoid a squabble. He could talk one-on-one with Suhonen after the meeting.

"I didn't realize we had ever gotten off," said Kulta.

"Right," said Takamäki dryly. "Tomi Salmela was shot in the middle of the forehead. We know Nyberg is the trigger man, but the motive is unknown. The victim has a bit of a record, too…" he said, glancing at Suhonen. The recap felt pointless, but it was important for Suhonen to be on the same page as the others.

Takamäki paused and an absent look came over his face. "The footage," Joutsamo prompted.

"Right," he said. "The outdoor camera on the convenience store recorded a dark Mazda 323 arriving around 4:27 P.M. Nyberg immediately gets out of the passenger side, and enters the building through an entrance next to the store. Six minutes later, he returns, gets back in the passenger seat and the car takes off. We couldn't identify the driver from the footage. Obviously, whoever it was has to be tracked down."

"We get the plate?" asked Suhonen.

"Too fuzzy. Kannas promised to try some image enhancement software once they get done with the crime scene."

"Was Salmela in the apartment alone?"

"As far as we know, yes," said Joutsamo.

"Did you find anything else there?"

"Nothing out of the ordinary. Some dope, a couple bikes and some electronics," she said. "Just based on a quick look, anyhow. We haven't received the report from Forensics yet."

"No money?"

"None."

"Do we know whether Nyberg took anything?" Suhonen asked.

Takamäki shook his head.

"Well," Suhonen reflected for a moment. "I suppose you all know who this Nyberg's been hanging out with for the last few years."

"We do. That's why the buzz over this case," said Joutsamo, as she took a printout off the table. "Korpi, Risto Mika. Age 35, first-class career criminal. Spent fifteen years of his life in prison so far, mostly on drug and assault charges. Did his first stint for manslaughter at the ripe age of eighteen. Been out on the streets for the last three years."

Suhonen nodded his head. "You might add that he has no remorse, is incapable of empathy and extremely dangerous. A complete shithead if you want it straight up."

"So we should send him straight to jail," said Kulta. "Without passing Go."

"That's right," said Takamäki.

* * *

Suhonen sat drinking coffee in Takamäki's cramped office on the third floor of Pasila police headquarters. Outside, the yellow streetlights were just now flickering to life. The birches on the distant slope still clung to their leaves. Takamäki was hastily tapping something out on the computer. Nobody else was in the room.

Kulta, Kohonen and two other on-duty officers had gone knocking on doors in the buildings near Porvoo Street to ask if anyone had happened to see the Mazda, perhaps even part of the plate number. Anything that would help them move the search along.

Joutsamo had stayed back to draw up the paperwork for the wiretap—surveillance was to start immediately. First permission from the court, then send the papers to the NBI's wiretapping central, which would reroute any calls directly to the wire tap room of Pasila police headquarters.

A couple of phone numbers belonging to Korpi had been found in the police databases. Most likely the phones had been ditched long ago, but it was worth a try.

"Listen to this," said Takamäki, and he began to read the text on his screen: *"Helsinki Police Department Press Release. Homicide on Porvoo Street. On Sunday, September 17, at about 4:30 P.M., a young male was killed in an apartment located at Porvoo Street 21. The crime is being investigated as a murder and the police have arrested a suspect. The suspect was observed arriving in front of the building in a dark colored car, which remained parked there during the time of the murder. Anyone with information on this matter or on the car in question should contact the Helsinki Police Department Violent Crimes Unit.* And then the contact numbers. Sound OK to you?"

"Pretty standard fare. Won't win any literary awards."

"Eyewitnesses are what we really need," said Takamäki as he glanced at the clock. Half past eight. The copy would make the morning papers by a nose. The TV stations wouldn't be interested in an ordinary shooting, at least not one based on such a lackluster press release.

The release was a purely tactical tool to fish for witnesses. If the driver of the Mazda wasn't still at large, they wouldn't need to release any information for several more days. Any eyewitness accounts would need to be screened for accuracy, which is why he had omitted the exact make of the car. Takamäki clicked "Send" and the report went out to media outlets automatically.

"Going, going, gone," said the lieutenant before falling silent for a while. "So, coffee at the Teboil station, huh?"

"Right," said Suhonen, flicking his ponytail as he turned away from the yellowed, dimly lit landscape

17

out the window. "I bought the kid a donut too."

Takamäki waited in vain for him to continue. For some reason this case was a sore spot for Suhonen, and of course the lieutenant wanted to know why. The man walked a fine line between the worlds of cops and criminals.

"Glazed or jelly-filled?"

Suhonen chuckled. "Pretty sure it was glazed, maybe even some sprinkles. But this comes on condition of total confidentiality. I'm serious, what I'm gonna tell you can't get out to anybody else, not even Joutsamo. I guess that meeting at Teboil is already out there, but we gotta keep the background under wraps. Agreed?"

"Of course," said Takamäki.

"This Tomi Salmela's dad Eero Salmela was also there at the Teboil. Eero is an old buddy from my stomping grounds in Lahti. We're still friends, but these days, or years, actually, we've been on opposite sides of the law. He hawks stolen goods so he's privy to a lot of street talk."

"So one of your informants then?"

Now Takamäki understood the reason for Suhonen's long deliberation. These sorts of relationships were highly guarded secrets, and rarely divulged to anyone.

Suhonen nodded. "One of the best."

"Is he involved in this case somehow?"

"Don't know. I've tried calling a few times, but no answer."

"That doesn't sound too good."

"Well, no, but not necessarily terrible either. In his line of work, it's not always a good idea to carry a cell."

Takamäki thought momentarily. "Wonder if the shooting has something to do with the dad? Seems like Korpi's style to bump off an informant's kid for revenge."

"Who knows, but I doubt anyone knows about our connection. Aren't you the one who's always telling us not to assume? Just make conclusions based on the facts."

"Has he said anything to you about Korpi recently?"

Suhonen shook his head.

"I think you'd better look a bit further into what Eero's kid was up to."

Suhonen was about to answer when his phone rang. The caller was anonymous. "Yeah," said Suhonen into the receiver.

Takamäki couldn't make out what was said on the other end. Suhonen nodded, "Yeah, I called earlier...right, right. I understand...let's meet soon. Right...but not the Corner Pub. Someplace quieter... OK, sounds good. Half hour. Later."

A sober-faced Suhonen slipped the cell phone back into his jeans' pocket.

"It was Eero."

"I figured as much. Does he know?"

"If he does, he didn't let on."

Both were quiet for a moment.

"I don't suppose you'll want the police chaplain along," said Takamäki.

CHAPTER 3
SUNDAY, 9:15 P.M.
THE PARKING LOT AT THE HELSINKI ICE ARENA

Suhonen backed his Peugeot 206, an unmarked loaner from the station's garage, into a spot at the south end of the ice arena's parking lot. He killed the engine and headlights, but left the keys in the ignition. An old U2 hit was playing on the radio.

The parking lot was nearly vacant: only a few cars remained, and of those, the nearest was a hundred feet from Suhonen's Peugeot. No pedestrians were about.

Suhonen glanced at his watch. Salmela was late. The undercover cop listened to Bono singing about Bloody Sunday. This Sunday hadn't been much different, even if on a smaller scale than the namesake of the song. In 1972, British soldiers fatally shot thirteen demonstrators in Northern Ireland. Suhonen had no memory of the incident, since he had only been four at the time, but it got him thinking of the first time he had met Salmela. Suhonen couldn't remember exactly, but he had been younger than ten for sure.

He spotted a rusty blue Toyota van turning into the parking lot, the same kind Salmela usually drove. Suhonen had never bothered to find out who it belonged to, but it was unlikely it was Salmela's, at least not on paper.

Salmela parked the van a few spaces away, cut the engine and hopped out, his cigarette already lit. The forty-something's hair was short and raked back over the top of his head. His features were rugged. A brown leather coat with a graying lambskin collar hung from his shoulders.

Suhonen flicked off the radio and rolled down the window. The cool autumn air swept across his face.

"Can't smoke in the van—wouldn't want you guys lifting DNA off the butts," said Salmela as he took a drag.

"We can get it off of a lot less nowadays."

"Still, wouldn't want to make your job any easier."

Salmela seemed nervous, which made Suhonen wonder what was in the back of the van.

"Rough day?"

"Nothin' I ain't used to. Had to help a buddy move," said Salmela with a grin. The tip of his cigarette glimmered in the darkness.

"Why don't you have a seat in the car here."

"Can I smoke in there?"

Suhonen knew it was against the rules. "Sure," he said.

He'd been trying to figure out how to break the bad news to Salmela, but there was no easy way. Salmela rounded the car to the passenger side, swung in, cranked the window down halfway and ashed his cigarette on the rim of the glass.

"Nice Pug."

"Just a rental. They must wax it pretty regular."

"Yup. Keeps the value up." Salmela drew his cigarette down to the filter and flicked the butt out the window. "So why the big rush? What's up?"

Suhonen was quiet for a moment. A green tram went gliding down the track toward downtown. Suhonen kept his gaze locked on the glow from the windows of the tram. "Eero…bad news."

The softness in Suhonen's voice got Salmela's attention. "Sounds pretty bad… Since when do you call me Eero? There a warrant out on me, or what?"

"I wouldn't be this serious about something like that."

"What then?"

"Today there was a homicide…"

Suhonen watched the muscles in Salmela's face ball up.

"Don't tell me. Can't be…"

"Tomi's dead. I'm sorry."

Salmela was visibly shaken. He took a deep breath and buried his head in his hands. Suhonen patted him on the back a few times, but the gesture seemed pitifully small.

"How?" Salmela asked, straightening his back. His hand scrambled at his jacket pocket for a cigarette.

"He died quickly…didn't suffer."

Salmela's voice became icy. "How?"

Suhonen had initially intended to stand behind confidentiality laws, but quickly changed his mind. "He was shot in the entryway of his apartment. A bullet to the forehead."

"Execution style or what?"

"Crossed my mind." Suhonen wanted to ask about any enemies Tomi might have, but Salmela would surely bring that up himself.

Salmela's hand trembled as he raised a fresh cigarette to his lips, then abruptly withdrew it.

"Damn, he was a good kid, even if a little down and out last couple years. Fuck yeah…I used to be so proud when I'd take him to soccer practice. Kid could score whenever he damn well pleased."

Suhonen didn't know what to say, so he listened. That was probably best.

"Then I wound up in prison for a year, and the wife found someone else. That kind of meant game over for the whole dad thing… But those soccer games were really something. Sunk four goals in one game once. And he was playing on defense. When he got the ball, ain't nobody was gonna stop him." Salmela's voice began to break up. "He stuck 'em in the net like Maradona at his best…"

Salmela put the cigarette between his lips. This time he lit it. "Maybe it's best to shut up so I don't get emotional."

"The memories will never fade," said Suhonen.

"You met him too once, over there at…"

"The Ruskeasuo Teboil station. A year ago. Seemed like quite the kid."

Salmela laughed. "I dunno about quite the kid at that time. More like quite the crackhead. He was hooked on speed and moved here to peddle some dope for some friends from Lahti. He got enough money from that to pay rent. I helped him out a few times with a C-note or two."

"Did you keep in touch?"

"Not so much. We met up a few times, but we were running in different circles. Last time I saw him he tried to sell me a hit of coke. Just about beat the shit out of the kid… Heh, tried to gouge me too."

The mention of cocaine got Suhonen thinking. "When was this?"

"Don't remember exactly. Two, three weeks ago."

Suhonen waited for Salmela to connect the dots.

"You sayin' the coke had something to do with it?"

"I didn't say that."

"But that's what you're thinking."

Since Salmela had brought up motive, Suhonen decided to up the ante. "We have the shooter in custody."

Salmela's body stiffened and he flicked the remainder of his cigarette out the window. "Gimme his name."

"I can't, actually," said Suhonen, though the moment he brought up the subject he had already decided to reveal it.

"Bullshit. Who is it?"

"Esa Nyberg."

Salmela fell silent. "Shit... What the fuck was Tomi mixed up in for them to send that kind of firepower after him? That Nyberg is a militant psycho. Apparently talks about joining the Foreign Legion all the time. He can go ahead as far as I'm concerned... Shoulda gone long ago."

"Back up a sec. Who do you mean by *them*?"

Salmela looked at Suhonen with a stupefied expression. "Them. Don't you know?"

"Nyberg could've switched employers."

"In other words you don't. Well let me fill you in. Nyberg is Risto Korpi's godchild. He ain't gonna switch employers."

* * *

Fifteen minutes later, Suhonen was striding down a long, quiet hallway at the VCU. Takamäki's door was open and the lieutenant was sitting in front of his computer.

Suhonen stepped inside and Takamäki looked up. "Well?"

"He took it hard."

"Figured as much. Who wouldn't." Takamäki thought of his boys. The death of one's own child would just as easily break a seasoned homicide cop.

"This Tomi hasn't been close to his dad since he was a kid, though. The divorce split them up long ago. But I did get some intel," said Suhonen, and he told Takamäki about the godchild relationship.

"So Korpi's our target," said Takamäki. "Unless Nyberg had side projects Korpi didn't know about."

"What about the surveillance?"

"We got the warrant and tapped the lines. According to records, the numbers have been inactive for two months. We'll have to figure out Korpi's current residence and means of communication."

The power of phone taps was rapidly waning. Professional criminals knew how to avoid them by cycling through prepaid SIM cards and cell phones. The police didn't bother to tap prepaids that were older than six months, since they automatically expired after that.

"Yeah, that'd be a nice surprise," Suhonen remarked. "What'd Forensics find in the apartment?"

"Kannas promised..." Takamäki managed to say before a gruff voice boomed from the hallway.

"Did someone say the holy word?"

Suhonen moved aside to make room for Takamäki's old friend, who soon filled the entire doorway.

"Tsk, tsk. Thou shalt not take your lord's name in vain," Kannas growled as he came into the room, a small briefcase tucked under his arm.

"Oh, really. A lord?" said Suhonen.

"Inspector Suhonen decided to show up for once, eh? And here I figured your type would just be stumbling out of the sack so you could go bar hopping and raiding whorehouses till dawn," said Kannas with a wink.

Suhonen had a comeback at the ready, but Kannas never gave him the chance. "Just so there aren't any misunderstandings, though, I should say I'm no god. *Forensics* is god. Everybody believes in it. Me, I'm just a humble servant of that god. A slave, I should say."

"A lowly worm of the earth," Suhonen went on. Takamäki smiled.

"Naah. No worms yet," said Kannas in a more serious tone, "the body was still warm. Worms and other critters need a bit more time. That's how it usually is, depending on the temperature, of course…"

"We get the picture," Takamäki cut in. "What did you find?"

Kannas dug a stack of photographic printouts from his briefcase and handed them to Takamäki. "Here's a little taste of blood for the paper-pushing lieutenant."

As he reached for the printouts, Takamäki shot a hard enough look at Kannas that he thought better of his comment. "Sorry, long day. Plus it's my day off. But a corpse beats the mother-in-law's birthday party any time, no matter what the wife might think of it."

"A milestone?"

"Luckily not."

Takamäki looked over the photos. Tomi Salmela's body lay on its back on a rag rug. The floor looked like grey linoleum. There wasn't much blood, which was typical, since sudden death stopped the heart's pumping immediately.

"The body's at the coroner's now, but based on experience and the diameter of the entry hole in his forehead I'd say it's a nine-millimeter round. Not to mention the bullet tore off half his head when it came out the back. We dug the slug out of the far wall of the entry. Still at the lab, so nothing more on that for now."

Takamäki nodded. They had found a nine-millimeter pistol on Nyberg when he was arrested.

"We found the casing too," said Kannas. "There among the shoes. Based on the location of the casing and the blood splatters, I'd guess he was shot right at the door or just inside. The door was intact, so the victim had apparently opened it himself. We got plenty of fingerprints, which we're sifting through right now. That doesn't cost much, but what about running some DNA? We found all kinds of cigarette butts, bloody kleenexes and a bunch of other junk that might tell us who's been there."

Takamäki thought for a moment. "I don't think it's necessary, at least not yet. Since the shooter is already in custody and apparently never entered the apartment I think we can save the NBI some time and money. But obviously we should archive the evidence in case we run into any surprises."

Kannas approved. "My thoughts exactly."

"Anything else of interest?"

"Not really. Just your typical drug hole: a bunch of stolen junk. We'll see if we can find the original owners if we get around to it… Oh yeah, I almost forgot." Kannas' lie was deliberately transparent. "The hiding spot was pretty unoriginal, but I suppose they figured the dogs wouldn't find the drugs in the toilet tank. And they never do either, which is why we always look there. Found half a pound of coke."

"Half a pound," said Suhonen.

"We don't have an official weight yet, so it might be a bit more or less."

The drugs got Suhonen thinking. Half a pound of cocaine was nothing to sneeze at. Maybe this Tomi Salmela wasn't such a small-time dealer after all. That much coke was enough of a motive to get him shot, but if that were the case, the killer certainly wouldn't have left the drugs in the apartment.

MONDAY,
SEPTEMBER 18

CHAPTER 4
MONDAY, 7:45 A.M.
MARI LEHTONEN'S APARTMENT,
ALPPILA, EAST HELSINKI

"Laura, put your coat on! It's cold out there," shouted Mari Lehtonen from the kitchen as her daughter tied her shoes. Twelve-year-old Laura had on jeans and a college sweatshirt. Summer had turned to autumn just the previous night. The thermometer in the kitchen window of their two-bedroom flat read forty-six degrees Fahrenheit. Gray clouds skirted swiftly over the gray apartment building opposite theirs.

"Yup," said the blond-haired girl as she grabbed her backpack off the floor. "Bye."

Before Mari Lehtonen could make it to the entryway to check, the girl was out the door. Her parka was still hanging from the hook next to the door.

"Figures," she laughed. Laura was a quiet and kind girl. Perhaps this was just how her teen rebellion would manifest itself.

Mari went back to the kitchen and sat down at a smallish dining table where the morning paper was spread out. Dark hair fell across her narrow face and reached her thin shoulders. She took a gulp of coffee from a mug that read "Mom's Joe," followed by a smiley face. Laura had painted the mug herself and given it as a gift the previous Christmas.

Mari and Laura shared an apartment on Porvoo Street. The interior was neat and clean, with a feminine décor. When Laura was six, Mari had divorced her husband for the usual reasons: alcoholism and the threat of violence. Anton had actually never hit them, but she had always suspected that it was just a matter of time. Life was unpleasant then and Mari had taken the necessary action.

Fear of violence had made her think about what she'd do when the first blow came. She loathed the thought of resorting to a kitchen knife. Best to throw the drunk out before it was too late. The divorce hadn't been easy, but a couple prior house calls to the police were enough to convince the judge to grant Mari sole custody. This had aggravated the situation to the point of threats and harassment. Finally, she had had enough and sought a restraining order on him, and he had relented. As far as Mari knew, Anton Teittinen had no idea where his ex-wife and daughter were now living.

Mari picked up the front page of the *Helsingin Sanomat* with an article about a company that was starting labor negotiations to eliminate 170 positions. She read only the headline and a couple of the first paragraphs. The article was written solely from the perspective of the firm, with employee comments made to sound like a lot of rabble-rousing. Mari knew what it was like to be fired. After earning an associate's degree in business, she had landed a job at the Jyväskylä Savings and Loan; but during the banking crisis of the '90s, she had been laid off and moved to Helsinki. Now she was thirty-seven and working in the finance department of a mid-sized office supply retailer. The job was alright and the pay adequate for rent and hobbies.

Perhaps Alppila was not the best neighborhood for a girl on the cusp of puberty, but at least life here was better than their previous situation. Once a vast cow pasture, Alppila was now largely an industrial district filled with working class apartments. It drew its name from the rugged bedrock prevalent in the area—a cheeky comparison to the Alps. They liked the area, as the school was nearby and there was plenty to do. Laura attended theater classes twice a week. Mari also liked the location because her office in Vallila was only a few hundred yards away. The cultural delights of Helsinki were almost as close.

Mari took a bite of a ham-on-rye sandwich with a single leaf of lettuce. She paged through the paper and made it to the Metro section before her phone rang. The number belonged to her boss, Essi Saari. "Hi," said Mari into the receiver.

"Where are you?" asked Saari, in a voice half anxious, half angry.

"Still at home."

"You forget?"

Shit, she thought, remembering the meeting invitation she'd received the previous afternoon. One of the higher-ups had been demanding some report and Saari had asked Mari to help. Saari wasn't much for computers, so Mari was supposed to have run the report.

"Yeah..." said Mari as she walked back into the kitchen. "I'm sorry."

"Well...it's alright. We still have time. Have your coffee, but let's get started as soon as you get here."

"Gimme fifteen minutes," she said, knowing full well it would take her longer with dressing and makeup.

With no time to sit, Mari raised her mug to her lips. That's when she noticed a small article: "Young Man Gunned Down in Alppila." Police were asking for information from potential eyewitnesses about a youth who'd been killed on Porvoo Street. Mari checked the address to be sure she hadn't read it wrong. She hadn't. It was the building just across from them.

Her thoughts stopped and a stream of images flickered through her memory. She shook her head faintly, tore out the article and hurried into the bathroom.

* * *

"What exactly did you see?" asked Essi Saari. The finance director was sitting at her computer in her sleek modern office, dressed in a white—and considering her weight—excessively tight pantsuit. Mari had shown her boss the newspaper clipping and mentioned to her that she had seen something.

"I saw a dark car and a man. It's like the picture is engrained in my head. License plate and all."

"I know you've got a good head for numbers, but…"

"But the police are asking for eyewitnesses."

"Come on. It's not like you saw the murder."

"But they're asking for information on the car. Shouldn't I…"

This time it was Saari's turn to interrupt. "Not a chance. No point getting mixed up in these kinds of things. The cops have their DNAs and phone taps. That's how you solve murders. There's really no point in getting involved. You've already had enough problems, given your ex and all. You'd wind up testifying in court, you know."

"But shouldn't I at least…"

"No," said Saari. "Should we get that report done now? Getting to be crunch time here."

"Alright, let me see it. You just tell me what you want me to run."

* * *

Half a dozen officers had already sampled the coffee Joutsamo had made. As usual, she'd made tea for herself. Suhonen yawned while Kulta sipped his coffee.

The meeting was supposed to have started at nine o'clock sharp, but Takamäki was late.

"So did you get drafted to play in the Elite League yet?" Joutsamo asked Suhonen, as he smothered a seemingly endless yawn.

Suhonen smirked. He regretted telling his colleagues that he had begun playing hockey again.

"Yup, by the Blues after their flop last season," Suhonen laughed.

"You played quite a bit when you were younger, didn't you?" asked Kulta.

"In Lahti till I was sixteen."

"Why'd you quit?"

"Uhh," Suhonen stretched and took a sip of coffee. "If I said I just got more interested in other things, I'd be lying. Truth is, I just wasn't good enough," Suhonen lied.

"So why are you back on the ice now?" said Joutsamo, genuinely interested.

Suhonen smiled. "I already bought the Harley. Can't change the wife, since I don't have one, and I can't complain much about my job, but I gotta do something about this imminent midlife crisis, right? I guess senior hockey is macho enough for me."

Joutsamo laughed. With the killer behind bars and the case all but closed, the mood was light. Locating the driver would only be a bonus, though a big one, of course. But that didn't put on much additional pressure. Risto Korpi, on the other hand, was a stressful target, one that they knew would take a lot of work and time to connect to the shooting. None of Korpi's goons would squeak, so the case would come down to phone taps or some other technological means. Provided Korpi was found, his apartment could be wired. Then it was just a matter of time before his tongue slipped. Incriminating evidence might surface by accident as well. Something significant could come up in a Narcotics operation.

"Good morning and my apologies," said Takamäki, who had swapped yesterday's sweater for a collared shirt and blazer. He had stashed his lightweight overcoat in his office.

A murmur of good mornings went around the room.

"Have we gotten the autopsy report from the coroner yet?"

"No," said Joutsamo. "But I doubt there's anything of interest there. No mystery on the cause of death."

"I'm mainly interested in the victim's blood alcohol level and any traces of drugs," said Takamäki. Since not everyone had been updated yet, he recapped last night's forensics briefing from Kannas. Takamäki had stayed on until eleven o'clock, when the officers who had gone to canvas the neighboring buildings returned. Nothing new there. No eyewitnesses.

"If there was coke in Salmela's system, I bet the stash in the toilet was his," said Kulta. "Though that's probably the case anyway."

"I saw a little blurb in the *Helsingin Sanomat*; what about the other rags?" asked Takamäki.

"Two columns each for *Ilta-Sanomat* and *Iltalehti*. No photos," said Joutsamo. "They probably couldn't make it out to the crime scene before deadline."

Takamäki gave a snort. "Doubt that has anything to do with it. The top photographer from *Ilta-Sanomat* must be out of town. The guy gravitates to corpses like a vulture. Have we gotten any calls to the hotlines?"

"A couple callers said they saw a car but couldn't recall the make, driver or plate. One of them thought it might have started with an X or a K," said Joutsamo.

"So nothing, then. What about the phone taps?"

Joutsamo went on, "We stayed until midnight. Figured the numbers were probably old. Voice-activated recorder didn't pick anything up overnight."

"So," Takamäki sighed. "Same cards as yesterday. And nothing new on Korpi either?"

"No," said Suhonen. "Got all the traps and trawlers in the water, but no hits yet."

"Alright. Doesn't look so good right now, but we have time. Let's focus on Korpi. Find out everything you can from the databases, and let's get a warrant to review any cell tower records in the area of the murder. Maybe the driver had a cell phone. If we find one, we can trace it right to the guy's hand. I want footage from any surveillance cameras in the area in case the car shows up in one of them. And let's contact the neighboring precincts, the NBI and any informants out there to see if we can dig something up. Anything else?"

Nobody said anything.

"Let's get to work, then. Plenty of footwork to do here."

* * *

Mari Lehtonen's hand was resting on the telephone, and had been for some time now. The newspaper clipping lay in front of her on the desk of her cubicle. The clock in the lower corner of her computer screen read 10:56 A.M.

Lehtonen had finished the computer reports in about an hour, and devoted half an hour to email triage afterwards. One was from Laura's theater instructor, who considered the girl a promising young actress and was asking for Mari's permission for Laura to take on a larger role in the upcoming fall production. Mari couldn't help but smile at her rather extravagant use of the word "production," but she felt warmed by the message. Mari consented on the condition that Laura's studies would not suffer. Rehearsals would consume three evenings a week, and opening night was in December.

Her mood, however, was unsettled. The image of a dark Mazda with its driver and license plate flitted continually through her mind. If only she could simply upload the image from her brain to a computer and send it to the authorities in an anonymous email.

She had to report it to the police, she thought. Maybe they wouldn't find her information useful, but it said right there in the paper that it was needed. She shuddered at the thought of someone being murdered in the neighboring building. The killers should be held responsible. *No point getting mixed up in these kinds of things*, Essi Saari had said. But her boss was wrong. If Mari didn't act, the criminals would win.

Mari picked up the phone and punched in the number listed in the newspaper.

* * *

The hotline phone was closest to Joutsamo's workstation in the office she shared with Kohonen, Kulta and a couple of other officers. Suhonen also had a desk, a chair and a telephone, but had the janitors not visited daily, spiders would have surely overrun it with their webs. The topmost item on Suhonen's desk was a year-old newspaper.

Joutsamo rolled her desk chair over to the phone and was just lifting the receiver when Kulta blurted, "Betcha three shifts of coffee-duty it's some wacko."

Joutsamo accepted and grinned as she flicked on the voice recorder.

"Helsinki Violent Crimes Unit, Anna Joutsamo speaking."

"Hello," said a hesitant female voice. "I'm calling about the incident on Porvoo Street. Is this the right number?"

"Yes, it is," said Joutsamo in a cordial voice. "Do you have any information on it?"

"Yeah. Not sure if it's important, but I was coming out of the convenience store and saw a Mazda parked there."

Joutsamo snatched a pen. The woman had the make of the car right despite its lack of mention in

the press. The sergeant scribbled out, *knew Mazda*.
"You're sure it was a Mazda?"

"Yes. A blue 323, as I remember. Not too old. The sort of rounder-looking sedan style. Wasn't it then?"

"Uuh," Joutsamo stalled intentionally. "Maybe I should get your name."

Witnesses often wished to remain anonymous. Joutsamo was confident the woman would reveal her name since her number was clearly visible on the caller ID. She had already written it down.

"Mari Lehtonen."

"What did you see there, Mari?"

"The car, driver and license plate. Nothing more."

"Do you recall the plate number?"

"Yes," said Mari, and she recited the number. It started with a *K*.

Joutsamo was ready to celebrate. The other officers had gathered around as well. Below the plate number she scratched out another message: *Kulta, put some coffee on! And tea too!!*

"Was the driver the murderer, then?"

"It's best if you don't ask any questions. What do you remember about the driver?"

"Male. About forty. Angry-looking eyes, though he never looked directly at me. He kept his hands on the steering wheel and stared straight ahead. Maybe that's why it stuck in my head. He was clearly waiting for someone in the store and seemed irritable."

"Listen, Mari. We should meet up as soon as possible. Where are you now? Could I come there so we could talk?"

Mari hesitated for a moment. "Uuh, maybe it's best if I came to the station. We have secured entry and all that, and I don't think the management would appreciate if the police came. I can get there by bus just fine."

"How about if I pick you up."

"That works too. Won't take too long, will it?"

"What's the address?"

Mari told her and Joutsamo promised to be there within fifteen minutes. She hung up the phone.

Joutsamo was beaming. "Just hit pay dirt. Almost too good to be true. Not only was she able to describe the driver, she remembered the plate number, too." Joutsamo handed her notes to Kohonen. "Kirsi, you track down the car. Kulta, I want every photo you can find of every guy connected to Korpi, but toss in ten or so extra photos for a control group."

* * *

Twenty minutes later, Joutsamo was returning to police headquarters with Lehtonen. She had parked her unmarked Volkswagen Golf in front of the station rather than its reserved spot in the underground garage. She didn't want Lehtonen feeling intimidated on account of their grim, claustrophobic parking accommodations. This might be their key witness, after all, and it paid to foster a buoyant, talkative mood. On the way, Joutsamo had avoided talking about the case, opting instead to ask about Mari's background. Mari had talked about her current job, her layoff at the Jyväskylä Savings and Loan, her alcoholic ex and her daughter, who was clearly an important figure in her life.

Mari Lehtonen seemed to Joutsamo to be a well-balanced woman and first-class eyewitness material.

Once on the third floor of the station, Joutsamo led her down a hallway and into a small interrogation room that was somewhat different from those used for suspects.

The room was plain, but not too dreary. On one wall, a map of Helsinki added a splash of color. A table, three chairs and a worn leather couch were neatly arranged about the room. If Joutsamo had had any say, she would have decorated with a bit more warmth, but perhaps a bit of barrenness helped to remind witnesses and plaintiffs of the importance of honesty. Only suspects had the right to lie without consequence.

"Would you like some coffee?"

CHAPTER 5
MONDAY, 12:05 P.M.
KAARELA, NORTH HELSINKI

Risto Korpi sat in a small, dimly lit room, browsing through electronic equipment websites on a laptop computer. Chat rooms provided a trove of valuable information on police methods along with pictures and license plates of unmarked squad cars. Korpi never posted messages; he only read them.

He stroked his head. It was smooth, freshly shaved that morning as it was every other day.

The websites contained information about surveillance microphones, their operating frequencies and how to detect them. Korpi's hard face cracked into a smile. The post was sufficiently interesting that he copied it, signed into an anonymous French email account and pasted the text into an email draft. A friend of Korpi's in Sweden knew the password to the same account, which allowed him to read the drafts on his own computer. This way, emails were never actually sent, which minimized the risk that the authorities could read them.

But the procedure wasn't foolproof either. Korpi knew the police had the capability of infecting his computer with viruses that would make his every move visible to them.

Real business had to be conducted the old-fashioned way, and even then, communications had to be coded in such a way that they revealed nothing to outsiders. The language had to be ordinary enough so as not to attract attention.

Years in prison had taught Korpi to be careful, to leave no trace.

A knock came at the door and Korpi barked out something unintelligible. The door swung open.

"Risto," said a young man in an uneasy voice. The man was powerfully built, with prominent cheekbones and a ragged scar beneath his right ear. Jere Siikala went by the nickname of Guerrilla and had actually come to prefer it over his former, a bastardization of Siikala to Sikala, meaning Pigsty.

Korpi wheeled suddenly and shouted, "Fucking idiot! How many times I gotta tell you not to use names! Goddamn shit for brains. Never goddamn learn."

"Sorry," Guerrilla said, shrinking back a bit. He knew better than to cross Korpi, but he had forgotten the rules.

Korpi massaged his jaw. He shouldn't have blown up, but sometimes he failed to smother his own fuse. Stupidity piqued his wrath more than it did most. Korpi struggled to quiet his voice. "Do you understand why we can't mention names?"

Siikala was prepared. He tried to offer the newspaper, explaining, "Of course I do, but it says here…"

"I wanna hear the reason."

"Well, cuz the cops might be listening."

Korpi nodded. "Good. And how do they do that?"

"They got the technology and all…room could be wired…mikes that work through the windows."

"Exactly. So tell me again, why no fucking names?"

Siikala was confused, not sure why Korpi was still hassling him. Was it just another of his endless tirades, or was something worse coming? "So the cops can't figure out who's talking."

"So you know all about this…"

Siikala nodded.

"Then why the fuck…" Korpi snatched an empty beer bottle off the floor and launched it at Siikala. The bodybuilder managed to dodge the missile and it shattered against the door frame. "…don't you do what I tell you?"

Guerrilla knew anything he said would only further irritate Korpi. Now it was wise to remain silent. Were anyone else to have thrown a bottle at him he'd have snapped their neck, but Korpi's psychotic streak made the man seem invincible. Sure, occasionally Siikala had felt like fighting back, but fortunately what little sense he had outweighed his penchant for fists, knives and firearms.

"Now then," said Korpi. "Is there something I can do for you?"

This sudden change of mood was no surprise to Guerrilla. Korpi's mind routinely reeled from one extreme to another.

Without saying a word, Siikala handed him a folded newspaper clipping with the headline "Young Man Gunned Down in Alppila."

Korpi took the clipping, wrinkling his brow as he read it, "Shit," he hissed. "Fucking idiot!"

* * *

Mari Lehtonen sat at the table inspecting a couple of dozen photos, which were spread out in front of her. She put her finger on one. "No question about it. That one's the driver," she said. The man in the photo wore a dour, angry expression. "I'd recognize those eyes anywhere. He had the same look then."

"I just want you to be sure," said Joutsamo. "So take some time to look over the others once more."

Lehtonen scanned the photographs, studying each one for about ten seconds. Joutsamo was satisfied with the care she devoted to each. She studied the collection for nearly three minutes before tapping Korpi's again.

"And you're certain?"

Lehtonen nodded. "Absolutely."

Joutsamo raked up the photos and stood up. "Okay, Mari. I need to go talk with my lieutenant for a while. Go ahead and pour yourself another cup of coffee from the thermos over there."

"Okay."

"I'll just be a few minutes," said Joutsamo, and she headed off for Takamäki's office. There, Takamäki and Kohonen were discussing the surveillance operation. Not much to discuss, as no phone activity had been detected. The police had obtained a warrant for a list of all cell phone activity from the area surrounding the crime scene. Takamäki had ordered Kohonen to go through the list to look for any interesting phone numbers.

"Sorry to interrupt," said Joutsamo from the door.

"What is it?" said Takamäki.

"Our witness recognized the driver. Korpi himself."

"Huh?" Takamäki seemed surprised. "She sure about that?"

Joutsamo nodded. "Positively. I showed her more than twenty photos of guys who've been connected to Korpi, plus Korpi himself. Lehtonen barely hesitated when she fingered him."

"And she's pretty levelheaded?"

"Yup. Even remembers the plate number on the Mazda. Said it herself—she's got like a photographic memory."

"Why would Korpi put himself in that kinda situation?" wondered Kohonen. "He's got plenty of guys to play getaway driver."

"Wondered the same thing myself," said Joutsamo. "He's not the type to do anything that stupid, even for his godchild."

"I guess we'll just have to ask him, if we can find him. Anna, did you discuss safety measures with Lehtonen?"

Joutsamo shook her head.

"Okay, you'll have to do that. But do a proper interview first and make sure to document in writing which photo she identified. Once we find Korpi, we'll organize a lineup," said Takamäki. His phone rang. Before answering, he asked Joutsamo if there was anything more. There wasn't.

"Yeah," Takamäki barked into the receiver. If he ever used his name, he certainly didn't for unidentified callers.

"Hi, it's Sanna," said a woman's perky voice.

"Hi there," said Takamäki.

Sanna Römpötti was a long-time crime reporter who had recently moved from newspapers to TV. She was friends with Joutsamo, who Takamäki trusted not to leak any information to the media.

"So, you guys got a new murder to solve?"

Takamäki smiled. Typical Römpötti. Her interviews were like a page out of a police textbook. Throw out a casual, open question and let the subject ramble on. Afterwards, if Römpötti heard anything interesting, the real grilling would begin. In most instances, she had already familiarized herself with the case in advance.

"Yeah. In Alppila."

"I saw the bit in the paper, but what's the backstory?"

"If only we knew."

"Don't play games, Kari. You know what I'm looking for here. Anything newsworthy?"

"Well, sure, if we solve the case."

Römpötti was quiet for a moment. "Organized crime?"

"You said that. Not me."

The reporter laughed. "Will you say it on camera?"

"Hey, you're the talking head. How about you say it," said Takamäki. "According to our sources and all that."

"So that's your working assumption then?"

"If we get somewhere with it, yes, but it might not stick." It never paid to lie to reporters, though occasionally information had to be withheld. Besides, getting the case on TV would help them angle for more witnesses.

"You have somebody in custody?"

"Yes."

"Who?"

"The murder suspect."

"How?"

"Can't say."

48

Römpötti sniffed. "That doesn't help much. Any biker gangs involved?"

Takamäki was about to say 'no comment,' but Römpötti would only have interpreted that as a yes. "No. No bikers."

"Alright. Does one-thirty work?"

"For what?"

"An interview, of course."

"Did I agree to one?"

"Of course. You sent out a written press release, so in the interest of fairness, you have to appear on camera, too."

"Alright," Takamäki laughed. "One-thirty, then."

CHAPTER 6
MONDAY, 12:45 P.M.
PASILA POLICE HEADQUARTERS

Joutsamo smiled as she hit "Save" on the computer. Mari Lehtonen was still seated on the other side of the interview table. Though it took more time, Joutsamo had opted to transcribe Lehtonen's account as she gave it rather than tape it.

"I'll just print this out so you can have a look and sign it," said Joutsamo, as she clicked the mouse. The printer whirred into action. "I'll sign every page, too, and then we'll be all done."

"That easy, huh?"

The printer pumped out four pages, which comprised the entirety of the interview.

"Yup."

Joutsamo handed the papers to Lehtonen, who began poring over them. "Looks OK," she said, and Joutsamo handed her a pen. "A few minor typos, but I don't suppose it matters."

"No. Not like it's a novel."

After Joutsamo showed her where to sign, Lehtonen leafed through the document, signing each page as she went. Joutsamo did the same.

"Just a couple more things," said Joutsamo. "I should remind you that you're prohibited by law from speaking with anybody else about anything we've discussed here."

"Okay," said Lehtonen. "I wasn't going to."

"The other issue has to do with security. All your personal information will be kept confidential, so that's why I left your address and phone number off of the transcript. We are, however, required to include your name and birth date. Since the case is linked to organized crime, do you think anyone would be able to track you down based on that information? There's no danger, it's just a precaution."

Lehtonen was quiet for a moment. "Why would you need a precaution if there's no danger?"

Joutsamo sidestepped the question. "What I'm asking is whether your name, number or address are listed in the phone book?"

"No. Some years ago I had problems with my ex-husband, so my daughter and I ended up moving and getting an unlisted number."

"Good," said Joutsamo. Removing data from electronic directories was quick and easy, but printed phone books presented a problem. Not in this case, however.

"Should I be afraid…or something?"

"No. Just go on with your life as usual. At some point, hopefully soon, we'll ask you to come back for a lineup. You'll look at a row of five men from behind mirrored glass and tell us if one of them is the driver. After that, some months down the line, you'll tell the court the same thing you told me today. And that's it."

"I see…are we are all done here, then?"

"Yes…and thank you. Your information has been very helpful."

Mari Lehtonen nodded as she took her coat off the hook.

"I can give you a ride back to work," said Joutsamo.

"No, thanks," she said. "I'll catch the bus." The policewoman seemed nice enough, but Lehtonen still felt strangely unsettled. It wasn't fear or nervousness, just an unpleasant feeling. Maybe it was just the atmosphere of the police station.

* * *

Suhonen was sitting in the passenger seat of Salmela's van.

Salmela was at the wheel, the only other spot to sit in his junker Toyota. He turned onto the entrance ramp heading toward Hämeenlinna and Tampere. They passed a massive bus depot.

A few light raindrops hit the windshield, and judging by the color of the sky, there would be plenty more.

Salmela flicked on the wipers, or the wiper, since the one on the passenger side didn't work.

"You had this thing inspected lately?" said Suhonen. "Or ever, for that matter?"

"Sure. All's in order… Least that's what the guy told me when he took my three hundred euros for it." Salmela smirked.

"You got gouged."

They passed Hotel Haaga on the left, and on the right, a forested arm of Helsinki Central Park, where scores of homeless people lived in ramshackle huts. The scene was hardly an uplifting one. Suhonen had pulled plenty of corpses out of these same woods.

Salmela ground the gears as he jammed the shifter into fourth. He had called Suhonen about half an hour earlier and invited him along, supposedly to show him something. Beyond that, Salmela wouldn't elaborate.

"Get any sleep last night?" asked Suhonen.

"Some. Once I finally got to bed. I had to take care of something first."

"What?" said Suhonen. He wasn't prying, just keeping up the conversation.

"You'll see," said Salmela, and he shut his mouth. The van was doing about fifty miles per hour, just over the speed limit.

Salmela exited the freeway and followed the signs for Kaivoksela and Myyrmäki. The van circled the cloverleaf and went under the highway. The Kaivoksela shopping center lay on the right and a large car dealer on the left.

"We picking up a new van for you?" said Suhonen. The game was getting old, even if Salmela had something important to show him. Thankfully, the rain had stopped, so Suhonen could at least see out the window. The sun was hidden behind a thick layer of gray clouds, and the flags at the dealership rippled in the wind.

"Nah. Just wanna show you this place."

The van turned left at a stoplight, followed a curve gently to the left, then to the right. The small houses on the passenger side gave way to tall apartment buildings. Suhonen knew that the road led to the Vihti Highway, but he doubted they would go that far.

At the intersection, Salmela swung left onto a side road and pulled into a small parking lot on the right. "The moment you been waiting for," said Salmela.

Suhonen said nothing, not that Salmela had expected him to. The lot had spaces for maybe fifteen cars but now there were only five. Nobody else was around.

"You did right by me last night…just like a friend ought to. First I figured I'd just get hammered, but then I got a taste for blood in my mouth. That's why I picked this up…" Salmela pulled out a stout, short-barreled pistol.

"What the hell have you done?" Suhonen hissed. Salmela's gaze was cold and unflinching.

* * *

Mari Lehtonen was sitting in her cubicle, her mind still at the police station, her work piling up on her desk.

A smiling Essi Saari popped her head around the corner. "Hey, you eaten yet?"

Lehtonen shook her head.

"Wanna go? Salad bar today."

"Not hungry."

"What is it? Something wrong?"

Lehtonen paused just a bit too long. "No…it's nothing."

"Come on…I know you," she said, as she came round the partition and approached Lehtonen. "So, what is it?"

Lehtonen didn't respond.

"So you told them."

"Yes, but don't start with your lectures, I didn't…"

"I'm not gonna lecture you. Actually, thinking back, I think you were right. If you hadn't already called, I would've made you."

Her words were comforting. "Really?"

"Yep, we gotta side with the good guys... So what was it like?"

"They said I can't talk about it." Her mood seemed to lift somewhat.

Saari seemed disappointed. "Come on, you can tell me *something*."

"I don't really know what's so secret about it. They showed me some pictures and one was of the guy I saw in the car. So I told that to the cop, and she typed it out on her computer and then had me sign it. That's all it really was."

"Who was the guy?"

"I dunno. The lady cop seemed really surprised when I pointed at him."

"So it must be one of their repeat customers if they already had a picture of him."

"I guess."

"Is he dangerous?"

"She didn't really say anything about him."

"Well, you already have some experience with psychos," Saari laughed.

"I guess." Lehtonen couldn't bring herself to smile. "Anyway, I doubt anything bad will happen. He'll probably just go to prison."

"Yeah. Should we go eat now?"

Mari got up. "Sure."

Then she stopped. "What do you think I should tell my daughter?"

* * *

Takamäki scrolled through his cellphone directory till he landed on the number. He pressed "Call."

"Nykänen," answered a raspy voice. Lieutenant Jaakko Nykänen had been a detective on Takamäki's team until a few years ago, when the walrus-whiskered veteran had been promoted to lieutenant in the neighboring city of Espoo's narcotics unit, and then last spring to the intelligence unit at the National Bureau of Investigation. A number of these units were established throughout the country in 2004 to help gather and coordinate actionable intelligence on organized crime. In addition to the police force, the border patrol and customs were also involved.

"Hey, it's Takamäki."

Due to the interdepartmental squabbling of the last few years, Takamäki's relations with the NBI were rather cool, but when it came to his old colleague and family friend, they were still quite warm.

"Hey there."

"You in a hurry?"

Nykänen gave a dry laugh. "What, in this job? We're never in a hurry. Intel just rolls in and we mull it over and hatch our clever theories. How's the boys' hockey going?"

"Fine. No games yet, but they were at camp last weekend. Gets pretty crazy with soccer and hockey doubled up in the fall."

"The coaches pushing them into one or the other yet?"

"No. Kalle's definitely better at hockey, but they're both doing well."

"Yeah. Keep 'em in hockey. It's a fine sport. I'll have to come to a game sometime." Nykänen guessed that Takamäki was probably busy, so he wrapped up the chitchat. "So?"

"We're on the hunt for one Risto Korpi," said Takamäki. He outlined the main points leading up to

Nyberg's arrest. Nykänen was tapping on his keyboard on the other end.

"Sounds like a tough case," said Nykänen. "I remember Korpi from a drug case back in Espoo. We got a tip about his involvement, but the case dried up because no one had the balls to testify against him. Out of several pounds of dope, we couldn't pin any of it on Korpi."

"Yeah. Apparently a pretty violent guy."

Nykänen kept typing. "Makes good on his threats. Says here he rules by fear. Only reason people respect him is because they're afraid, not because he's a born leader. Looks like nothing acute going on with him at the moment."

"What's acute mean in your language?"

"None of our units have any open investigations on him. He lands in the three-to-five-year bracket here. In other words, we're looking to open a case and bust up his little outfit within that time frame. His gang is classified as organized crime, though..."

"So why such a long time frame?"

"Not enough boots on the ground. Resources are slim and we gotta set priorities. Maybe things will improve next year. Apparently the interior ministry's making organized crime the big theme for next year. Might actually get some funding."

"That's ridiculous."

"Gotta set priorities," said Nykänen, his voice filled with sarcasm. "We got about a thousand criminals in the database that make up these gangs. About a hundred and fifty are behind bars and about the same number are foreigners. Just think how much manpower we'd need to track them all."

"I know. The numbers are never pretty."

"Say we need ten cops minimum for every bad guy. That makes about ten thousand cops over here at the NBI. And I'm talking good street-smart cops."

"Yeah," Takamäki grumbled.

Nykänen returned to Korpi. "Yeah is right. Anyway, I did get a couple hits. Korpi was spotted in June in a Kannelmäki liquor store with the same Nyberg you got in the cooler. Then in early August he was seen with a gangster by the name of Jere Siikala meeting some Estonian guy in the West Harbor."

"So you have him under surveillance, then?" Takamäki wondered.

"Nah...just stuff we've gotten in connection with other investigations. Our guys were after someone else and Korpi just happened to be there."

"You don't have an address, do you? We've got a couple questions for him."

"Sorry. Don't see anything here."

"So nobody has an open case on Korpi?"

"No, but I'll put a note here that you do."

"Good. We might be able to get a life sentence... Anything to help clear your logjam."

Nykänen knew his ex-boss meant business.

* * *

Suhonen and Salmela stepped out of the van just as a light drizzle began to fall. The fine mist didn't have the weight to penetrate their coats, but the men could feel it on their faces.

"This way," Salmela said, as he circled a gray office building toward the rear.

"Where we going?"

"Patience. You'll see."

Suhonen's hand found its way to his hip pouch where he could feel the butt of a Glock 26 through the fabric. Salmela's reticence had started to make him suspicious, though Suhonen doubted his old friend would set him up.

The two high-stepped through a thicket toward the rear of the building. Once past the office building, they continued on between two houses and into a small forested area.

Salmela looked back. "Kinda reminds me of playing cowboys and indians in the woods back in Lahti."

"More like cops and robbers," said Suhonen. Salmela laughed.

The underbrush grew thicker as they advanced a couple hundred feet further. The ground was littered with fallen leaves and small branches, which crackled beneath their feet.

"You know people were already living here six thousand years ago?" said Salmela.

"How you know that?"

"Read it in prison in some history book on Helsinki. Poor saps probably lived in mud holes and loafed around in the dirt daydreaming all day."

"Uh-huh," said Suhonen. "How 'bout we cut the shit. Like now."

Salmela stopped and squatted down. "Well, this is it. Come on over here, but get down low."

Suhonen did as he was told and clambered up into a shallow depression along the ridge of a small hillock.

"Look over there. The house, and especially the car."

Through the trees, Suhonen could make out a dingy, ramshackle two-story house and a dark Mazda sedan in the yard. The car was nearly a hundred yards away, and without binoculars, Suhonen couldn't make out the license plate.

"Korpi's place. Not sure if he's there, but he was last night. Saw him through the window."

"You sure?" said Suhonen with a stern expression.

Salmela nodded. "Positive. Korpi took the house as payment for a twenty-thousand-euro dope haul that a low-level pusher lost somehow. Who knows if it's true, but apparently this dealer got the house when his mom died. Her estate has never been closed, so the house couldn't be foreclosed."

"And you heard this yesterday?"

"Yeah. I happen to know one of the dealer's buddies. Anyway, I was pissed off about Tomi last night so I started asking around about Korpi. Came here last night thinking I'd put a bullet through the fucker's brain, but then it started to seem like a dumb move. Maybe I got cold feet…I dunno. I ain't afraid to use a gun, but I didn't want to study any more history in the joint. And that's exactly where you would've put me. So I figured I'd let the cops handle the payback."

Suhonen was silent, his gaze fixed on the house. What he wouldn't do for a pair of binoculars. He took his phone out of his pocket.

"Later," said Salmela, and he set off back toward the van, flipping up his collar as he went.

CHAPTER 7
MONDAY, 2:00 P.M.
PASILA POLICE HEADQUARTERS

The mood in the SWAT team conference room was tense.

"It's a tough location. Dead-end street and all," said SWAT team commander Turunen as he examined a computerized map projected onto the wall. Three roads came together to form a sort of stylized K with the target residence at the terminal point on the lower leg.

Turunen was wearing the SWAT team's trademark black coveralls. Helmets and weapons lined the walls of the conference room, which resembled a sort of classroom. In addition to Turunen, Takamäki, and Joutsamo, ten other black-garbed SWAT officers were sitting at the table. Kulta was leaning against the wall with his arms folded over his chest.

"So where exactly is Suhonen?" Turunen asked.

"Not completely sure, but I'd guess somewhere around here," said Takamäki, pointing to a spot about halfway down the lower leg of the K.

"It's pretty wooded there but he has a visual on the house. Hasn't seen any movement."

Half an hour earlier Takamäki had been interviewed by Römpötti, but he had stuck to the basics and managed not to mention the upcoming raid.

"Can Suhonen scout out the terrain for us?" wondered Turunen.

"I can ask him."

Joutsamo cut in. "Why don't you just use the net?"

"That's where the map's from," said Turunen.

Joutsamo strolled over to the laptop and pulled up Google Earth on the browser. After loading for a moment, an image of the earth appeared. She rotated the image to the Eastern Hemisphere and closed in first on Finland, then Helsinki. In less than twenty seconds they were viewing an aerial photo of the house where Korpi was believed to be. "There's terrain for you," said Joutsamo. "You can zoom in and out right here."

Joutsamo showed them how detailed the image could get. Once the viewing altitude dipped below a hundred and fifty feet and only the target residence remained in the image, the contours of the image began to pixelate. "If this is a free service, just think how detailed the military satellite photos must be."

"Hmm," said Turunen. "You're always full of surprises. Let's go with it." Turunen began to plan the raid based on the aerial photo. On screen he could see a field on the north side of the house, while the other three quadrants were forested. A gravel path that wasn't marked on the map appeared to cut through the woods on the eastern end.

* * *

Suhonen lay on the damp leaves, half-sheltered by a tree trunk, examining the house. The rain had soaked through his leather jacket and clothes. Initially he'd been squatting, but his knees had started to hurt. Salmela's words about ancient Finns lying in the dirt had started to sink in—the bastard had known full well what Suhonen would end up doing. Suhonen suppressed the urge to curse his friend. Without Salmela's help, they'd have no idea where Korpi was.

Suhonen hadn't seen any movement in the house. The Mazda was still parked in the driveway.

He heard some rustling behind him and whirled around. Turunen was advancing in a crouch, while Joutsamo and Kulta were lagging back. Suhonen motioned for Turunen to get down on all fours. He didn't intend to be the only one to get wet, even if all the SWAT officers had waterproof gear.

Turunen covered the final thirty feet scrambling along the ground. "What's the status?"

"The wood house there. No sign of life."

"Any dogs?"

"No barking. Not sure otherwise."

Turunen drew a pair of binoculars from a case strapped to his back and quietly surveyed the house. The binoculars were military-grade with a built-in laser rangefinder. "Doesn't seem to be any security cameras, though nowadays they can be small enough to hide just about anywhere." He read the license plate on the Mazda. "That match what our witness said?"

"No idea," Suhonen answered.

Turunen switched on his headset. "Joutsamo. Here's the plate," and he read the number. Joutsamo confirmed the match.

"Hold on a sec. Let me call Takamäki for the go-ahead," said Joutsamo. Conducting a raid without probable cause was not a mistake they wanted to make. Takamäki could give them the green light.

Turunen kept his binoculars trained on the house as he dispensed orders to his men. Almost everyone was already in position.

"Turunen," Joutsamo's voice came over the earpiece. "The matching plate is all we needed. It's a go."

"Good. Two minutes till showtime. Everyone in position?"

The other officers checked in over the radio.

"Look!" Suhonen rasped. A faint wisp of smoke rose from the chimney of the house.

"Someone's inside."

"Or we got a new pope," said Suhonen. "Though I'm more interested in what they're burning."

* * *

Korpi and Siikala sat round the fireplace, a few fresh newspapers burning under the grate, the flames just beginning to work their way through a pile of birch splits. Beads of sweat glistened on Korpi's bald head.

Siikala bent down and blew into the stack, keeping his ponytail away from the mounting flames. Smoke wafted into the room.

The fireplace was situated in a small room on the first floor. For the most part, the interior looked just as dated as the building, with its old sofa, television, bookcase and a broken grandfather clock. A rag rug lay on the worn hardwood floor and pale, sun-faded floral curtains hung in front of the windows.

Both Korpi and Siikala had a sheet of paper and pen in hand. No notepads, since the cops could discern what had been written by the indentations on the lower sheets. Korpi had forbidden speaking because of the possibility of microphones. Speech was only allowed in the most random of places where it would be impossible to plant a mike.

Siikala scratched out a message and showed it to Korpi: *Should I ditch the car?*

No need, Korpi scribbled. *I didn't do nothing.*

Nyberg's in jail!

His problem. He won't talk.

Sure?

Korpi nodded as he tossed his sheet into the fire. Siikala did the same, pushing them around with the poker enough that no forensic scientist could ever discern anything from the ashes.

Korpi's philosophy was simple: leave no trace. Speaking out loud was a great way to wind up on tape. Since phones left a digital trail, they were only used in emergencies; and even then, only on anonymous phones with new, prepaid SIM cards. Korpi even took to wearing Levi's since reading that their fibers were too common for the police to use as evidence.

Korpi had structured his organization so that only he understood its entirety. Siikala routed the domestic drug traffic, while Nyberg and Matti Ahola were mainly debt collectors. Ahola was also responsible for hiding the inventory. Beyond that, there was the import racket, but that was for Korpi to run himself. Each of his men knew only his own role, and nothing more.

Though Siikala, Nyberg and Ahola knew each other, only Korpi knew the entire organization. The trio's minions weren't even aware that Korpi was the man in charge, though naturally many had heard rumors. But for every weak link he could think of, Korpi had a safeguard.

Siikala thought Nyberg had made a surprisingly dumb move, but it was none of his business. Nyberg could run his own crew as he saw fit, though he wondered why Korpi had been behind the wheel during the hit.

Korpi rubbed his bald head. "You want coffee?" he said without expecting an answer. The coffeemaker had recently sputtered out its last few drops, and Korpi was the one that wanted some. He was on his way to the kitchen when the front door smashed open.

"Police!" boomed a voice from the door.

* * *

Officer Dahlman repeated the warning. "Police!"

When raiding a gang's hideout, it was wise to make it very clear who was entering. From the gangsters' standpoint, the game the cops played was fair, at least at the outset. The cops weren't out to kill, but the same could not be said of rival criminals.

The SWAT officers wore composite helmets and black masks. Their eyes were protected with shatterproof goggles.

"On the floor! Hands on your heads!"

The first officer through the door, the point man, was wielding a big, black ninety-pound ballistic shield heavy enough to stop a handgun bullet. A small window in the middle the shield was reinforced with bulletproof Plexiglass. Just after the point man was Dahlman, holding a Heckler & Koch

MP5 submachine gun in firing position. The shield provided good cover in the narrow entryway. Just behind Dahlman were two other SWAT officers.

The men stayed in a tight stack behind the shield. Only the barrel of Dahlman's gun jutted out from the side.

"In the entryway," Dahlman barked over the radio. "We're moving in."

"OK," said Turunen. The units outside had to be aware of where the team was in the house, so they wouldn't accidentally fire on fellow cops through the windows.

Dahlman heard the dog bark behind him a few times—a message to those in the house that fleeing was futile.

The shield bearer advanced to the entrance of the living room. Dahlman noted the empty room and the fire in the fireplace, then spurred the shield bearer onward.

"Living room clear. We're heading into the kitchen toward the stairs."

"Copy."

The shield bearer pressed on toward the kitchen with a shuffling gait. His left foot always led, the right coming just abreast with every step. In this stance he was always ready to withstand a blow, and the shield came in handy for forcing a suspect up against a wall.

"We're entering the kitchen," Dahlman reported. "Let's go."

The shield bearer inched through the doorway, and when the shield was halfway through, he saw a man sitting at the table. "Suspect in sight," he rasped, still moving forward. Dahlman pushed the machine gun barrel between the door jamb and the shield.

"Police! On the ground!" he shouted, but the man at the table didn't move. That's when Dahlman noticed a second man sitting on the opposite side of the table.

Both appeared to be drinking coffee.

"Get on the ground!" Dahlman shouted, again with no result. The men sat motionless, not even glancing toward the door. Dahlman recalled a training scenario in which a deaf man couldn't hear their commands. He quickly eliminated that possibility, since he could see their mouths moving and hear them talking.

"Can't a man drink coffee in his own house," said the bald one, whom Dahlman recognized as Risto Korpi, their prime target. The other man laughed.

"Get your hands in the air!"

Korpi turned his head toward the door and asked in a calm voice, "With or without the coffee cup?"

Dahlman kept the dangerous one in the crosshairs. The shield bearer stayed in the middle of the passageway while another sharpshooter rounded to his other side. The situation seemed to be under control, but Dahlman paused for half a second before answering, "Put the cup down and your hands on your head."

Korpi took a final gulp of coffee before lowering his cup to the table. "What seems to be the problem, officer?" he asked with a doe-eyed stare. "Here we are, having a nice cup of coffee and the Gestapo barges in."

"Shut up and put your hands on your head!"

Korpi complied with a wry smile. "Well, for chrissakes. The whole SWAT team and everything."

Dahlman knew his partner on the other side of the room had his MP5 trained on the second man, so he kept his eyes riveted to his target. A quick glance was enough to tell him that the man was Jere Siikala. Dahlman prodded the shield bearer forward enough that he was able to squeeze into the kitchen.

"Keep your hands where they are," he shouted, advancing about six feet toward Korpi. With his finger nuzzling the trigger, Dahlman hoped the blowhard would stop provoking them with those sips of coffee. One sudden movement could trigger a bloodbath.

Dahlman wanted to minimize the risks. The suspects, though outmanned and outgunned, were extremely dangerous. He came around behind Korpi, and with his wing man behind Siikala, gave a nod and they jerked the chairs backwards.

Korpi reeled back and crashed to the floor before Dahlman flung him onto his stomach, drove his shoulders into the floor with his knees and slapped the cuffs round his right wrist first, then his left, the backs of his hands trapped against one another.

Just as quickly, the wing man cuffed Siikala, while the shield bearer and the fourth man in the stack covered the stairs leading to the second level.

"Anyone else in the house?" Dahlman asked the men, but neither responded.

He repeated the question, but when silence prevailed, he reached into his pocket, pulled out a black hood, and pulled it over Korpi's head. The others hooded Siikala in the same way.

"Two suspects in custody in the kitchen," Dahlman said over the radio. "We're going upstairs."

Dahlman signaled for the fourth man in the stack to stand watch over the two suspects on the floor. The others would continue on up the stairs.

* * *

Korpi could feel the pitted hardwood floors through the coarse hood against his cheek. His wrists were throbbing. The pig had slammed the cuffs on him so hard that his fingers were beginning to tingle from lack of circulation.

The awkward position compelled him to relax, as tensing up only made him more uncomfortable.

He knew Siikala was lying on the other side of the table, though he couldn't see a thing. From the sounds in the room, he could tell one of the officers had stayed back to stand guard while the others went upstairs with that shield-wielding shithead.

Korpi had little appreciation for cops, but he felt a certain respect for the SWAT team's approach: cold and professional. He had no doubt they would have shot him at the first sudden movement. Their protocol was utterly controlled and predictable. Every man knew his task. Nothing like the bungled jobs of strung-out criminals that only ended in needless corpses and life sentences. Korpi decided he'd need a hit squad just like the SWAT team. One capable of the most demanding jobs. Maybe he could even piggyback on their reputation, their uniforms, their sinister presence. It would shock his rivals, at least.

But how in the hell had they found him so quickly? Not that it was much of a surprise. His working assumption, after all, was that he was under constant surveillance. Had the cops rented the house next door? Was there a bug in the wall? But that was an issue for another time. Korpi was more interested in why, and he couldn't think of any other reason than Nyberg's hit job.

He worried briefly about it, but the worry faded quickly. Either someone had talked, or the cops knew about his connection to Nyberg from previous surveillance.

"Jesus," he groaned. "Getting gangrene over here. Your boss put these cuffs on too tight. Can't you loosen 'em up a bit?"

His wrists were throbbing and drool was spilling out of the corner of his mouth onto the hood.

The cop in black didn't react in the slightest. No compassion, thought Korpi. Just like the TV images of American soldiers with Iraqi POWs.

"Relax a little, will ya?" said Korpi. The cop didn't. Korpi pictured the barrel of the MP5 sweeping back and forth between Siikala and himself before deciding to take his own advice.

* * *

Suhonen and Turunen were still lying low in the woods. "Nobody upstairs," came Dahlman's voice over the radio. "House is clear."

As he stood up, Turunen nodded at Suhonen. "We can go in now."

Suhonen struggled to his feet, his right arm now numb. His pants and jacket were soaked. "Good, but I think I've had enough fun."

"You're not coming in?"

"Nah," said Suhonen, wiping the mud and leaves off his jacket. "Gotta go find you guys some more work."

Joutsamo caught up to the two. "Should we go in?"

"Let's go."

Turunen noticed the gentle way Joutsamo patted Suhonen on the shoulder. He could have used a pat too.

Joutsamo and Turunen covered the distance to the house quickly. On the way, Joutsamo notified Takamäki of the arrests and requested that Forensics inspect the house.

A few SWAT officers had filtered out of the woods toward the house. "I want the whole place taped off along the property lines," shouted Turunen. Kannas and the Forensics team would have to comb the lot for footprints. If the rain didn't get any heavier, they might still be able to find some around the Mazda.

Joutsamo considered whether she should go in. Inside, there was the possibility of tarnishing any potential prints, but a quick breeze-through could also turn up something to go on. In the end, curiosity prevailed and she asked Turunen to wait outside. Joutsamo mounted the short flight of stairs to the front door, drew a pair of blue plastic booties from her pocket and slipped them over her shoes. Once inside, the smell of smoke mingled with a stuffy odor. Either the house had mold issues or it hadn't been cleaned or ventilated properly.

The narrow entryway led into the living room, where Korpi and Siikala had been moved. Four SWAT officers were standing guard.

"What should we do?" asked Dahlman as Joutsamo came into the room.

"Let's take 'em in."

Korpi protested from beneath his hood. "Uhh…on what grounds?"

"You're suspected of murdering Tomi Salmela."

"Who's that? And who killed him?"

Joutsamo stopped in front of Korpi. A sharp kick in the ribs would do the scumbag some good, but the sergeant let him be. "We'll talk about it at the station," she said.

When Korpi launched into a whistled rendition of Leevi and the Leavings' "Would you shed tears of joy," Joutsamo recognized the verse.

"Would you shed tears of joy, if I banged you right and proper?"

With a smirk, she made up the next verse, "The whole damn town surrounded, the culprits in the hopper."

The SWAT guys were amused.

"Let's take these leavings downtown in separate cars," ordered Joutsamo.

Dahlman nodded to the others and they dragged the suspects to their feet. "You searched 'em, right?"

One of the SWAT officers who'd been standing guard the entire time nodded. "When we moved 'em out of the kitchen."

Joutsamo glanced into the fireplace where the flames from a couple of logs were dying down. Nothing else of interest in the living room.

She continued on into the kitchen. It wasn't very big. There were dirty dishes piled in the sink. A faded photograph of what was perhaps a ten-year-old boy fishing off the dock on a sunny summer day was taped to the window. Judging by the boy's clothing, the photo was taken sometime in the eighties. He didn't look like Korpi, so apparently the photo was part of the old woman's estate. Strange sense of humor for Korpi to just leave the pusher's picture there. Or maybe it just never occurred to him to move it.

Joutsamo looked out the window toward Suhonen's stakeout spot. It was far enough away that she wouldn't be able to make out anyone from here. Nice spot, she thought.

She inspected the downstairs bathroom, but nothing in particular caught her attention. She continued up the stairs to find a couple of bedrooms and a small chamber lined with bookshelves. The bedrooms proved uninteresting and the only remarkable item in the chamber was the computer, but Joutsamo left it alone. That was for the pros.

Hmm, thought Joutsamo. No bodies, no dope, nothing. She hadn't expected to find much, but of course there was some disappointment in raiding what appeared to be an empty house. Perhaps Kannas' men could turn up something.

CHAPTER 8
MONDAY, 4:00 P.M.
PASILA POLICE HEADQUARTERS

Korpi sat dressed in green coveralls in a bare, windowless interrogation room. The vents hummed. A computer and recording equipment rested on a worn veneer table. There were four chairs, two of which were empty. Joutsamo was seated opposite Korpi. Mikko Kulta was standing behind Joutsamo puffing on a cigarette.

"Shall we begin?" said Joutsamo as she pressed the record button. She recited the date and time. "Risto Korpi, you're being held under suspicion of the murder of Tomi Salmela, which took place yesterday afternoon. This is a preliminary interview. Do you have anything you'd like to say?"

Korpi started whistling the same Leevi and the Leavings song.

"That was funny once. Not anymore."

"Still funny to me," said Korpi, rubbing his bald head. He burst into a fit of artificial laughter, "Ha-ha-ha-haa!"

Joutsamo waited for him to finish. "Right. Do you wish to make a statement?"

Korpi's face hardened. "First off I'd like to state for the record that this preliminary interview is illegal according to the criminal statutes. It's a violation of my civil rights. Second, I want a lawyer. Third, as the homeowner, I demand to be a part of the search being conducted on my home in Kaarela at this very moment."

Joutsamo had initially intended to stop the recorder, but she decided to let it roll. "Alright, then. That concludes the interview. But I should note that preliminary interviews are indeed permitted under chapter 38 of the criminal statutes. Secondly, you should know that a lawyer will be provided when such can be procured. Thirdly, according to the deed on file, the house in question is not yours, but it's owned by the estate of Marjatta Saarnikangas. The attorney in charge of the estate has been notified of the search, and has not demanded anyone be present. But let me ask once more, do you have anything to say about Tomi Salmela's death?"

"No. Nothing. I'm done talking."

"So you won't even claim that you're innocent?"

"I'm done talking."

Joutsamo stopped the recorder and rose without a word. Outside the interrogation room she turned to the guard, "Take him to his cell. Don't let him talk to anyone."

* * *

It was nearing eight o'clock when Kannas came into Takamäki's office. The lieutenant was slaving away at his computer.

"Hey," Kannas growled.

"Hey."

Takamäki noticed the large plastic bag in the forensic investigator's hand. "Well?"

"Right. Interesting place," said Kannas, as he stepped inside and sat down. "Where to begin…"

"Hold on a sec." Takamäki got up and shouted down the hallway, "Joutsamo! My office!"

Joutsamo came in shortly.

"OK, go ahead," said Takamäki.

"Well, let's start with the car. Pretty shitty set of wheels at any rate, but preliminary evidence strongly links it to Korpi and Nyberg. Both of their fingerprints were found inside. We also found a third set of prints belonging to Jere Siikala, aka Guerrilla, who was arrested today. Found plenty of fibers, too, but since these guys are such fans of jeans, I doubt they'll get us anywhere. Too common."

"The fingerprints are a good thing. Jibes with our other evidence," said Joutsamo.

Takamäki wasn't so convinced. "Obviously the car has been in Korpi's possession for some time, so the significance of the prints to the murder case is questionable. What about the house?"

"Our investigation is still ongoing, but we found the same prints there, needless to say. We also turned up their arms stash." Kannas reached into the plastic bag and drew two smaller transparent bags. In one was a sawed-off shotgun while the other held a large caliber handgun. "The pistol's an interesting old classic. A Russian Stechkin M1951. Capable of firing on full automatic. I saw some of these for sale at the Hietalahti flea market in the early nineties, so one of the undercover boys and I picked one up. Not a bad piece. On full automatic you can't hit a damn thing, though. Recoil kicks the barrel up..."

"Ahem," Takamäki cut in. "What else?"

"Right. What I was getting to is that we don't know the history on these weapons. Yet. But we found a couple other interesting things. On the wall above one of the wardrobes was a sort of secret compartment where we found these." He held up two plastic bags. In one of them was a large quantity of cigarette butts, and in the other were several small Ziploc bags, each containing some dark flakes.

"What are those?" asked Joutsamo.

"Well, these are cigarette butts. But that there in the little bags is dried blood."

"Huh?"

"We haven't analyzed it yet, but I'd bet this stuff was intended to throw us off at some point when the time was right. In other words, Korpi or one of his goons has been collecting butts at the bars so they can muddle up the DNA trail. Same thing with this dried blood."

Takamäki shook his head. "He's pretty paranoid."

"Pretty clever, too. If DNA from fifty random people is found at the crime scene, then it's pretty easy to claim yours was intentionally planted too."

"And what about the laptop?" asked Joutsamo.

"Haven't looked at it yet. The IT guys get it tomorrow morning. But it only had Korpi's prints."

Takamäki thought for a moment. "So the only thing we have pertaining to the case is a blue Mazda and some fingerprints. Whose name is the car in?"

"Registered to the same Marjatta Saarnikangas that owned the house. She's dead and her son Juha is doing a four-year stint on drug charges," Joutsamo explained.

"We're taking it to a Mazda dealership to have them plug into the on-board computer and see how it's been driven the last few days," said Kannas. "At least it's new enough that we can get that."

Takamäki stroked his chin. "Good. We'll have to put together a lineup for Mari Lehtonen tomorrow. Then we can decide whether to hold onto Korpi."

"What about this Siikala?" asked Joutsamo.

"Did you interview him?"

"Couldn't get anything out of him. Said he was home all day Sunday watching TV."

"Did he say anything about Korpi's whereabouts?"

"Couldn't remember if he was there or not. So he's playing the same game as the rest of them."

"Right. Obviously we won't crack the case on interviews," said Takamäki, "The witness is our key. Let's meet with the prosecutor tomorrow. You round up the fillers for the lineup—plenty of bald cops to choose from."

* * *

Mari Lehtonen and twelve-year-old Laura Lehtonen were strolling along West Brahe Street toward Sture Street around nightfall. The rain was coming down hard enough that Mari had taken out her umbrella. Laura flipped up the hood of her raincoat.

The wind had stripped the wet leaves from the trees and scattered them on the sidewalk. A soccer team was practicing under the lights on the artificial turf at Brahe Field. The 3T streetcar rattled past, but otherwise, traffic was light.

Mari had been watching TV, but something had told her she should pick up Laura from theater rehearsals herself tonight. She couldn't quite place what it was, she just went. Probably just on edge after her visit to the police station.

Laura had been surprised when her mother appeared.

"Wanna stop for tea somewhere?" she asked hopefully.

Mari didn't hear the question. Her eyes were fixed on a couple of men in leather jackets approaching from the opposite direction. Now about fifty yards off, the men said nothing to one another, just stared at mother and daughter as they drew nearer.

Mari felt her pulse race as she considered her options. Should they cross the street?

"Did you hear what I said?" asked Laura, annoyed. "I wanted to tell you about the production—we got the framework ready today."

The gap had closed to thirty yards, close enough to make out the men's faces. The one on the left had a long ugly scar across his cheek. The other kept his hands in his jacket pockets.

The men were coming straight for them, and fast. Mari pulled her daughter to the edge of the sidewalk.

"What's this?"

She didn't answer. Ten yards now, and the men were looking straight at them. It occurred to Mari that she could jab them with the umbrella, and maybe shout for help from the soccer players.

They came within arm's reach when one of them turned to Mari and said, "Boo!"

Both roared with laughter as they continued on their way.

Idiots, she thought, suppressing her urge to cuss them out. She glanced back. The men were still walking.

She took a deep breath.

"What was that about?" asked Laura.

"I dunno. Couple idiots."

"Can we get some tea somewhere?"

Before Mari had the chance to respond, her cell phone rang. The caller was Anna Joutsamo.

TUESDAY, SEPTEMBER 19

CHAPTER 9
TUESDAY, 10:30 A.M.
PASILA POLICE HEADQUARTERS

Mari Lehtonen was standing behind a mirrored window. On the opposite side stood six men with shaved heads.

"Number one, could you please step forward to the line," said Lieutenant Ariel Kafka into the intercom. Takamäki had asked his colleague to conduct the proceedings. The protocol for police lineups explicitly stated that the officer conducting the proceedings must not know which of the subjects was the actual suspect.

Takamäki wasn't sure if Kafka knew Korpi. He certainly might, but he hadn't said anything, and his demeanor was perfectly impartial.

Number one stepped forward and Lehtonen shook her head.

Joutsamo was also in the room taking notes. Two video cameras were capturing the event, one trained on the lineup, the other on Lehtonen and Kafka.

"Thank you. Number two, please."

Lehtonen shook her head again, and did the same over the next minute as numbers three, four and five stepped up to the line.

"Number six, please," said Kafka.

Lehtonen nodded. "That's the one. He was in the car."

Number six was Korpi.

"Are you sure?"

"Absolutely positive."

Kafka returned to the microphone. "Thank you for participating. Please exit through the door on your left."

On the other side of the glass, the men filed out slowly.

Joutsamo finished off the last few words of her notes and Kafka stopped the video cameras.

"Alright. That's that," said Joutsamo, as she offered Lehtonen her hand. "Thanks again."

"What happens now?"

"We'll finish up the investigation and then send the case to the prosecutor. As I said before, you'll receive a summons from the court informing you of the date and time of the trial."

"That's it?"

"Yep. In court, the prosecutor will ask you a few questions and possibly show this video."

Kafka handed the tape to Joutsamo as he left. "No need for me anymore?"

"Nah. I'll just type up my notes and bring them for your sign-off."

"Sounds good."

Joutsamo turned to Lehtonen. "I'll show you out. You need a ride?"

Mari shook her head.

* * *

Helena Muuri, district prosecutor, was sitting in the VCU's conference room, her expression grim, as

84

usual. Takamäki didn't know if she was capable of a smile, at least he had never seen one on her.

Muuri was wearing a black-collared shirt and a gray blazer with a red bird-themed brooch. Takamäki likewise wore a blazer and tie. He always dressed up for meetings with district prosecutors.

Joutsamo came in wearing a sweater.

"Do you two know each other?" asked Takamäki. "Anna Joutsamo is my lead investigator on the case."

Muuri stood and the women shook hands. "Seems like we've met somewhere," said Joutsamo.

"Well, anyway, let's get to it," said Takamäki, and he explained the events of the last few days, as well as the highlights of the investigation from the time of the murder to the interrogation of the suspects. Muuri took notes in her notepad.

Takamäki was encouraged that the prosecutor was getting involved with the case before the investigation was closed. This way, she'd know the details much better than if a pile of paper just appeared on her desk.

Takamäki went over the police lineup as well.

"Tsk, tsk…" said Muuri. "Didn't you mention that you also showed Lehtonen photographs before the lineup?"

"Yes. Is that a problem?"

"Well, nothing serious, but you can only ask a witness to identify a suspect once. That happened when you showed her the photographs. The lineup is irrelevant since the witness already identified the suspect earlier."

"That we didn't know," said Joutsamo. "Normally once is enough, but we just thought we'd double check."

"It just means that the police lineup is inadmissible. It doesn't really matter, since the witness had already identified the suspect from a photograph."

"Alright," said Takamäki. "Though I'd imagine using a lineup would better ensure due process for the suspect, since photographs tend to be older and less accurate."

"True enough, but the rules are explicit. Do you have a motive for the crime?"

"No," said Takamäki. "Nobody's talking. We found cocaine in Tomi Salmela's apartment, which could be a possible motive."

"Could be, but motives aren't always clear cut, either. The forensic evidence against Nyberg is pretty unambiguous, but with Korpi there are still quite a few question marks. Mari Lehtonen's account puts Korpi near the scene of the crime, but what level of involvement did he really have? It's a difficult question."

"Right."

Muuri continued to reflect, "What we know is that Korpi was in the car with the killer, who left the vehicle, committed the crime and returned to the car. Korpi then drove away and dropped off the murderer somewhere else in the city. We have no information on Korpi's activities after that. Essentially what we need is proof that Korpi was complicit in the crime, or even ordered Nyberg to commit it. The problem is that Korpi's a professional criminal, so it's unlikely you'll get a single word out of him in the interrogations."

"Same goes for Nyberg."

"Right," said Muuri, returning to her papers. "With that in mind, we can assume that Korpi must have something to hide. His activities would likely cross the threshold for a murder charge, and he'd certainly be an accessory."

"He's the leader of a criminal organization where nothing is done without his approval," said Takamäki. "And he has a long record."

"Good points," said Muuri. "And this is a good angle to focus on in the investigation. Can Korpi be tied more closely to Nyberg? Do we have evidence from previous investigations clearly indicating that Nyberg takes orders from Korpi? What about Nyberg's weapon? Can it be tied to Korpi? Did Nyberg ever live in the same house in Kaarela? What about the drug trade in Korpi's organization? His funds and other assets?"

Joutsamo was jotting everything down in her notepad. This was plenty to go on, thought Takamäki. They'd need help from Narcotics and the Financial Crimes Division. Takamäki knew from experience that the drug bosses commonly moved their assets abroad, while keeping some funds in the form of loans to street pushers and others. This way, the police wouldn't be able to confiscate them, but the money was always accessible with the help of hired muscle.

Muuri went on, "This is also important because Nyberg will almost certainly try to exonerate his boss in court and shoulder the blame for everything. At that point we'd need some facts to sling at Korpi. Something that will stick, not just generic observations about criminal organizations."

"We'll do our best," said Takamäki.

"I have to wonder, though. If this Korpi is such a high-ranking boss, why is he chauffeuring some guy around on a hit job. Why didn't they take care of this

Tomi Salmela by some other means if it was so important?"

"You got me," said Joutsamo.

"Is it possible he truly wasn't aware of Nyberg's intent?"

"Possible," said Takamäki, "but if that were the case you'd think he'd say so instead of insisting on keeping his mouth shut. We'll try to find out in the interrogations and otherwise."

A momentary silence fell over the room.

"About your witness, this Mari Lehtonen…"

"Yes?"

"You haven't promised her anonymity, have you? Or that she could testify behind one-way glass or anything?"

"No," said Joutsamo. "She's understandably a little nervous, but who wouldn't be. We haven't talked about anything like that. All I promised was that no address or personal information would appear in the case files."

"That's fine. But in court we'll need her to show her face and point out who she saw in the car."

"Then that's what she'll do," said Joutsamo.

"And what about her safety?" Muuri asked. "She's so central to the case here that we have to consider whether Korpi's gang represents a threat to her. They'll know her identity once they receive the case files."

"Right," said Takamäki.

"You'll certainly have to keep an eye on that. Witnesses have been threatened and blackmailed for much less. And if this organization is capable of killing competing dealers, then I'd think there's potential for violence toward the witness."

"That'll depend on how good a chance Korpi thinks he has at an acquittal," said Takamäki.

"Well, I'll chat with Lehtonen about it."

"But don't scare her, of course."

"Will do," said Joutsamo. "Won't do, that is."

* * *

Suhonen was driving a rustbucket VW Golf eastbound on Helsinki Avenue. He passed Brahe Field on the right. The Corner Pub wasn't far off, but he wasn't headed there. Maybe he'd stop by later in the evening to see what he'd find out. The lunchtime crowd was just a bunch of blowhards anyway. Loose talk on last night's petty thefts didn't interest him.

Actually, his intentions had nothing to do with work. Maybe in a way they did, since Suhonen had met her while on a stakeout at a downtown pub on Friday night. Deputy Chief Skoog had decided to crack down on the Subutex street trade, so Suhonen had volunteered to help bust a drug ring that was hawking it out of the bars. The operation targeted a number of dealers across various locations where the pills were known to be peddled, and Suhonen wound up staking out a Belgian pub. No traffic in Subutex that night, but at the bar he had met Raija.

Raija was about five years Suhonen's junior, and an employee of an insurance agency on Aleksander Street. The evening had culminated in a long kiss at around midnight before Suhonen had to go back to the station for a wrap-up meeting on the sting. They had arranged to meet again for coffee on Tuesday.

Back at the station, Suhonen had checked her background. Such caution was necessary, since gangs were constantly trying to infiltrate the police by putting women into bed with them. Nothing in Raija Mattila's background gave reason for alarm. All that turned up was a speeding ticket from a few years back; and she'd been telling the truth about not being married.

Suhonen parked his car near the coffee shop where they had agreed to meet. The spot suited Raija just fine, as it was only a couple of minutes from the Kaisaniemi subway station.

Suhonen arrived ten minutes early, but Raija was already at a table, waving him in. She smiled and whisked back her blonde hair. Suhonen gave a nod and walked to the table. "Hey," he said.

"Hi," she chirped.

"You're early."

"Yeah, nothing pressing at work. But so are you."

"Yeah, pretty slow on my end, too." He hadn't told her what he did, but neither had he lied. "Can I get you a coffee?"

"Yes. Please," she smiled.

"Cream?"

"No, just black."

Good, he thought. He liked people who took their coffee straight. "Wanna sandwich or something?"

"No, thanks. I had some chicken salad at work."

A few minutes later, Suhonen returned to the table with two coffees and sat down. Raija started to dig some money out of her purse, but Suhonen stopped her.

"I had a nice time on Friday," she said, still smiling.

"Me too." Suhonen was about to complain about having had to leave, but that would leave an open question as to why, which he didn't care to answer. He sidestepped. "You make it home all right?"

"Yeah. No problem."

Suhonen tasted his coffee, clearly better than the station's. Or maybe it was her. She took a sip from her own cup, and he wondered if she found it better than the insurance company's. She must—office coffee was pretty much all the same, somehow tied to the workplace.

But so was Suhonen's life. There he sat, at a table with a radiant woman, and all he could think about was how to avoid talk of his job.

"You know," she said. "You're a pretty mysterious guy. I've been wondering all weekend about what it is you do."

Well, here we go, thought Suhonen. He didn't want to lie. "I'm a cop."

"Really? I thought so, but I wasn't sure." Her whole face was lit up now. "Were you working then on Friday? All you had was two beers all night."

"Not then, but I was over the weekend. Not smart to get hammered before a shift." A little white lie was okay, he thought.

"What kind of cop?"

"I catch bad guys," he said, grinning over the rim of his cup. In a way, it wasn't so bad that his job had come up, though talking about police work was always a double-edged sword. Some women were repelled by it, some attracted to it.

"Violent Crimes Unit?"

"Yep."

"You don't look like the kind of cops you see on TV."

"That's why they don't let me on camera."

Suhonen's phone rang, and he glanced at Raija. She urged him to answer. Not that his glance was anything more than a gesture, since he would've taken the call in any case. The caller was Salmela.

"Yeah," he answered. "Right... Well, no... It can't wait? Alright. I'll be there." He hung up the phone.

"Work?" she asked.

Suhonen nodded. "Yup."

"Urgent?"

"As always. But listen, I wondered if you might like to go to the theater sometime. A friend of mine has a part at the Ryhmä Theater and says they have some good stuff going right now."

"When?"

"When would work for you?"

"Whenever."

"There's a show on Thursday. We could go out for a beer afterwards, and maybe some pizza beforehand or something," Suhonen said, sort of hesitating.

"Sure. That sounds good."

"Good. I'll get the tickets and give you a call."

"You gotta go?"

Suhonen nodded. "But I'll see you on Thursday."

"Mmm-hm," she said, taking a sip of coffee as Suhonen got up. She looked down at her watch and shook her head.

* * *

Two guards brought Korpi into the same interrogation room where Joutsamo had interviewed him the previous day. One of them was waiting in the room when Takamäki stepped in. He gave Takamäki an inquiring look, wondering if he should leave, but Takamäki signaled for him to stay.

"Hello," said Takamäki.

"Pig," Korpi snorted.

"Takamäki, rather. I'm the head investigator on your case."

"I ain't saying nothin'."

"That so? Well, let me brief you anyway... You're being held on suspicion of the murder of Tomi Salmela."

Korpi narrowed his eyes. "On what fucking grounds?"

"I thought you weren't gonna say anything. I'd think you'd know by now that all we need to detain you is reasonable suspicion. Your lawyer's waiting out in the hall. I'll let him in."

Korpi sat sulking behind the table. Takamäki stood and signaled for the guard to open the door. On his way out, he passed Korpi's defense attorney, Mats Martin. The tall, thin man was nearing fifty and had on a gray tailored suit with a well-chosen navy blue tie and crisp white shirt. His hair was blond and his skin still bore a hint of summer bronze.

Takamäki nodded as he exited.

"Just knock on the door when you're ready," the guard told Martin as he shut the door.

Martin set his briefcase on the wooden table and sat down. He looked Korpi sharply in the eyes. "Haven't seen you for a while."

"Guess not."

"What's this about?"

"Just found out they're trying to pin me with a murder. Which I didn't commit."

"What have you told the police?"

"Nothing."

Martin opened his briefcase and took out a notepad. "Well, you know me well enough to know my first question."

Korpi nodded.

Martin continued, "No use playing games. That just wastes everybody's time. I want you to answer honestly so I can build your defense. And let me be clear: I won't ask this question again, because if I find out you're lying, I'll drop the case." Martin's eyes met Korpi's. "Did you do it?"

"No."

"Did you have any role in it?"

"No."

"And that's the truth?"

A seasoned attorney, Martin had developed his own style. It didn't bother him if a killer got off the hook, but he himself had to get the suspect's honest account of what happened.

"This is important. I want the truth. Because if you lie, it'll backfire on you later, and then I won't be able to help you."

"That's the truth."

Martin nodded. "Okay. So in principle, there's nothing to worry about. All we need to do is find out what they have on you."

"Nothing," Korpi snorted.

"With all due respect, cut the bullshit," said Martin. "Get real. These cops are hardened pros, just like you. Sure, they want you in prison, but they know damn well it's not gonna happen without clear and convincing evidence. The fact that you're in custody means they have something on you, but they're not gonna let us in on it because that could mess up their case. Our number one priority is to figure out what that something is, and the only person who would know is you."

"I told you, I don't know."

Korpi had always known what a hardnose Martin was. Still, he didn't much like his pushy style, even if the guy might have a point from time to time.

"Well, I'll tell you what the police just told me. On Sunday, one Tomi Salmela was shot in his home and the police suspect that Nyberg shot him. Nyberg has his own counsel, but I haven't consulted with her—yet. So tell me what happened after the arrest."

"Not much. They gave me a grilling yesterday and put me in a lineup this morning."

"Which tells us they probably have an eyewitness. Maybe you and Nyberg were seen together somewhere," said Martin, and he searched his memory for past murder cases involving accomplices.

"Maybe. So what?"

"With your record, the fact that you know the shooter is sufficient grounds for arrest."

"I had no idea Nyberg…"

Martin didn't let him finish. "That doesn't interest me. You already told me you had nothing to do with the shooting."

"Fuck. The car Nyberg's been driving was there in front of the house in Kaarela. If I had anything to do with that junkie's murder, that car would have been toast in about two seconds. And why the fuck would I be driving someone around on hit jobs? Goddamnit!" Korpi slammed his fist down on the table.

The lawyer looked Korpi smartly in the eyes, "So were you in that car with him on Porvoo Street?"

"No."

"Are you lying?"

"No."

"Well, then you have two choices. Either you tell that to the cops now, or to the court later."

"I ain't telling the pigs a damn thing, that's for sure."

"Then it'll have to come up in court. But this lineup means someone thought they saw you, though we still don't know if they actually picked you. If you weren't there, then nobody could have recognized you anyway."

Korpi kept his eyes locked on Martin's. "So who supposedly saw me?"

"I don't have that information, but it'll come out in due time, once we get the case files."

"The son-of-a-bitch will never make it to court."

"Now there's a stupid idea. Again, we don't really know what the lineup was about, and if something happened to the witness before your court date you'd definitely take the fall for it. The cops will figure out a way to pin it on you for sure.

"I always like to be honest with my clients. Nyberg is a member of your outfit, so if he gets convicted for murder, your odds are about fifty-fifty of taking the rap too. The police will bust their asses on this case, but if you say you're innocent, we have a good chance at winning an acquittal, eyewitness or not."

"So you're saying leave the witness alone."

"Absolutely," said Martin. "Eyewitness accounts are pretty easy to poke holes in once we're in the courtroom."

CHAPTER 10
TUESDAY, 2:10 P.M.
KULOSAARI HARBOR

Salmela tossed Suhonen a red life vest from the bottom of a small fishing boat.

"Put it on."

"Fishing?" said Suhonen, eyeing the rack of rods on the gunwale. The sixteen-foot aluminum boat was docked just off the East Highway. The rain had stopped, but the clouds still lingered.

"Why, you busy?"

Suhonen considered briefly. "No, not really," he said. At least not anymore, since he'd already ditched Raija at the coffee shop.

"We'll just troll around for a few hours."

Only now did Suhonen notice that the rods were stouter than the usual ones. He stripped off his leather jacket and proceeded to pull on some coveralls. Salmela was fastening what appeared to be a fish finder and GPS unit to the rear side of the windshield, just adjacent to the wheel.

"Whose boat?"

"A friend's," said Salmela. "Borrowed it for the day."

Suhonen got his coveralls on and glanced over at a nearby concession stand. "What about something to eat..."

"No need. I got coffee and a few sandwiches."

Suhonen climbed into the boat and looked at the rods. "Deep sea fishing, or what?"

"Yup. The big boys—salmon, maybe."

"What's the weather gonna be like?"

"Nothing to worry about." Salmela started the forty-horse outboard. "Not blowing too much. Untie the rope, will ya?"

Suhonen did so and Salmela backed the boat away from the dock, swung it around and headed out.

"I don't have a license," said Suhonen.

Once outside of the harbor buoys, Salmela opened the throttle and the wind bit against Suhonen's face. "Doesn't matter. Neither do I."

"You know some good spots?"

"Nah, but the GPS does. My buddy saved the coordinates for some nice underwater gullies. The fish like to hang along the rim where the cool water rises up. The gullies are tough to find, and there's still no guarantees."

"That's for sure."

"Could be the water's still too warm. Hey, grab some coffee if you want."

Suhonen nodded and rustled a thermos out of Salmela's rucksack. He filled the cup only halfway because of the pitching of the boat.

Within half an hour, Salmela had managed to pilot the boat to the outer islands west of Helsinki. She was planing smoothly now in the shallow chop. On a few occasions, the boat hit the swells at just the right angle to shower Suhonen with water. It felt good. He had never been an avid boater. Cars and motorcycles were more his style. But this wasn't so bad.

The GPS unit beeped, signaling that they had arrived at the first spot. Salmela eased up on the throttle to a couple of knots and switched on the fish finder. Suhonen watched as Salmela dug a planer board out from beneath a bench, tossed it into the water and rigged it to the boat with some plastic line.

"We'll rig the line to the leader on the planer with these clips…" Salmela muttered as Suhonen looked on. The idea was for the planer board to keep the lines far enough apart that they wouldn't get tangled as they trolled along. "You take the wheel. Just hold the course."

Salmela took the first rod and dropped the lure into the water. It fluttered along easily next to the boat. He let out the line about fifty feet, made a small loop and clamped it with a spring-loaded clip that had a ring for the planer leader. Salmela let out the line till the ring reached almost to the planer, then he propped the rod up in the holder.

Within five minutes, all four lines were in the water. "Once you get a hit, the fish will jerk the clip off the line and you just reel him in. That's it. You take the first hit, I'll take the next. Just remember to brace yourself when you take the rod out of the holder."

Suhonen began to suspect that this wasn't a friend's boat after all. Salmela seemed to know his way around it well enough. Or maybe he had more than borrowed it.

"What's next?" Suhonen asked as Salmela took the helm.

"We troll around for a few hours and hope for a bite."

"You brought a knife, right? If we catch something?"

"Figured you could do the honors with your Glock. You brought it, right?"

Suhonen smiled. The boat was cruising along smoothly at a couple of knots, the planer keeping the lines neatly spaced outboard of the gunwales.

"Heh," Suhonen began. "So this one time one of our detectives ends up in a foot chase with this guy who must have been some kinda track star or something, and slowly but surely he starts losing the guy. You know, it's really embarrassing if the bad guys get away on foot, so he starts cursing the fact that there's never a dog around when you need one. So he barks real loud a few times and hollers, 'Stop! Police K-9! Stop or I'll release the dog!'"

"He barks?"

"Ruff! Ruff!"

"You're shitting me."

"He really did. So the runner stops in his tracks and lays face down on the pavement in the X-position, all on his own. Detective comes up, slaps on the cuffs and hauls the guy up. He goes, 'Where's the dog?' The detective says, 'They already took him back to the wagon...he's got a mean streak.'"

"Ohhh. That's rough," said Salmela with a laugh. "I like dog stories. I ever tell you about the time I was lifting stuff from this grocery store about ten years back? Might have been earlier, but anyhow this security guard almost busted me. I managed to split just in time, but he spots me heading into the woods on the other side of a little field. So I dive under a tree and hide. Just then this squad car pulls up and they start talking to the security guard. The guard opens the hatch on his wagon and out pops this huge fucking dog. I still remember its name because the guard kept going, 'Search, Nemo, search!' So the dog takes off straight towards me, just jerking at his leash. The cops come slogging through the mud after them and I think one of them lost a shoe in the muck. I'm pretty much scared stiff and about to give myself up when the dog stops about thirty feet off and takes a shit. Once he finished up, he just wanted back in the wagon. The slack-jawed cops just watched the whole show and finally headed back to the road cursing up a storm. So then the security guard's petting the dog and one of the cops asks him, 'So…you train him all by yourself?'"

Both men laughed.

Salmela dug a small silver flask out of his breast pocket and offered it to Suhonen, "French cognac."

"No, thanks."

Salmela took a swig.

"So how you been?" asked Suhonen. Already at the dock it had been obvious that Salmela had set up the fishing trip so they could have a little privacy to talk. Suhonen also knew Salmela wasn't going to bring up his son's death himself. He would have to be the one to ask.

Salmela took another swig and sighed. "Like shit. I spent all day yesterday trying to play detective… With Korpi and all, but then last night it hit me hard. That's why I…"

"I know." Suhonen nodded as he looked his friend in the eyes. Salmela thumbed away a tear.

"Just got to thinking about all the shit I should have done. What I could've done to keep this from happening. How I could've been a better dad. Not that I had much choice with the ex and me always going at it. But I could've tried harder. Or should have, at least."

Suhonen had encountered many people grappling with the death of a loved one. For some, the grief spiraled into overwhelming emotional problems.

Salmela seemed ashamed of neither having been the kind of father he would have wanted to be nor having taught his son the ways of the criminal world. But the past was gone.

Suhonen thought for a moment. Salmela had spent time in prison, had seen the darker side of life. Maybe it was best to just be straight with him. That was Suhonen's style anyway.

"Yeah, grief ain't easy," he said. "Some struggle with it their whole lives. For you it's just starting. But there's one thing you need to keep in mind: letting go of grief is hard because you can't help but think it's an insult to the dead. You shouldn't stop grieving today or tomorrow, but soon. And that doesn't mean you have to forget your boy. Those memories will always be with you."

"They were pretty good times," said Salmela, wiping tears openly now. "Damn, this fucking wind…" he said with a sad smile.

Suhonen nodded.

"But the more you get to thinking, the more you start to regret," said Salmela. "I've made a lotta dumb decisions."

"And that's what they'll always be," said Suhonen, as he put his hand on his friend's shoulder. "You can't think like that…in hindsight. Life is pretty random—some days are good, some bad."

"Feels like the bad have been coming outta my ears lately."

Suhonen kept his hand on Salmela's shoulder. "Well, then they are. That just makes the good that much better…like this fishing trip."

Salmela laughed. "Yeah, right. But tell me this…"

"What?"

"You say it's all random…"

"Right, and nothing you can do about it. No point blaming yourself for what happened to Tomi. You didn't get drunk and drive him off a bridge. You didn't bounce his head off the pavement. Nyberg came to the door and shot him."

Salmela looked Suhonen sharply in the eyes. "I know all that. I'm talking about something else. Back when we did that attic job in Lahti. I got busted and you didn't, 'cause you were sick at home. How you make sense of that?"

"Pure chance. Had I gone with you guys, I doubt I'd be alive right now. It would've changed the course of my life. No doubt about it."

"Yeah. Sometimes I wonder how you're still kicking, being a cop and all."

"I'm not so sure I'm better off for it, either. At least you got the memories of your son. All I got are a bunch of random women and motorcycles."

"But you're a hero, a police officer."

"It's a shitty job... Ain't much different than a criminal's—except the government gives us the guns, so we don't have to buy them off the black market."

Salmela waited a while before responding, "I've always considered you a hero."

Suhonen laughed. "Right."

"If there's anything I can be proud of, it's that I can call you a friend."

Suhonen gulped. "Getting kinda serious here."

"Gotta be serious sometimes. If you don't, you never realize what really matters."

"Yeah...you're right."

Slowly, the forty-horse engine pushed the boat onward through an empty sea. The fish weren't biting, but the coffee was good.

* * *

Takamäki was on the phone when Joutsamo stepped into his office at Pasila police headquarters. "Hockey? Sure, I can bring him," Takamäki was saying as he glanced at Joutsamo. "Least I think so... Let's see, one-thirty now. I suppose around three I'll know for sure... Yeah, I'll be there... Bye."

"Driving the hockey shuttle?"

"Among others. How's things with our interview subjects?"

"Neither one's much of a talker."

"No surprise."

Joutsamo sat down on the opposite side of Takamäki's desk. "What about Guerrilla? Hold onto him or let him go? The twenty-four-hour holding period will be up soon."

"The prosecutor's position on that was pretty clear. And I'm not arguing, either. He wasn't in the car and nobody's fingered him, but still, if he's not Korpi's right hand, then he's his left. If the hit was planned, then what are the chances he would've known?"

"I'd say pretty good."

Takamäki looked his best detective in the eyes. "How good? What standard of proof are we looking at?"

"What, this the lieutenant-level test?"

"No. You already know I think you ought to go for lieutenant. Just mulling some things over."

"Like what?"

"Like might Siikala cross the threshold of reasonable suspicion for murder based on the fact that the NBI classifies Korpi's outfit as an organized crime ring and Siikala is high up in the ranks."

"So you want to keep him?"

"Well, no, actually. If he's not talking, he's no use to us. But might he talk to someone else?"

Joutsamo nodded. "I see where you're going. Phone tap or bug?"

"Why not both? Let's start with a phone tap and see how far-reaching Korpi's outfit really is. That might tell us if there's any cross-over between their contacts and Tomi Salmela's."

"With Korpi and Nyberg both in jail, it stands to reason Siikala might be up for a promotion. That might put him more in the jurisdiction of Narcotics, though."

"I'll have a chat with them. If it starts looking more like their case, then they can have it. But as long as you're in agreement, I'll say we have reasonable suspicion to suspect Siikala and that we're only letting him out for strategic purposes. Then we'll get a warrant for a phone tap and see who he calls."

That made Joutsamo pause. "And what if he just gets a new prepaid SIM card?"

"Didn't he just have some old beat-up Nokia? Least that's what I remember seeing in the report."

"Yeah. I don't remember the model, but it was old."

"Well, at any rate, if he bought a new SIM card he'd still have to turn on his old phone to save the numbers onto it, so the phone will connect to the network then. Once we see that, we'll just wait for the new prepaid number to come up in the same location and get the new number."

"I already copied all the numbers from his cellphone directory."

"But the court won't grant warrants for those numbers in relation to this case. Maybe Narcotics could get one, but not us. So based on the info we have so far, the trail seems to end with Siikala."

Joutsamo nodded. "OK. Fair enough. So you'll get the warrant for Siikala's phones and I'll set up the tap. You think Siikala's phone calls for round-the-clock surveillance?" she asked, conscious of the resources such an operation could devour.

"Let's assess it on a daily basis. Initially, at least in the daytime, we'll have someone listen in live so we can see when he changes his SIM card, but no need to burn the midnight oil. The case is not at a critical stage at this point," said Takamäki. All conversations and call data would be saved on a computer hard drive anyway.

"Alright. In other news, Kannas says they're still working on the laptop, but that they did pick up some information from the Mazda's onboard computer."

"What's that?"

"The engine was started on Sunday afternoon about three o'clock and ran till almost five. Went about thirty miles."

"So that supports our case."

"It sat idling somewhere for a while, but we don't know where."

"And the gas tank?"

"Half full, so I don't think we'll find them on any service station cameras."

"Well, we'll have time to think about that for a day or two. Some other places might have got them on camera. But this isn't the kind of case where we'd really need to determine the car's route. We have Nyberg's picture from the store by Salmela's apartment and a statement from an eyewitness that puts Korpi in the car. That'll take us a ways."

"Hopefully far enough for a conviction," said Joutsamo.

"Well, sometimes it's a sprint, but just as often it ends up being a marathon. Anybody heard anything from Suhonen, by the way?"

Joutsamo shook her head. "Nope. One more thing: I'm having a chat with Mari Lehtonen this evening. She wanted to meet."

CHAPTER 11
TUESDAY, 5.30 P.M.
GULF OF FINLAND

The bait had been in the water for three hours already without a single bite. No coffee left, either.

"You got anything going on tonight?" asked Salmela.

"I'm in no hurry," said Suhonen, despite the boredom that had set in after the novelty of a majestic, desolate sea had faded. His life vest kept out the cold and he could piss in the sea—all was well.

They didn't broach the topic of Salmela's son again, nor any other difficult subjects. On their last coffee break, Suhonen had promised to help with the funeral and other arrangements, but that having been settled, he didn't care to bring it up again. Of course, he was more than willing to continue that conversation if that was what Salmela wanted. But Suhonen had said his piece about grief and getting over it, and there wasn't much more he wanted to add.

"Let's give it another hour," said Salmela. "Should make land before nightfall."

"Fair enough."

"Who knows, might even get something once it gets a little darker."

"What, like a fine for fishing without a license?"

Salmela was quiet, which made Suhonen pensive.

After a minute, Salmela spoke up again. "About Tomi…"

"Uh-huh."

"I heard some things that might interest you."

Now it was Suhonen's turn to keep quiet. Of course it interested him, but not more than his friend's grief. He allowed Salmela to continue.

"I heard Tomi had got mixed up in some… Well…why the fuck should I sugarcoat it—only fair I give it to you straight. He was selling coke to a bunch of soap stars. Business was booming, and he was looking to expand. Heard that from one of his buddies."

"What buddy?" said Suhonen. The tip could be related to a possible motive, so Suhonen tried to ferret out a bit more. He doubted Salmela would reveal his source, but he wouldn't lie either.

"Can't tell you, but it came direct from the source. Put a piece to the guy's head last night. Pretty sure he was telling the truth."

"Okay. What'd he say?"

"Tomi had somehow managed to buy two pounds of coke. The guy didn't say where, but it was all on credit. Up till then he'd been buying maybe a half pound a pop max, so he was pretty damn psyched. He'd managed to sell some of it to the same soap stars; word got around, you know, and he started selling to others, too."

Suhonen nodded. "So someone was using Tomi to get a piece of the market."

"Pretty fucking reckless if you ask me...to think that's gonna fly. You can bet they ain't pros. Probably some yuppie fucks, or maybe a foreign operator testing the market."

"And wound up stepping on Korpi's toes."

"Exactly. Sold better shit for less. Coke's a hot commodity."

"Finland must be getting rich."

The theory made sense. Tomi Salmela had started to compete with Korpi's outfit, so they had to get rid of him. In this light, his murder was hardly surprising. Korpi and Nyberg had no choice but to make an example of him.

"Shitty deal."

"Damn right. That's why I should've taught the kid how the drug trade really works... Taught him to shoot. Not that many dealers got the balls to pull the trigger, and the ones who do are the badasses like Nyberg."

"Quite a few crime bosses got their start as hit men."

"But they ain't that smart. They might have balls, but they ain't got brains. That's why the cops got it so easy. If criminals had some actual intelligence, maybe they wouldn't..."

"Break the law," said Suhonen with a smile. For a moment he entertained the idea of trying to turn Salmela from the dark side. Likely a naive notion. Not that Salmela had ever had a choice in the matter. Anyways, he didn't care to lose his best informant.

"Or they'd start a company."

"Some have."

"So which one am I?" Salmela asked.

Suhonen declined to answer because he had a more important question. "So who told you this? If we can get him to testify, Korpi would get life."

"Can't tell you…no way."

"Can you ask him?"

"Uh-uh."

"Lean on him?"

"No," said Salmela, visibly irritated. "He's not an idiot. You don't testify against Korpi if you wanna live… That would just be fucking stupid."

"You're actually a victim in this case, you know. You could testify."

"I don't think so. My ex can sue Korpi if she wants, but as long as the asshole rots in a cell I'm OK with that. I had my chance to face him over in Kaarela the day after the murder, and I made up my mind—I never want to see him again."

Suhonen nodded and glanced at the lines. Guess the fish weren't biting.

* * *

The sky was growing dark as Joutsamo strode down the street toward the mammoth concrete structures of Merihaka, the drab, gray pinnacle of early 1970s civil engineering. A cold wind swept briskly off the sea. The sergeant had parked near the Häme Street intersection in the first available spot. On the left were the glowing green signs of the employment office.

Joutsamo pushed on toward the north end of a tall red-brick building that had originally been a munitions factory. Off and on it had served as the offices of a construction company, and then as an immigration office. The building had suffered from severe mold problems. Now it housed various firms and tax administration offices, but Joutsamo was only interested in the Czech restaurant on the north end.

It was ten minutes till eight and the meeting was set for eight o'clock sharp. Joutsamo had initially had doubts about the location, before deciding it was fine.

She stepped into the vestibule of the Milenka Restaurant and paused as she came through the door. The bar was on the right and two adjacent dining rooms on the left. She unzipped her coat, walked up to the bar and ordered a cup of tea from the thickly-whiskered bartender, who brought over a cup of steaming water. After paying him, she chose a packet of orange tea from a large basket of assorted flavors. The atmosphere in the bar was nothing short of torpid.

Joutsamo scanned the restaurant for Lehtonen and spotted her wearing a pale sweater at a corner table on the left. She looked up and nodded at Joutsamo.

The interior of the restaurant was a shade nicer than your typical pub. Some art was hanging from the walls and a massive window formed the back wall. Maybe it lent a more artistic air.

Joutsamo steadied her cup as she walked to the table, then took off her jacket and sat. Lehtonen had her paper open to the sudoku page. Joutsamo had done a few of the puzzles herself, but complained that the easy ones were too easy and the difficult ones ridiculously hard.

The women greeted one another.

"You have kids?" asked Lehtonen once Joutsamo was seated.

"No. Why?"

"You're single?" she asked, glancing at Joutsamo's ring finger.

"You're not wearing a ring either, but yes, I'm single."

"Why?"

Joutsamo had no interest in being cross-examined about her private life, but neither did she want to rile their star witness. She bought herself some time with a sip of hot tea. "I don't know. There have been some guys…but…I don't know. Sounds kinda dumb, but I just don't think I've met the right one."

"Well, nothing wrong with that. You should be glad, actually. My ex-husband was a very good actor. Knew how to pretend like he really loved me. And I bought it. Toward the end he didn't bother acting anymore. And when I stopped loving him, his genuine hatred came out. The change was sudden for both of us."

Joutsamo knew the guy from police records. She had checked into Lehtonen's background and found Anton Teittinen's name. The man had a laundry list of petty crimes, which revealed a lot. Smart criminals didn't commit petty offenses, so when there were a lot of them, it usually meant drugs or booze— probably both. A mug shot of a mean-looking, slightly bloated man with a pockmarked face seemed to support the assumption.

"You mentioned a restraining order earlier."

"I did finally get one. Oddly enough he obeyed it, especially after the police picked him up around the corner a few times for getting too close. That's when we moved."

"Good to hear the system works every now and then. Not always the case."

Joutsamo sipped her tea. In a way she was glad the conversation had shifted to Lehtonen, which was the point of the meeting anyway. Not to mention that she hated talking about her own life. As to why, well, that was a sore subject.

"The only good thing that came out of my marriage was Laura."

"I hear that a lot…that kids are good."

"The jerk threatened to beat me up a couple times. Naively, I thought, well, the girl needs her dad and, oh, it's all right, after yet another of his perfectly-crafted apologies. Some women apparently tolerate it for years. Twice was enough for me. I've always believed that you can forgive anything once. The first time, okay, maybe he was just being stupid; could've been a misunderstanding, or he was high or something. But the second time is my limit. End of story. And when I make up my mind, it stays that way."

"Sounds pretty smart to me. How's his relationship with your daughter?"

"She never had any problems with him. Actually, he was really involved in her life when she was a pre-schooler, but after the divorce I cut off their relationship. No Christmas, no birthday presents, no Father's Day cards. We just sort of melted out of his life."

Joutsamo got the impression this was a woman who never looked back, and such a mindset may have been the only way to escape such a situation. "How old was Laura then," said Joutsamo, though she already knew the answer from the records. Laura was born in 1994 and the divorce happened in 2000.

"She was six. She didn't understand, and I didn't explain. I lied to her face, actually. I mean, she knows about the divorce, but I've kept the details under wraps. We don't have a single picture of him anywhere."

"That's understandable, in a way."

"Did I tell you why we had to meet here?"

Joutsamo shook her head.

"Laura has theater practice next door. Over there at the Theater Academy. She's really excited about acting. One of the instructors at the academy actually started the group to research how twelve- to sixteen-year-old kids learn acting. She's worked with school kids before and now she's writing a dissertation about the play. Doing interviews and such. Getting kids to memorize the lines from some random play can be tough, but the idea here is for the kids to write the play themselves and kind of internalize their lines that way. Opening night is in December."

"Sounds good," said Joutsamo, though it didn't much interest her.

"I know. But the problem is that the project started at the beginning of August, and before this police thing, Laura used to walk home from here every night. Now I feel like I have to come meet her."

Before Joutsamo could respond, Lehtonen stood up, "Can I get you a beer?"

Joutsamo shook her head. "No. I'm driving."

"I'll just get one for myself."

A minute later, Lehtonen returned with a beer and a glass. She sat back down and continued before Joutsamo could say anything. "Well, I was honest with you about my story. Now you can be honest with me…so do Laura and I have anything to be afraid of?"

Joutsamo looked her keenly in the eye. She was glad they had gotten back to official business. "To be honest, I don't know."

"Would you tell me if there was?"

"If I really wanted to lie, I'd just say there wasn't. But you're a key witness in the case and this Risto Korpi is a professional criminal. That's not a good combination, but from experience I can tell you that these types go after informants first. Then of course the cops, the prosecutors and the judges. It's extremely rare for someone to target an ordinary citizen."

"Rare…" said Lehtonen. "How rare?"

"I'll be honest with you. At this point, neither Korpi nor anybody else knows anything about you, but the defense will get the case files once they're ready. That might take a couple months. At that point, they'll have your name, but since your address and other personal information are confidential, finding you would be difficult. Not impossible, but difficult, and at that point, Korpi will still be in jail."

"Okay. At least you're being honest."

"And once they finally get your name, the bitterness has usually lost its edge."

"Usually?"

"Usually. I couldn't put it more frankly."

"You seem pretty serious about this."

"You better believe I'm serious about these things. You saw the mugshots when you were down at the station the first time. If you remember, there were about twenty of them. From what we know, that's Korpi's entire gang. Except for the upper ranks, none of them even know they're working for him. In his outfit, the only person anybody knows is their direct boss. With the biker gangs and other street gangs it's different, of course."

"But twenty guys is quite a few."

"And you've got a good ten thousand police officers on your side," said Joutsamo. She took a sip of tea to let her words sink in before continuing, "We have specific procedures in place for just your kind of situation. I gave you my card, and of course you can call my cell at any time of day, but we're also going to mark you down as a high-risk target."

"High-risk target?"

"That means that if you call the police for any reason, they'll immediately send out a fleet of cruisers."

"And that's supposed to comfort me?"

"Well, that's the intention. We're on your side. There's no reason to be afraid."

Mari Lehtonen glanced at the clock: a quarter after eight. "Oh, Laura's probably waiting already."

"I can give you a ride home."

"Why? Is that necessary?"

"No, but I have a car and it's raining." Joutsamo smiled. The wind-driven raindrops were just beginning to beat against the restaurant windows.

"Alright. But only because of the rain. I'm not afraid."

"You shouldn't be," said Joutsamo, despite a vague feeling of uncertainty that for some reason had begun to plague her.

WEDNESDAY, DECEMBER 13

CHAPTER 12
WEDNESDAY, 8:45 A.M.
COURTHOUSE BASEMENT, HELSINKI

At least the coffee's hot, thought Mari Lehtonen as she sat with Joutsamo in a basement witness room of Helsinki District Court. The long, three-hundred-square-foot room, with its pale gray walls, was every bit as ascetic as the interrogation rooms at police headquarters. In the middle of the room was a long veneered table surrounded by ten chairs. A lone Christmas-themed centerpiece lay on the table: a ring of elves cut from red cardboard.

The only sound was the hum of the ventilation system.

Lehtonen picked up her paper cup, but her hand was trembling enough that she had to steady it with her left.

"Are you scared?" asked Joutsamo.

Lehtonen shook her head. "No. Nervous, yeah. Never been a witness before."

"Just tell them what you saw. That's all that's expected of you."

"I guess so," said Lehtonen. Over the past few months, the whole September episode had been gradually fading from her memory, and a semblance of normalcy had returned to her life. But two weeks ago, a summons from the court had snapped her back to reality. Lehtonen had had to go to the post office to pick up the registered letter. Inside the envelope was a summons in cold officialese, demanding that she appear in court.

"Laura was really good in the play the other night. She was probably nervous, too," said Joutsamo. Mari had sent her a ticket to the show.

"Well, that was a play."

"Not to Laura. It was real to her."

"What do you think is gonna happen?" asked Lehtonen, still clutching her paper cup with two hands.

"We've done our job, and we have a good prosecutor. You tell them what you know and Korpi will get life."

"Today's paper had a little different take."

Joutsamo snorted. "The papers can print what they want but it won't sway the court. The judge and jury will look at the facts and nothing more. And that's all they'll need to convict him."

The door opened and in stepped District Prosecutor Helena Muuri, dressed in a dark gray pantsuit. She exchanged nods with Joutsamo then introduced herself to Lehtonen, and the two shook hands. Muuri had left the door open, and the faint sound of music drifted in from the hallway: the voice of the late Curt Cobain, "*I love you, I'm not gonna crack.*"

"Is everything alright," Muuri said, more as a statement than a question, though her words were directed at Lehtonen.

"Uhh...sure."

Muuri nodded. "A couple of tips for you. Please tell the court only what you know. If you don't know something, please say so. Avoid eye contact with the suspect. Korpi's attorney is going to ask you some questions, but please keep your eyes on him alone. A few other witnesses will come to the box before you, so it'll take a little while."

Muuri's overly courteous style was irritating to Joutsamo. It only made the situation more tense.

"When..." Joutsamo began to ask.

"I don't know. The judge on the case is the decisive type, so before lunch in all likelihood."

"And you still want Mari to testify on the witness stand?" asked Joutsamo. The alternative was for Lehtonen to stay in a separate room adjoining the witness room and give her testimony from behind tinted glass.

"Yes. There's no evidence of any credible threats. A witness who is present in the courtroom is always more believable to the jury." Muuri looked at Mari. "Your testimony is key to the case because it links Korpi to the crime scene."

"Do you think he'll be convicted?" asked Lehtonen. Joutsamo hoped Muuri would say something encouraging.

"I don't know. That's for the court to decide."

No such luck, thought Joutsamo.

"So he might go free?"

"It's always a possibility," said Muuri coldly. "Neither of the suspects have said anything to the police during the entire investigation. Today, they'll spin some tale for the court about how events unfurled. What that tale might be, we don't yet know."

Lehtonen fell silent. With a nod, Muuri got up and left.

* * *

TV reporter Sanna Römpötti was seated in the waiting area of the courtroom where Korpi was about to be tried. The long, plainly furnished room had five rows of seating, each composed of five banks of airport-style seating units. Forty-year-old Römpötti was dressed in jeans, sitting with a few other crime reporters from various media outlets. A couple of uniformed officers, white-shirted guards and a few lawyers were also in the room. No photographers were present, since cameras were prohibited in the courtroom. Römpötti's cameraman was waiting in the courthouse cafeteria.

"Did the prosecutor offer copies of the charges?" Römpötti asked a mustached *Ilta-Sanomat* newspaper reporter with a fox-pattern tie.

"Yeah," he nodded. "You can get 'em from the bailiff on the first floor once they get started. I can bring some for everyone."

"Great, thanks," said Römpötti. The Porvoo Street murder, as it had come to be called in the newsrooms, wasn't headline material anymore. Nobody from National Public News was even on location. In addition to Römpötti and the fellow from the *Ilta-Sanomat*, reporters from the *Helsingin Sanomat*, The Finnish News Bureau and *Alibi* crime magazine were on site. The usual cast.

Römpötti had been following the case since the beginning. She had done a couple of spots on it then, and as the court date drew nearer, the case began to gather attention again. Much of the interest had to do with Risto Korpi's background and status in the underworld.

The fledgling conversation hit a lull. Nobody had anything worth saying, not even about last night's adventures at the downtown bars. Römpötti was tired.

In a way, the case seemed fairly routine. She had ordered the case files from the police, which included security camera photographs from the front of the building where the murder occurred. She could easily build her news story based on those, along with interviews from the prosecution and defense. Martin, Korpi's attorney, was not a well-known lawyer, but Römpötti had already managed to request an interview. That had been fine with Martin, as was often the case with lawyers who liked free publicity. The key points of the case could be easily explained in a minute and a half.

The sleepy tenor of the waiting room was abruptly shattered by a voice over the loudspeaker: "The court calls prosecution versus Korpi and Nyberg."

Martin and the other lawyer grabbed their thick briefcases, and the reporters let them go in first.

* * *

Mari Lehtonen and Joutsamo were sitting alone in the witness room when a middle-aged, spectacled bailiff cracked the door open and informed them that court was now in session and that he would come for Lehtonen when it was time. There were no loudspeakers in the witness room.

"Thank you," said Joutsamo with a strained smile.

Lehtonen sat in silence with a pensive expression on her face.

"We won't...that is...*I* won't be coming in. It'll just be you," said Joutsamo.

Lehtonen looked hard at her. "Uhh..."

"What is it?"

"Well, I don't really know about this. I mean...I'll go, of course. Just got a bad feeling about it."

"I know," said Joutsamo, not really sure how to respond. Should she break out the pep talk or just sympathize? Neither option seemed very sensible, nor did quoting legal clauses about mandatory testimony and potential prison terms for perjury.

Lehtonen waited for a response.

"What do you want me to say?" said Joutsamo.

"I guess there's not much to say. If Korpi gets acquitted, he'll be out on the street."

"True, but we probably won't have a verdict today. Usually takes a couple weeks. Besides that, we're in good hands with Muuri. I'm very confident in the case we've built."

Joutsamo too had begun having doubts after their talk with Muuri. It was clear that Nyberg would try to shoulder the blame—he'd do everything he could to whitewash Korpi. By now, the defense knew exactly what evidence the prosecution would present, and they could simply tailor their testimony to that.

* * *

District Prosecutor Muuri clicked onto the final slide of her presentation. The heading read "Summary." All eyes in the courtroom, some twenty or so people, were on the screen projected over the judge's bench. Each of the judge and three jurors had their own private screens in front of them. Judge Tuomela, presiding, was seated in the middle.

At least *almost* all eyes were on the screen, for the two guards next to Korpi's table kept their eyes firmly on him, as did the two assigned to Nyberg.

Muuri had read the charges, which Korpi and Nyberg had denied. Muuri then took about half an hour to make her opening statements, which were just now coming to a close.

The high-security courtroom was about seventy-five feet long and forty-five wide, exceptionally large for a courtroom at the Helsinki district court. The wainscotted walls and wooden floors were stained light brown, and the room was bounded by four crested columns. All in all, there were forty seats arranged around six tables, in two rows of three, for defendants, plaintiffs and lawyers.

For security, or at least supposedly so, the room had no windows to the outside. A four-foot-tall iron railing stood between the defendants' table and the bench, as did an identical one between the defendants and the spectators. Behind the bench also stood a door through which the judge and jurors could make a quick exit if needed. On the other wall, to the judge's left, were two blackened windows. From behind one of them, security personnel could survey the crowd without drawing attention to themselves. The other was reserved for witnesses who chose to remain anonymous.

Muuri's opening statement was quite brief. Forensic evidence indicated that Nyberg had been in the apartment and shot Tomi Salmela. She contended that a turf battle between competing drug dealers had been the motive, and mentioned that a narcotics officer would be testifying more on that later.

She also emphasized that the murder was carried out in collaboration with Korpi.

"As we later found from file fragments on his computer, Korpi has been running a drug-dealing operation. A narcotics officer will be testifying as to the victim's role in a competing drug ring. As we all know, competition in the illicit drug trade is fierce, and gangs will stop at nothing to curtail competition, case in point," said Muuri, gesturing toward the screen. "For committing the murder, Nyberg would certainly gain status in Korpi's organization. Moreover, we know that Korpi is Nyberg's godfather, also indicating a close relationship between the two men. Clearly, the two are co-conspirators."

"Taking all of the evidence into account, I intend to show before this court, beyond any reasonable doubt, that Korpi planned Salmela's murder, and that Nyberg carried it out. Despite the fact that Korpi was in the car at the moment of the murder, he is every bit as culpable for Salmela's violent death as Nyberg is."

Muuri shut off the projector.

"All right," said Judge Tuomela, a stern-faced, fifty-something man in a gray suit. "Nyberg's defense, please."

Counsel Hanna Aaltonen was wearing a black pantsuit. When trying a homicide, an unspoken code among lawyers demanded a certain reverence be reflected in their dress. The brunette's black pantsuit made her seem much older than her thirty-five years, though this impression was partly due to the tightly wound bun she wore her hair in.

Nyberg sat quietly next to Aaltonen in a dark green T-shirt and camouflage pants. A fucking military tribunal, he thought.

"My client pleads not guilty to the charge of murder, but admits to aggravated assault and manslaughter in excess of justifiable self defense. My client did in fact go to the apartment that Sunday, not with the intention of murdering Salmela, but to collect four hundred euros for a television that Salmela had purchased. My client will comment more about this later on the witness stand. Salmela did not wish to pay the sum and threatened my client with a gun, leaving my client no other alternative than to draw his own weapon and attempt to frighten Salmela by shooting him in the foot. Unfortunately, in the confusion, the shot didn't hit him in the leg, but elsewhere. This was an accidental shooting, which regrettably resulted in Salmela's death. There was no motive related to drugs, and Risto Korpi was not involved in any way. That is our opening statement—we will provide further details when my client takes the stand."

Muuri asked for permission to speak, which Judge Tuomela granted.

"Your client hasn't said a word in any police interview. If it happened as you claim, then why is that?"

"He has his reasons."

"And what are those?" Muuri persisted, pleased that the defense had taken the bait.

"He doesn't trust the police to conduct an objective investigation."

"And why not?"

Judge Tuomela interjected. "Prosecution, do you have anything else?"

Muuri kept her gaze fixed on Nyberg and Aaltonen.

"Just one small thing for now. Counsel Aaltonen neglected to mention whether, according to her client, Korpi was in the vehicle or not. Was he?"

Aaltonen turned to Nyberg, who shook his head. They whispered briefly. "We'll touch on this when my client takes the stand, but for now I can say that according to my client, Korpi was not in the vehicle."

"Who was, then?" asked Muuri. The value of Lehtonen's testimony was going up by the second. But Korpi's defense would try to derail it by any means necessary.

"My client does not wish to answer that."

No surprise there, thought Muuri, but she kept her thoughts to herself. The modern courts appreciated more temperate prosecutors—the days of aggressive, unrestrained badgering were over. Judge Tuomela turned to Korpi's counsel. "Defense, go ahead."

Martin took a last glance at the papers on the table where he had outlined his relevant points. Korpi sat next to him in a pale gray sweater, trying to appear calm. With little effect—he seemed overly calm.

"My client denies all charges. He was not in the vehicle, as the prosecutor mistakenly claims. Vague observations of one individual witness during a random encounter are patently unreliable. Korpi does indeed know Nyberg, but he has no knowledge whatsoever of this incident. As Nyberg said, he shot at Salmela in self-defense, which my client had nothing to do with. Neither has my client had anything to do with drugs since his last conviction. I'd also like to point out on my client's behalf that he has no obligation to prove his own innocence. The points outlined by the prosecutor in this court are pure speculation and based on assumptions rather than reality."

CHAPTER 13
WEDNESDAY, 10:35 A.M.
SELLO SHOPPING CENTER, ESPOO

Christmas Eve was still eleven days off, but Takamäki had decided to get his shopping done early for once, and at a time of day when the malls weren't teeming with crowds. The idea had struck him after leaving the Espoo police station nearby, and with nothing pressing at work, it seemed a good time for a shopping excursion. No problem, he had thought.

But once inside the atrium of the Sello Shopping Center, he was struck by the true dearth of his ideas. What to get his wife? The boys? Joutsamo? Suhonen? Takamäki felt like turning around and taking the elevator back to the parking ramp. Surely there would be time for this later. But he forced himself to take a step forward, and then another. Clothes? Hockey gear? Books? What would they want? Damn, maybe even this operation required a plan, thought Takamäki as he spotted a coffee shop. Maybe he could think about it over a cup of coffee. And maybe a list would help? Wandering aimlessly through the mall was hardly his idea of enjoyment.

The lieutenant sat at a table drinking his coffee from a paper cup. A few other customers were scattered about.

He had thought to buy a paper at the register, but decided to leave it on the rack. Time to concentrate on gifts, not tabloid news. All the headlines were about the antics of a member of parliament on the ferry to Tallinn. Takamäki wondered if it was all a publicity stunt for the upcoming elections. Not likely, though someone had once claimed that any publicity is good publicity when it came to politics.

Christmas presents, he reminded himself...still at a loss. Maybe some jewelry or a book for Kaarina. Something like that. And the boys? Some books, video games or sports stuff? Toys? Maybe...but what kind?

Takamäki finished off the last of his coffee. Christmas shopping was not his cup of tea. He decided to return to the station, knowing he'd come to regret it. The shopping wouldn't do itself. Urgency was his best motivator, and with eleven days to go, that was still lacking.

He decided to drop the car off at home, which was within walking distance of the Leppävaara train station. His team would be gathering for an informal Christmas party that evening, and a few beers were probably in the cards. This way, he could head straight to the restaurant from work.

* * *

It was almost eleven-thirty, and Joutsamo and Lehtonen were sitting in the witness room quietly reading. Joutsamo had the memoirs of a foreign legion soldier and Lehtonen a translation of a novel based on the lives of a group of New York women. An hour earlier, the bailiff had stopped by during a recess to tell them that several witnesses had already testified.

Joutsamo knew that a financial crimes officer had testified on the significance of the fragments of data found on Korpi's computer. Another officer had testified on the crime scene. Among the prosecutor's witnesses was a narcotics officer who had investigated Korpi's cocaine business based on the initial intelligence that Suhonen had gathered. An organized crime specialist from the National Bureau of Investigation had also made the list.

The door opened and both women startled. "It's time," said the bailiff. "The court calls Mari Lehtonen. Room 001."

"Alright, then," said Joutsamo as Lehtonen rose. "Just try to relax."

"Yeah. I will."

Joutsamo was glad to see a display of resoluteness from Mari. The sergeant remained seated as Mari followed the bailiff out.

At the end of a short hallway they came to the door leading into the courtroom. The bailiff opened it and let Lehtonen inside. She felt confused, lingering at a small wooden table by the door, her eyes scanning the courtroom. In addition to the judge, there were three jurors behind the bench. Prosecutor Muuri stood straight ahead, about thirty feet away, while the defendants and a group of guards sat behind the iron railing. A crowd of onlookers were seated in the back of the room.

"Good morning," said Judge Tuomela. "Are you Mari Lehtonen?"

"Yes."

"Could you please approach the bench?"

Lehtonen did so. Just in front of the bench, resting on its own lectern, was a large, open Bible.

"Do you belong to the church?"

"Yes."

"Then typically you would take the oath, but you can also choose a secular affirmation."

"The oath is fine."

"Good. Repeat after me. I, Mari Lehtonen."

Before she began, she wondered if she should put two fingers on the Bible like they did on TV. Apparently not, since the judge hadn't mentioned it. Lehtonen felt a mixture of confidence and self-doubt. She was confident she could relate what she saw, but the circumstances made her doubt herself.

"I, Mari Lehtonen."

The drill was a familiar one for the judge and he rattled it off at a quick pace. Lehtonen repeated dutifully. "Swear by Almighty God…that the evidence I shall give…shall be the truth…the whole truth…and nothing but the truth."

"Keep this oath in mind and tell the unvarnished truth," said the judge, and he directed Lehtonen to take the stand. "Please sit. We'll be recording your testimony, so speak clearly into the microphone."

Lehtonen looked at the microphone, the same kind used by Formula One drivers in post-race interviews: a stand with a long stem and a small capsule. A red light on the base popped on.

"Prosecution, go ahead," said the judge.

Muuri began, "Mari Lehtonen, you were on Porvoo Street on Sunday, the seventeenth of September, at four-thirty in the afternoon. Tell us in your own words what you saw."

"Okay. Well, I was going to the convenience store and there, kind of in front of it, was a blue Mazda that was double parked. I wondered what it was doing there and so I looked inside. There was a man behind the wheel, so I figured he was just waiting for someone from the store. Then I went home."

Muuri cringed a little at that last part—Lehtonen had just revealed that she lived nearby. At least she hadn't recited her address. Muuri brushed it off and continued, "Take a look at the individuals in this courtroom. Is the man you saw in the car present here?"

Lehtonen let her gaze wander until it came to rest on Korpi.

"That's him," she said, nodding.

"Which one?"

"That one, right there." Lehtonen extended a finger in Korpi's direction and their eyes met. She disliked his cold stare. It was the same stare he had in the photograph, the same bald head and rigid features.

"Let the court note for the record that the witness is pointing to Risto Korpi. I'd like to ask again, are you absolutely certain? And remember the oath you just took."

"Yes, I'm absolutely certain."

"What was the man doing in the car?"

"Nothing. He was sitting in the driver's seat with his hands on the wheel."

"How did you get in contact with the police?"

"I saw an article in the newspaper and I remembered the car. The police were asking for eyewitnesses, so I thought I should call."

"How did you identify Korpi once you were at the police station?"

"The police had me look through a bunch of photographs. Then the next day I came in for a police lineup."

"In those two instances, were you just as certain as you are now that the man in the car was Korpi?"

"Yes."

"Then I have no further questions."

"Defense, your turn," said Judge Tuomela.

Martin stood up. "I have a few questions, too," he said in a plucky tone. "What sort of work do you do?"

Lehtonen was somewhat taken aback. "Uhh, I work in an office."

"For what company?"

Muuri interjected before Lehtonen could respond. "The question has no bearing on the case."

"Yes, it does. It's my responsibility to evaluate the reliability of the witness. A janitor can work in an office, too."

"A janitor's testimony is every bit as reliable as anyone else's," said Muuri.

"She said that she works in an office—that will suffice," said the judge dryly.

"I noticed that you're not wearing eyeglasses. Do you wear glasses at work?"

"No. I don't need them."

Martin paused briefly and glanced at his papers. "When was the last time you went to an optometrist?"

Muuri cut in before Lehtonen could respond. "Objection. Irrelevant."

"Sustained. Let's stay on topic."

"Well, then," Martin grumbled. "How can you be so certain that the man in the car was the same as this man here, sitting next to me?"

"Uhh, well… Because I saw him."

"Just like that, you saw him?"

"Yes."

The lawyer's questions were beginning to annoy her, but she tried to stay calm like she had been told.

"Would you say you have a sort of photographic memory?"

"I'm not sure how to answer that. Maybe."

"In psychology, the term 'photographic memory' refers to an ability to remember an image in vivid detail. Some people can memorize a page of a telephone book in minutes. Do you have that ability, Ms. Lehtonen?"

"I don't think I could memorize a telephone book."

"So you *don't* have a photographic memory."

Muuri spoke up again, "Objection, leading. The witness never claimed to have a photographic memory."

"Martin, get to the point," the judge said.

The attorney fixed his eyes on Lehtonen's. "Keep your eyes on mine for the time being. If your memory is as good as you claim, you should be able to describe Ms. Muuri's clothing, right? Go ahead, no peeking, please."

Muuri tried to object, but Lehtonen had already begun. Her eyes never wavered from Martin's, "She's wearing a gray pantsuit with a white shirt and a necklace with a reddish stone. She's not wearing glasses and her hair is brown and medium length."

Martin was dumbfounded by her answer— there was a pause of a few seconds. "What was the license plate number of the Mazda you saw?"

Lehtonen recited a plate number beginning with K.

"How many stacks of paper does Ms. Muuri have in front of her?"

"Three."

The judge interjected this time. "I think we've had enough of your memory games, Martin."

"Then I have no further questions."

"Alright," said Judge Tuomela, turning to Nyberg's counsel. "Aaltonen, would you like to cross-examine?"

"No, thank you."

The judge nodded and turned back toward the witness stand. "Do you require any compensation for expenses or loss of wages? You're eligible for half a day's pay."

"No, thank you," said Lehtonen, though she could have used the money. She felt a wave of relief, and all she wanted was to get away from the tension of the courtroom.

"Alright, then," said the judge. "In that case, the court thanks you. You are excused."

Lehtonen nodded and rose. Before she closed the door behind her, she heard Judge Tuomela saying, "The court has now heard testimony from all witnesses and will take recess for lunch. Court will be back in session at one-thirty to hear closing arguments. The verdict will be delivered later on today."

Joutsamo was waiting in the hallway. "How did it go?"

"Good, actually," said Lehtonen. Only now did Joutsamo detect a slight tremor in Mari's voice as her body defused the tension. "Did you hear? They're going to have a verdict today already."

"Really? That's kind of rare. Well, were you excused?"

"Yes."

"Then you're free to go. I can drive you home or to work, your call."

* * *

Takamäki arrived at work around twelve-thirty in the afternoon. Joutsamo was already there to report on the trial. Apparently, everything had gone smoothly, though according to Lehtonen, Korpi's counsel had tried to rattle her on the stand.

At this point, all the lieutenant cared about was the verdict. The case was out of his hands. Joutsamo's coaching of the key witness had been an apparent success. Naturally, hearing that the verdict would be delivered today made him feel a little anxious. In the end, verdicts were the only real measure of police performance.

No homicides had crossed Takamäki's desk since the Korpi case. Just as well. It was good to get a break every once in a while. Various assaults were abundant, of course, but recently they had had none of the tumult that came with a murder case.

On his desk were the case files for a few robberies. Some gangs that had been active around the Helsinki Central Train Station a year back had re-energized with the expanding nightfall of winter. Takamäki's team had joined in the investigation.

As cases came, they were comparatively insignificant. None involved violence—the wave of a knife was all that was required to relieve a drunk of his wallet or laptop.

But the spate of incidents had captured the attention of the Helsinki media, at which point police brass started yet another collaborative task force. Takamäki had gotten involved against his own wishes. Several suspects had been taken into custody. The interrogations were all through and the case files had to be forwarded to the prosecutor, though some of the DNA evidence was still pending.

A knock came at the door and Takamäki looked up. Suhonen had grown a full beard, and with his leather jacket he looked more like a biker thug than a policeman.

"Heard we'll get a verdict on that Korpi case today," said Suhonen, raking his fingers through his beard.

Takamäki nodded. "That's right."

"What do you think?" asked Suhonen, lingering at the door. Takamäki took that as an indication that Suhonen had no pressing business, at least nothing relating to an open investigation.

"Hard to say. These types of trials can be unpredictable. I suppose the speed of the verdict would indicate the evidence is pretty convincing one way or the other."

"So for the court, the case is cut and dried."

"Yup. You coming tonight?"

"Of course," Suhonen grinned. "High point of the year."

"Really."

"You don't think so?"

"Well, we've had a lot of fun. At least in the past. How's things with the future Mrs. Suhonen?" Takamäki asked with a smirk.

Suhonen shifted his weight to the other foot. "Like I said before, 'Mrs. Suhonen' is a bit of a stretch. No talk of that with Raija yet. You eaten?"

"No. Let's go grab something."

The lieutenant stood up, unable to suppress his smile, for one word in Suhonen's rebuttal had revealed a lot: yet.

CHAPTER 14
WEDNESDAY, 6:45 P.M.
CANTINA WEST RESTAURANT,
DOWNTOWN HELSINKI

"One more round before we move on?" said Suhonen.

Seven cops were crowded into the private dining room of a Mexican restaurant. On one side of the table were Suhonen, Takamäki and Joutsamo. On the other were Kohonen, Kannas from Forensics, Kulta the rookie, and as a special guest, the bushy-whiskered Nykänen, now with the NBI. Homicide also organized a larger Christmas party for the entire unit, but a few years back, Takamäki had started this tradition with a smaller group.

"I could be talked into one more," grunted Kannas. The table was littered with empty plates and a couple of wine bottles amongst the fajita toppings and baskets of tortillas.

"Fine with me," said Joutsamo, and she pushed a button on the wall to signal the wait staff. Joutsamo ordered a cider, Kulta a gin and tonic, and the others ordered more beer.

Once the waitress left, there was a brief lull in the conversation and Suhonen took the opportunity. "Those white-collar crime detectives might actually make something of themselves one day."

"Yeah," croaked Nykänen in his gravelly voice. "Heard you were giving them seminars on undercover work."

The others pricked up their ears. Suhonen hadn't mentioned teaching any classes. "Yep, instead of pushing paper, the financial crimes guys are actually out there actively looking for cases. Makes sense to me. They were pretty interested in tailing and infiltration."

"Ha!" said Kulta. "What'd you teach 'em? How to infiltrate the fat cats on the rooftop bar of the Palace Hotel?"

Suhonen laughed. "Sure, we touched on that too. But also how to get a job, say, on a construction site. Those guys actually have some interesting stories. Apparently, the gray market is really booming. You know, wages paid off the books, hidden revenue…that sort of thing. They say things will only get worse till our eastern neighbors start getting their affairs in order."

"Well, at least they're starting to catch up with the rest of the police force," said Joutsamo. "Actually, they use kind of an interesting tactic in their surveillance. First they set up all their wire taps, then they take the suspects in for questioning. But instead of arresting them, the suspects are released and then start calling each other, all on tape. Something for us to try, too, at least with some of our cold cases."

Takamäki drank the last of his beer and smiled. "Don't go getting too interested in this white-collar stuff. I don't want you going anywhere."

Suhonen smirked. "Might just be me, but I'd rather be posted on a stool in the Corner Pub than some swanky place like Savoy. You find a more honest crowd in the Corner Pub. Those financial guys were telling me about Morgan Stanley..."

"Morgan Stanley is a New York investment bank," Joutsamo cut in.

Suhonen grinned. "Right, that's the one. Anyhow, they were telling me the bank gives psychological tests as a part of their job interview process. Turns out that if the test shows a tendency toward dishonesty, you might want to consider a career on Wall Street."

"Doesn't sound much different from here in Finland," said Joutsamo.

"Business is global," said Takamäki.

"But seriously. We all need to cooperate on the big cases regardless of which unit or floor of the police station we find ourselves on," said Nykänen. "We have no other choice."

"Maybe so. Provided all units have the same objective," Takamäki hedged. His experiences collaborating with other units had been awful, and everyone knew it.

The waitress broke the tension at an opportune time as she breezed in with the drinks.

Kannas spoke up. "I ever tell you about the time way back when I was standing guard at the presidential palace and saw two people going at it in the Supreme Court building?"

"Yes!" was the unanimous response followed by chuckles.

Kannas grinned. "Well, this one I *know* you haven't heard. True story. A Helsinki rookie is out riding shotgun with a twenty-year veteran and he wants to show off what he's got. So they're driving around and the rookie spots a crowd of people standing on the corner. He cranks down the window and yells, 'Let's get off the corner, people.' They just kind of glance around, so he yells again, 'Get off the corner... Now!' So they kind of shuffle off and he turns to his partner and says, 'How'd I do?' 'Not bad,' says the vet, 'That'll teach 'em to wait at the bus stop.'"

The others chuckled, though the joke had been told a hundred times before. Even the waitress laughed as she served up the last round of beers.

"We'll take the check, please," said Nykänen. He turned back to his colleagues. "But here's an actual true story from Espoo. So a patrol car was kind of creeping along through this neighborhood, right? A cat runs out of the bushes, and the squad runs it over. So the officer stops the car and goes with his partner to take a look."

"And this is supposed to be true?" said Joutsamo.

"Didn't I already say so? Well, the cat was just barely alive and kind of twitching, so the guys didn't know what to do. They couldn't really shoot it, but they didn't want to let it suffer, either. So one of them suggests that they get back in the car and drive over it a few more times and that's what they did. The cat was pretty much smeared into the pavement when one of them noticed a little granny—the cat's owner—standing behind the bushes with her eyes like saucers."

"Ohhh, man," Joutsamo groaned while the others laughed.

Takamäki's phone signaled a text message.

"Couldn't be the wife yet," laughed Kannas, but the others grew quiet with anticipation.

Takamäki dug his phone out of his belt holder and looked at the screen. His face was impassive. "From Muuri. Better read this out loud: *Two life sentences. Unanimous decision. Lehtonen's testimony was key.*

Puts Korpi at the scene. Well done!"

Suhonen cracked a smile and raised his glass. "I'll drink to that."

The others joined in.

As he set down his glass, Suhonen took out his own phone and sent news of the verdict to Tomi Salmela's father.

* * *

Counselor Martin and Risto Korpi were in a tiny holding cell in the basement of the courthouse. The room had space for a table and two chairs. Korpi couldn't bring himself to sit, just paced around the cramped room like a caged animal: three steps one way, three steps back.

Martin, on the other hand, sat at the table watching his client. He couldn't help but feel afraid.

"Fucking idiot," Korpi hissed. "I trusted you. You said you'd take care of this."

"I never promised anything."

Korpi stopped and stared his lawyer in the eyes.

"Really? Think again."

"These are unpredictable cases. With your record it shouldn't…"

"Kiss my ass. You get to walk outta here and I get to walk into a cell. Damnit. How can you be so fucking stupid?"

Martin wanted to ask him how he could have been so stupid as to be waiting outside while his partner offed some minor dealer. But he didn't dare. He wasn't sure if Korpi had actually known about Nyberg's plan to shoot Salmela. According to the verdict, however, there was no doubt that Salmela's death was an execution. Nyberg's self-defense claim had been completely quashed in court.

"Maybe I oughta tell the cops about your nose candy…"

Martin cut in, "Keep it down! Might be a mike."

"Oh, that's right," Korpi sneered. "A client can't even have a private conversation with his lawyer anymore."

"I'd think you'd know there's no such thing."

"Fuck," Korpi kept ranting. He took his seat and tried to calm down.

"The appeals court could…"

"Fuck the appeals court. How is this possible? Hell, I had it all figured out—don't talk about nothin' on the phone. Everything gets taken care of off the grid…"

"Are you making a confession?" asked Martin. In all actuality, he wished that were the case, as then he could invoke ethics rules to get out of representing Korpi. That actually sounded like a pretty good outcome.

"Of course not. I didn't know anything about it— you know that. Do you think I'd have been in that car if I'd known? Not a chance in hell. Son of a bitch! What reason would I have to lie to you? And I sure don't trust the appeals court to change anything. They're all in bed with the pigs one way or another."

Martin started to say something but Korpi shut him up with a raised hand. "Don't say a word. Not a word. Just listen. I don't understand how it's possible some bitch with a photographic memory would just happen to see me and then go and call the cops. That's some bad fucking karma. Shit, I can't think straight with fifteen years hanging over me, but I'll figure it out. I know from experience you never sleep the first night after a sentencing, but that doesn't matter right now. I'll get things straightened out."

Korpi fell silent, and Martin was quiet too.

Korpi spoke up again, "Not sure if they're gonna move me to Helsinki Prison today or tomorrow, but you're gonna come meet me in the afternoon. By then my head'll be clear and I'll tell you what to do."

"I can't..."

Korpi narrowed his eyes. "You'll do what I tell you. Or you're the one I'll be thinking about tonight."

CHAPTER 15
WEDNESDAY, 10:05 P.M.
MARI LEHTONEN'S APARTMENT

Mari Lehtonen was at home watching the evening news with her daughter, Laura, at her side. Mari had opened a bottle of wine, which had now dwindled to about a third. The broadcast had begun with news from the Middle East, which had been grim for so many years that it wasn't interesting anymore. Next up had been some political story, but that too, at least tonight, held no charm.

The news anchor continued, "Tonight Helsinki District Court sentenced two men to life in prison for a drug-related murder that took place in September. According to the court, the motive for the murder was a turf battle between competing drug rings."

Laura glanced at her mother, who nodded.

The screen cut abruptly to reporter Sanna Römpötti, standing in front of the courthouse in the waning light. Römpötti proclaimed that the court's swift verdict was only as extraordinary as the murder: two dealers, who had been previously convicted of drug crimes, assassinated a competing dealer. It was yet another example of the ever more violent nature of organized crime.

Some photographs of the crime scene appeared on the screen and Römpötti described the murder. As the surveillance photograph of the Mazda in front of the apartment building appeared on screen, the reporter explained, "A crucial piece of evidence in the case came when a Helsinki woman testified to having seen this car, as well as the driver's face, at the time of the murder. In court the witness identified gang leader Risto Korpi as the man who was waiting in the car, while Korpi's henchman Esa Nyberg went into the building and shot a competing cocaine dealer to prevent him from taking business from Korpi's organization."

More crime scene photographs appeared on the screen. "Korpi denied allegations in court that he had been at the scene, and that he had given Nyberg the order to kill. But since a reliable witness had testified that Korpi was in the car, and Nyberg was a member of a gang led by Korpi, the court found him guilty of murder as well."

Mari's phone alerted her to a text message, but she ignored it. The broadcast moved on to the backstory and highlighted the recent spate of violence among criminals. The reporter concluded that the game was clearly getting more ruthless, and would continue to do so.

When the news anchor reappeared and shifted to a story on water quality, Lehtonen picked up her phone. The text had come from her boss, Essi Saari, and it was brief: "Nicely done!"

Lehtonen had time to take another sip of wine before the phone rang. The call was from an unknown number. Mari wondered if she should answer or not, but since the police also used blocked numbers, she decided to answer.

"Hello?"

"Yeah...so I hear you got a nice new black suit and red necklace," said a man's voice. Mari recognized her ex-husband all too well.

"What?" she managed to say as she stood up.

"Where'd you get the money for them fancy new clothes and jewelry?"

Mari stole into the bathroom and closed the door so Laura wouldn't hear. "What are you talking about? You're drunk."

"Fuck yeah, I'm drunk, but I still got ears. I hear you been hanging out with the cops in a fancy new suit and necklace puttin' an innocent man in jail."

"I don't have any... Where'd you get this number?"

The man's voice grew threatening. "Listen, whore. You done somethin' real stupid and you're gonna..."

Lehtonen hung up and turned off her phone. The jerk could leave a thousand voicemails and she wouldn't listen to a single one. She came back into the living room and Laura looked at her inquiringly.

"Nothing. Just a wrong number."

The girl shrugged. "What are we watching sports scores for?" she wondered, reaching for the remote control. The next channel up was airing some detective show.

"Change the channel," said Mari. "Or better yet, get your jammies on and get to bed. You'll be getting that feedback on your project tomorrow night."

She poured herself another glass of wine. The tremor in her hand had returned.

* * *

Joutsamo was crooning like an Idols star on the karaoke stage of the Ace of Spades Bar, "*And your day to day life is the torment of strangers. Day after day, restless Cinderella makes a martyr of herself.*"

The other officers were sitting around a table in the crowded bar.

"I didn't know homicide cops could sing," said Nykänen.

"Now you do. She's the one and only," said Takamäki, and he took a swig of beer. With five rounds already in his system, he was beginning to feel it.

"Least not here, anyway," Nykänen added. The Ace of Spades was the flagship of Finland's karaoke bars, and not just anybody could take the stage there. "I gotta say, though, she's not half bad."

"Yeah. Seems like she's good at everything she does. Either that or she doesn't do anything she stinks at."

"You know, I'm still a little bitter about you stealing her away," said Nykänen, not entirely joking. Nykänen had once worked with Takamäki's team, but had made lieutenant and taken a position with Espoo narcotics, where Joutsamo had been working. "She planning on going for lieutenant?"

"Not sure. That's what I've been asking her myself, but she hasn't hinted either way."

"It'd be a good position for her."

"I think her clock is ticking, too."

Nykänen gave Takamäki a blank look before he finally understood. "Oh, right. Yeah. Is she seeing someone?"

"Not to my knowledge."

"Strange. Maybe she's set the bar too high."

The music faded out, and the men changed the subject as Joutsamo came back to the table.

"I see you know your Dingo tunes. Nicely done," said Takamäki.

Suhonen had a fresh cider waiting for her. "Not bad," he said, handing her the drink.

"Thanks," she smiled.

Suhonen heard his phone ring through the opening bars of Don Huonot's, "Good Night, Good Morning." *"No such thing as a bulletproof heart yet,"* sang a forty-something man, well out of step with the music. After checking the number, Suhonen excused himself, got up and went into the bathroom where he could hear.

When he came back five minutes later, the conversation had turned to the Korpi case. The team was happy with the course of the investigation and the final verdict.

"I gotta go," said Suhonen without sitting down.

Takamäki looked at him inquiringly. "What is it?"

"My friend Salmela called. He's pretty trashed. Gotta make sure he doesn't do something stupid."

"Okay," said Takamäki, and the others wished him luck. Joutsamo got up and planted a wet kiss on Suhonen's shaggy cheek.

"What's that for?" he asked.

"I dunno," she said, smiling. "Just felt like it."

Suhonen shook his head with a grin. He slipped on his jacket and stepped out of the bar. The air was crisp and cold in contrast with the smoky confines of the karaoke bar. He coughed a few times to clear his lungs and decided the weather was nice enough to walk the one-mile-plus to Salmela's apartment on Helsinki Avenue.

He kept up a brisk pace as he turned up the hill toward the Hakaniemi bridge. Of course, he could have taken a taxi too, but a little walk might help him work off a few beers, or at least seem to. Salmela hadn't seemed suicidal at all--more lonely than anything. Maybe the verdict had stirred up old memories of his son.

The streets were quiet. A few cars were about at this hour, but almost nobody on foot.

Suhonen had gone to Tomi's funeral in October. The proceedings had been spartan, and Tomi's mother hadn't come. Suhonen wasn't sure if Salmela had talked about it with his ex at all. It was really none of his business.

At any rate, right now Salmela needed Suhonen's company more than his comrades at the bar did.

Suhonen decided to take a shortcut through a small park. Four- and five-story stone buildings flanked the park on all sides. A couple of street lights were burned out.

Suhonen noticed the movement a few tenths of a second before he heard the voice. "Hey man, you got a smoke?"

Three youngsters in dark hooded sweatshirts with stocking caps pulled low over their foreheads appeared from behind some bushes. Suhonen stopped about six feet short of the boys, "Sorry, not at the moment."

The kid in the middle had a thin face and straggly hair, about eighteen years old. He slipped a knife out of his belt and held it up. "Then gimme your money."

"Everything you got," said the one on the left. "So we don't have to kick your ass."

"Okay, okay…take it easy. It's all yours," Suhonen said, raising his right hand in capitulation. "It's right up here in my breast pocket. Just let me get it out."

Suhonen chattered on in hopes of keeping the knife man at bay. He considered his options at the same time. Not many...he was in too much of a hurry.

He opened the zipper of his jacket pocket with his right hand, his eyes locked on the knife man. Suhonen's unexpected calmness was beginning to make the kid nervous. "Cough it up you son-of-a-bitch," he hissed, thrusting at the air with his knife. "I'll cut your eyes out!"

Really, thought Suhonen, still fumbling in his pocket. "Just a sec here, let me find it," he said, wrapping his fingers round his Glock. He pulled it out and leveled it at the knife man.

Gun in hand, Suhonen's voice went cold, "Now get the fuck outta here you little pussies. And don't try this again."

The knife man turned to run, but tripped on his own feet and crashed down a few steps away. His friends didn't bother to stop and help him, and Suhonen was upon him before he could regain his footing. He threw the kid onto his back, pressed his knee into his chest, and put the gun barrel against his temple. "Next time I kill each and every one of you. Understand?"

The kid nodded.

"I didn't hear you!"

"Yes! I understand!"

"Good, you gonna quit this shit?"

"Yeah."

"Sure about that?"

"Yeah, yeah," he said, his voice shrill now.

Suhonen pressed the gun harder. "And you'll go to school? Do a little studying and start your own business...that's the way to make some real money."

Suhonen stood up and let him go. The gun went back into his shoulder holster. He could have called it in and had a cruiser come for them, but it was already too late. He glanced around quickly: nobody watching from the windows.

Suhonen continued on his way. At no point had he identified himself as a police officer, but there was no doubt in his mind that this was just the sort of preventive work that a police officer should be doing.

THURSDAY, DECEMBER 14

CHAPTER 16
THURSDAY, 8:30 A.M.
HELSINKI PRISON

A pudgy guard with a shaved head and wooden expression led Korpi to the entrance of his cell. Korpi was holding a small bag with some personal items, his prison-issue coveralls and bedclothes.

The third floor of the east wing, with its pale walls and potted plants, was more akin to a stalwart hospital than an ordinary prison. First built in 1881, Helsinki Prison was intended to project a sinister presence to the outside. That's what it still did, but after several remodels, the inside of the complex had begun to appear progressively more accommodating. Or at least as accommodating as a prison well over a century old can appear.

"Here's your cell," drawled the guard. Though not an imposing presence, Rauli Salo had plenty of experience as a prison guard. He knew Korpi from the con's previous stint, and he predicted what Korpi would say next.

Korpi stopped at the door and glanced inside. "This ain't gonna work."

"You don't have a choice."

Korpi had been quickly transferred from the new admissions block, where inmates sometimes spent weeks. Cell block three was in better shape than the others, but Korpi didn't intend to share a cell. He turned to the guard. "Lifers get special rights. I want my own cell."

"You think I have a say in that? It's a question of space. Two guys per cell is the bare minimum. Most cells have three or four, plus construction noise. You oughta be thankful I got you this much. Cell doors are open till eight here, too. Lockdown's at five on most blocks."

Not convinced, Korpi took another look at the cell. Some girly pictures were hanging on the walls and a guitar was leaning against the windowsill. Whoever occupied the lower bunk was either at work or class. "Who's got the bunk there?"

"Kaapo Nieminen. Mule. Doing a couple years for drug smuggling."

"So you're sticking me in a cell with some junkie. Fuck. Not gonna happen."

"No other choice."

Korpi looked at the guard in silence. "Well. Then you know how it's gotta go."

The guard shrugged his skinny shoulders. He knew all too well. By tomorrow morning at the latest, Nieminen would file for transfer to the protective ward under a barrage of threats from Korpi. And Korpi would keep going regardless of who they put in the cell with him. Salo couldn't be bothered by it—there was no changing inmate hierarchies. Certain inmates would give the orders, and the gangsters could terrorize whoever they wanted. Korpi would be in the pen for a long time, so it paid to get along with him, which is precisely why Salo had tried to arrange things beforehand.

Korpi stepped inside and slammed the heavy steel door behind him. The doors weren't locked during the day. Korpi tossed his bag onto the top bunk. He snatched the guitar by the neck and swung it hard against the metal frame of the bed. The instrument splintered in one hit. "Fucking junkie," he hissed, as he emptied the man's things onto the lower bunk.

Next up would be to find out which of his friends were on the block, and in that respect, this was a good place to be. Sometimes referred to as "Little Tallinn," the Estonian inmates held court along the gable end. There would likely be some familiar faces over there.

In any case, he had a meeting with Martin in the afternoon. Korpi's thoughts had crystallized overnight. He knew now what had gone wrong, and what he had to do.

* * *

At his computer, Takamäki was reading reports on last night's events. A few robberies had occurred in the early part of the evening, but nothing very serious. It had been almost noon before he made it to the station. The rest of the team had the day off, which is why they had chosen the previous day for the Christmas party.

Takamäki registered a movement out of the corner of his eye. Suhonen had walked past the door.

"Suhonen," Takamäki called after him.

Suhonen returned to the door with a smile. "Look who actually made it in."

"Well, I'm *supposed* to be here. You have the day off, so what's your excuse?"

"Just figured I'd go to the gym and check some emails. Those finance detectives invited me to play on their hockey team, and I couldn't remember when the game started."

"You taking up hockey?"

"Sure. Back in Lahti I played till I was sixteen. Haven't skated much since, but it'll be interesting to see how it goes."

"Pads and everything?"

"Seniors' rules. No checking and no slap shots. Otherwise, everything's the same. But I figured if I wore Kevlar under my pads I could be a bit more aggressive."

Takamäki was a bit surprised. Had the man's new relationship taken its toll? Takamäki had also played hockey as a kid. Maybe he could give it a shot again too. "How was Salmela?"

"Drunk as a skunk. We chatted and one of us cried. He was still taking it pretty hard, so it was good I went to see him. Ended up just crashing on the couch. What about you guys?"

"I hung it up at around midnight, but some people don't know when to stop. Once Kannas and Nykänen got to reminiscing there was no end to the chase stories."

Suhonen chuckled. The team had once rented a cabin for the weekend, and Kannas had brought a handful of Matchbox cars in order to better illustrate his best pursuits from the last twenty years.

* * *

Counselor Martin was sitting on the opposite side of a wooden table from Korpi. Between the two men stood a glass partition about sixteen inches high to prevent visitors from smuggling contraband to the inmates. The prison also had separate rooms partitioned off with thick plexi-glass walls and telephones for communication.

With the exception of a lone guard, nobody else was in the room. The guard kept his distance, since conversations between lawyers and clients were confidential. Martin had known of a case in which the police had illegally eavesdropped on prison conversations between a lawyer and his client, who had been convicted of financial crimes. But today, he considered the risk of audio surveillance to be insignificant. The NBI agents at fault had gotten a slap on the wrist from the parliamentary ombudsman, whose job it was to ensure that public officials observed the law. A repeat performance would undoubtedly lead to formal charges.

Martin and Korpi had been conversing for nearly half an hour.

"You're sure this is what you want," said Martin, his voice tense and worried. He felt reluctant to get mixed up in Korpi's affairs.

"You'll do just as I tell you."

"It could influence the handling of your case in appeals court."

"Appeals ain't gonna change anything, didn't I just tell you that? The cops got 'em in their pocket just like district. The more I think about it, the more sure I am I got convicted on my record. Had nothin' to do with this case."

"That's what I've been saying all along."

Korpi leveled a piercing gaze at his lawyer. He had seen glimpses of the man's weakness before, and now it was showing again.

"You said your piece yesterday in court. Now you'll do what *I* say. You get in touch with Guerrilla and tell him what he has to do."

Martin nodded. Maybe this once, he thought. He was only delivering a message, nothing criminal, just a bit unsettling. In a way, he understood Korpi, understood his anger. But he had to get something in return.

"Alright, it's a deal. I'll do it. But then this is over."

"What?"

"Using the old coke thing to blackmail me."

Korpi laughed. He hadn't even begun yet, but there was little point in telling Martin that. "Sure. It's a deal."

"Deal?"

"Yup. Oh yeah…and if you happen to need a little pick-me-up, just ask Guerrilla. But no phones. Same goes for the meeting—make sure the cops don't find out." He lowered his voice a little. "Shoot him an anonymous text saying, 'Wanna catch a hockey game?' An hour after he texts back, he'll be at the McDonald's by the ice arena."

Martin didn't respond. His face was expressionless. Obviously, the police were on the right track if Korpi's gang used these kinds of spy tactics to throw them off the trail. "Okay," he said finally.

"Good. The cops were probably out celebrating their victory last night, but at least one of them will be clearheaded enough to notice if someone's talking openly about the case."

"Right. So…you still want to go over this appeals form?"

"No," said Korpi as he stood up. He gestured to the guard, and as the man shuffled over, he said to Martin, "Send it straight to the court once you get it ready."

The guard approached. Korpi looked up, "I'd like some lunch now."

"Fine," said the guard. "Cabbage rolls today."

"My favorite."

Martin watched his client being escorted from the room. A steak dinner would hit the spot, he decided. With a couple of cold beers. But before he did anything else he would send that text. As soon as he got his phone back at the gate, anyhow. Yeah, and a new SIM card would be a good idea.

CHAPTER 17
THURSDAY, 1:50 P.M.
JOUTSAMO'S APARTMENT, HELSINKI

Joutsamo lay idly on the sofa of her two-room apartment. She had on an extra-large green T-shirt, baggy black shorts and a blanket draped over her legs. It was almost two in the afternoon. The worst of her headache had succumbed to ibuprofen, a sandwich and a soft drink, but her mood was still listless. Her only consolation was that she hadn't planned to get anything done today anyway, since it was the day after the Christmas party. So there was no reason to feel bad about being idle.

But there was one thing she had managed to do. She had sent a happy-name-day text to a friend of hers who had moved to London. A very cute friend by the name of Jouko.

The television was off—nothing of interest was on in the afternoon anyway. Something from Madonna was playing on the radio in the background. On top of the bookcase was a picture of Joutsamo's parents. With the two of them seeming to stare at her, she didn't care to look in that direction at the moment.

The evening had gone on right up until the last call at 3:30 at the Zetor Bar. Luckily, Nykänen and Kannas had been in the mood to dance. The more she danced, the less she drank.

She wondered if she should force herself to get up and clean. A fitting punishment for such overindulgence. Cleaning was too much to ask, but she got up nonetheless—if only because she was bored of lying down—and padded into the kitchen nook. She poured some water into the teapot and rubbed her weary face. She didn't need to look in the mirror to see how terrible she looked. Maybe she should take a shower and force herself outdoors. All she could see from the kitchen window was the greenish flank of the neighboring building, but at least it wasn't raining. According to the thermometer, it was twenty-five degrees. That would perk her up.

The tea water was just beginning to hiss when Joutsamo heard the phone ring. But where in the hell was it? She followed the ringing to the left-hand pocket of her overcoat, which still reeked of cigarette smoke, peeked at the caller ID, and answered with a smile.

"Well, hi," she said before clearing her throat. The deepness of her own voice startled her.

"Hi," said a perky woman's voice on the other end. The caller was Sanna Römpötti. "How's it going? By your voice I'd say not so well."

"Well, I'm fine now. The team had a Christmas party."

"I hope I didn't wake you?"

"No," said Joutsamo. The teapot began to whistle and she returned to the kitchen with the phone on her ear.

"Quiet day at the press room here. I thought I'd lure you out for a beer…er… lunch."

"I'm thinking probably not…" said Joutsamo, perhaps a bit too emphatically.

"Just wanted to congratulate you on the Korpi case. Well done."

"Well, it wasn't really all that complicated. Muuri did a good job on the prosecution."

Römpötti paused for a moment. "What else is new?"

Joutsamo looked at her bubbling teapot. "Figured I'd have a cup of tea."

The reporter laughed on the other end. "OK, get better. We'll talk later."

"Bye," said Joutsamo. She set the phone down on the table and took a packet of tea out of the cupboard, and a teacup from the drying rack. Her apartment didn't have a dishwasher.

Joutsamo was pouring steaming water into the cup when the phone rang again. She paid no attention to the screen, assuming Römpötti had thought of some hangover joke.

"Yeah?" she answered.

A second's pause passed. "Is this Joutsamo?" asked a woman's voice. Joutsamo recognized Mari immediately, and her fear.

"Yeah, it's me. Sorry, I thought you were someone else."

"OK, uhh…" said Lehtonen, trailing off.

"What's wrong?"

"It's really not that serious, but I thought maybe you could help."

"Of course. How?"

"Well, yesterday my ex-husband called to harass me out about that court case, and now this afternoon when Laura came home from school, the lock was all gummed up with some kind of glue."

"I see," said Joutsamo. She felt sharper already. "What did he say on the phone?"

"Called me stupid for talking to the police. You know, the kind of things exes say when they're drunk."

Joutsamo knew the type. "Are you at home now?"

"Yes. The locksmith changed the lock, so we're okay on that front, but I just wondered if you could do something about Anton so he doesn't start with his harassment again."

"Can't really take him to jail for it, but I can sure look into it. How'd Laura react?"

"Kind of confused. She didn't really understand because I haven't told her everything."

Joutsamo gazed out the window. Her head was already beginning to clear. "We'll try to do something about it."

"Just try. That's all I ask."

Immediately after hanging up the phone, Joutsamo dialed Takamäki's number.

CHAPTER 18
THURSDAY, 3:30 P.M.
KALLIO NEIGHBORHOOD, HELSINKI

Suhonen sat down in the front seat of a gray Peugeot parked at the intersection of Vaasa and Fleming, and took a folded piece of office paper out of the breast pocket of his coat. It was a mug shot printout of forty-year-old Anton Teittinen, Mari Lehtonen's ex-husband, his dark hair hanging over his forehead, eyes glowering at the camera from beneath his brows. His bloated face was serious enough without the scowl. The photo had been snapped a year ago, after Teittinen was arrested for a bar brawl. A search of his record had turned up several other petty crimes.

Suhonen was out in the field alone. He had begun his search for Teittinen at the man's home address. No luck knocking on the apartment door. He had listened through the mail slot, but heard nothing. Back outside, Suhonen had checked to see if any lights were on. The man could be hiding out in the dark apartment, of course, but that was unlikely.

He could be at work, but that was also unlikely. The police had his phone number, so in principle, Suhonen could have called and tried to set up a meeting, but that wouldn't have been as effective— the encounter should come as a complete surprise to Teittinen.

Suhonen started the car, drove a couple blocks and turned onto Helsinki Avenue. Not finding a single parking space, he pulled the car up to a bus stop.

He got out and walked the remaining distance to the Corner Pub. The pavement was slick and the cold seemed to be tightening its grip. It felt about ten degrees below freezing.

The stench of smoke hit him at the door, even with only a third of the seats in the pub occupied. A few tables boasted groups of three and four, while others were occupied by just one man and a beer. Suhonen's eyes quickly took in the room. The hands on the clock showed half past three.

Teittinen was sitting alone at a corner table reading a daily. Nothing on Suhonen's face betrayed the fact that he had found his quarry.

The bartender stood behind the bar with an inquiring look.

"Coffee," said Suhonen.

The man didn't say anything, just took out a cup and filled it. "One euro."

Suhonen put the coin on the bar and took a sip. Not bad. Metallica's "Nothing Else Matters" was playing softly in the background.

Teittinen had draped his dark, hooded jacket over the neighboring chair. He looked larger than Suhonen had expected, and was wearing jeans and a gray, paint-stained sweatshirt. His hair fell over his forehead in the same way it had in the mug shots. His skin was strikingly bad.

Suhonen took his coffee and strode over to Teittinen's table. "Looks like you got room," said Suhonen as he pulled up a wooden chair. The table was riddled with cigarette burns.

Teittinen sized up Suhonen. "Room over there too," he growled, but Suhonen had already sat down.

Suhonen remained silent and Teittinen started to get edgy. "What the hell?"

Suhonen just took a sip of coffee.

"What, you wanna piece of me? Here I am minding my own business and you come butting in. Look around, asshole. Plenty of seats to be had."

"I'm not looking for a fight."

"Well you're damn sure gonna get one if you don't start explaining."

Suhonen calmly drank his coffee. "Listen, Teittinen," he began, then paused briefly. Mentioning the man's name seemed to have the desired effect, as he flinched. Suhonen went on, "You've been harassing a friend of mine."

"How you know my name?"

"I know your shoe size, too."

That was no lie. He had gotten it from one of the case files, in which Teittinen had kicked a victim in a fight.

"Size ten."

"What the fuck? What is this?"

"Listen to me when I'm talking to you. I just said you've been harassing a friend of mine."

Teittinen had apparently come to the conclusion that he shouldn't mess with Suhonen. This was the kind of guy who could be packing, and he seemed to be in good enough shape. Teittinen didn't even have a knife. "What friend?"

"Mari Lehtonen."

"What, you banging that bitch?"

"No, just a friend."

"And who are you?"

"I already told you—I'm her friend. Use your

ears, idiot." Suhonen clearly had the upper hand, and was taking full advantage of it.

"Yeah, right. So what did I supposedly do?"

"You know."

Teittinen wrinkled up his brows. "I called her once and bitched her out for talking to the fucking cops about that shooting, and then taking it to court."

"So?"

"What do you mean, so? You don't talk to the cops...everyone knows that."

"What were you doing at her apartment earlier this afternoon?"

Teittinen looked genuinely confused. "Phh. Been drinking here all day."

"Bullshit."

"What are you a cop? This some kinda interrogation?"

"Fuck it," Suhonen grumbled. "You want to go outside or in here? Fists or knives?"

Teittinen sized him up once more and changed his tack. "Marko!" he shouted at the bartender. "Ain't I been here since noon?"

Marko appraised the situation at the corner table and shouted back, "Yup, been here all day."

Suhonen was confused. He didn't put much in the bartender's claim, but Teittinen's look of genuine surprise was perplexing.

"There you have it," said Teittinen in a triumphant voice. "Shit, tough guy, check your facts before you come hassling an innocent man."

Suhonen wondered who had glued the lock. "Whatever the case, you stay away from Lehtonen," he said.

"Fine. I've had more of her stinky ass than I care to remember."

Suhonen stood up and left, leaving the coffee cup on the table.

"Asshole," Teittinen stammered just loud enough for Suhonen to hear.

* * *

The corridors of the VCU were quiet tonight.

"Care for some coffee?" asked Takamäki.

Suhonen shook his head.

"Well, I'll skip it too, then."

The detectives were sitting in Takamäki's office. Outside the window, all was dark, save for the yellow glow of the street lights. The temperature had dipped to ten degrees Fahrenheit, and a light snow was drifting down from the skies.

"If it wasn't Teittinen, who was it?" said Takamäki.

"Well, he confessed to the drunken phone call, so why would he deny the glue job? It was just a little bullying."

Takamäki went on, "Think it was one of Korpi's guys?"

"That was my first thought."

"But why now that the trial is over? You'd think the point of any harassment would be to scare the witness out of appearing in court."

"It's possible that Lehtonen has another enemy," said Suhonen. "Or maybe her daughter's friends were just playing a prank."

Takamäki thought for a moment. "What do you think we should do?"

"Well, a little glue in a lock is a pretty innocent thing. And since we have no idea who did it, it's all guesswork anyway. No point in starting anything."

"Agreed. Korpi wouldn't be using a glue bottle for his payback."

"So we should just lay low?"

"Yeah. But let's keep tabs on it," said Takamäki.

"You want me to fill Joutsamo in?"

"No need. I'll tell her tomorrow when she gets in. Let her have at least a half-day off."

* * *

Laura Lehtonen was walking alone along Western Brahe Street toward home. Her face stung in the frigid air and she pulled her wool hat further down over her ears. The red of her scarf and parka was carefully matched with that of her hat. The snow creaked beneath her boots.

It was just past seven o'clock and her theater feedback session had just ended. The director had praised Laura's performance, hence her buoyant mood. The director had also mentioned a spring project, one much more demanding than the current one. Laura would play one of the main characters.

Skaters flocked on the ice rink. Laura hoped to go skating someday soon with her best friend, Mira.

Her thoughts turned to school. Her homework was done, but she still had to study for tomorrow's English test. Mom had said she could stay in theater as long as she kept her grades up. Her thoughts returned to theater. On Saturday, her mother was taking her to see the new musical at the Helsinki City Theater, for which they had bought tickets back in August.

The glue thing had been weird, as was Mom's court appearance. But they had talked it over enough that neither incident bothered her anymore. The director's positive feedback on her performance made her feel like skipping.

She didn't notice the dark-colored car until it was nearly upon her. It slowed just abreast of her and kept pace. She glanced over, unable to tell whether anyone but the driver was inside.

Laura felt panicked and she quickened her gait. The car did the same. "Laura," said a man's voice. "Stop. It's the police."

Laura thought for a moment before stopping. The car stopped too and the driver's window rolled down. A hand emerged with an envelope.

"I was bringing this to your mother," said the voice. "Could you please take it to her?"

Laura stepped closer to the car and took the envelope. On the front, the words *MARI LEHTONEN* were scrawled in marker.

The window slid up and the car zoomed off.

Laura was confused, but she continued on her way home. Still ten minutes to go.

Their 1930s seven-story building was situated at what used to be the end of the number 3 streetcar line, just opposite Porvoo Street 21, the site of the murder.

Laura dashed up the stairs. The new lock was still stiff, but she got it open. "Hi," she hollered from the door.

"Have you eaten?" asked mom from the kitchen.

"What do we have?"

"Pork sausage soup."

It wasn't really her favorite. She hung her parka on the entry hook and went into the kitchen with the envelope.

"Some policeman gave me this. It's for you," she said, handing over the envelope.

Mari stopped stirring the soup and took it.

"What policeman?"

"I dunno. I was walking home past the ice rink and this car pulled up."

"What car? A police car?"

"No, it was smaller. I didn't see what kind." Her mother's grilling was making her wonder.

"How do you know it was a policeman?"

"That's what he said. It wasn't?"

"I don't know. But how many times have I told you not to talk to strangers?"

"Well, he just handed it over and took off. What is it?"

Mari was still holding the envelope. She took out a kitchen knife, neatly cut open the flap, removed the letter and began to read.

"What is it?" said Laura. "Why are you shaking?"

Mari didn't respond. The letter was terse: *THAT'S HOW EASY IT WOULD BE.*

The paper slipped out of Mari's hand. She felt like screaming, but no sound came. She sunk to the floor and leaned back against the kitchen cabinets, her whole body seeming to tremble. She wrapped her arms around her folded knees.

"What's wrong, Mom?"

"Sweetie…uhh…my phone, please."

Laura dashed back into the entryway.

CHAPTER 19
THURSDAY, 8:25 P.M.
PASILA POLICE HEADQUARTERS

Takamäki glanced around the VCU conference room where Suhonen, Kulta, Kohonen, Kannas and a couple of men from Lieutenant Kafka's division had gathered. Kafka's men were currently on duty, and had come to listen to the briefing in case they were called to help.

"Okay, let's get started," said Takamäki. The briefing was primarily intended for Kafka's men. "I'll run through the key points of the case first so we're all on the same page, then we can talk about how to proceed."

The others nodded.

"A single parent by the name of Mari Lehtonen recently testified against Risto Korpi. I'm sure everyone is familiar with Korpi's gang?"

"Yeah," answered Kulta, and the others nodded.

"Good," said Takamäki. "Well, this Lehtonen testified that she saw Korpi waiting in the car while Esa Nyberg shot Tomi Salmela back in September. The trial was yesterday, and everything went smoothly. Since the verdict, we've had two incidents. Today, either late morning or early afternoon, somebody filled her door lock with super glue, and about an hour and a half ago, a man claiming to be a police officer gave Lehtonen's daughter Laura a letter as she was walking home along Western Brahe Street. The letter said, '*that's how easy it would be.*' Clearly referring to kidnapping the girl. Right now, Joutsamo is at their apartment and we have a patrol posted at the entrance of the building. Last I heard, the situation was secure."

"How are they doing?" asked Kulta.

"According to Joutsamo, they've calmed down. Just watching TV, but Mari is definitely scared, which is rubbing off on her daughter."

"So Joutsamo's spending the night?"

"Yes, same with the patrol. Kannas, what'd you find out about the paper and the marker?"

Forensics had done a quick analysis of the threat letter. "Standard 20-pound stationery. Same stuff you see everywhere. We found some fingerprints, but they all belonged to the mom. The envelope was also standard store-bought stock, and no fingerprints. As far as the marker, it was more felt-tip pen than marker. One-millimeter line width, which is about consistent with a Text Mark 700."

"With a what?" asked Kulta.

Kannas pointed to the flip chart in the corner, which held three different-colored felt-tip pens on the tray. "Those. Garden variety markers."

"So not much to go on, then," said Takamäki.

"Right... But the envelope was apparently sealed with moisture-sensitive adhesive, not the peel-and-stick type. If that's the case and somebody licked it, we can get the DNA. Same thing with the envelope itself if it has any hairs or sweat drops. We sent the envelope and letter to the NBI's lab for further testing with a rush on it."

"Good," said Takamäki. "Sounds like we could get somewhere on that." Still, they'd need a matching DNA sample on file. And of course, the envelope could have been sealed with water. "Anybody have anything else?"

"So the girl didn't catch the plate number?" said Kulta.

"Nope."

"I can look for the car on the surveillance cameras in the area," said Kulta. "Unless there's a better idea."

"Sounds good. Check the database for any cameras on Brahe Street, but be sure to look further out, too. The suspect was probably trailing her all the way from the theater academy on Haapaniemi Street."

Suhonen's phone rang. He glanced at the screen and excused himself from the conference room.

"Hey," said Suhonen in the hallway.

"Hey," said Salmela.

"What's up?"

"This is kind of a strange thing, but there's a lot of buzz going around about this Mari Lehtonen."

"What kinda buzz you talking about?"

Salmela paused for a while. "She seems to have found herself on someone's hit list…"

"Tell me more."

"Well, someone's got a lotta dime and wants to give her a real hard time. Damn, that was like a poem. Not exactly Tommy Tabermann, but not far off. I oughta pick up the pen…"

"Stick to the point," Suhonen snapped.

Salmela was silent for a moment. "What, something happened?"

"First tell me what you know. What kind of hard time, and who?"

"That's the whole problem. I don't know whether it's true or just talk…"

"Get to the point."

"Right. Well, word is you can make some good money for pushing her around."

"What kind of pushing."

"What do you think? Harassment…threats against the family…that kind of thing. Problem is, word's going around a bit too much."

Suhonen knew what he meant. In that case, it was probably planted. Such a rumor was bound to spread quickly in the bars with everyone wanting to crow about what they knew.

"What's your guess?"

"I dunno. I'm sure there's some truth to it, but it sounds more like a plant. True or not I figured I'd call."

Suhonen thought for a moment. "Well, thanks. All I can tell you is someone gave Lehtonen's daughter a letter threatening to kidnap her."

"No shit."

"Nothing happened, but we got our hackles up over here."

"No kidding…"

"And then earlier someone squirted glue in her door."

"In the lock?"

"Right."

Salmela didn't respond.

"Helloo," said Suhonen after a while.

"Well, if this someone's already doing it, then why would they trumpet it all over the place. Unless these things happened because of all the talk?"

"Good question. Did you have a particular 'someone' in mind?"

Salmela smiled. "Well, someone someone... Isn't it pretty obvious?"

"Well, yeah. But still, why all the talk?"

"Either this someone's recruiting more guys or he just wants to extend his reach. You know. A little guerrilla marketing, right?" said Salmela, with emphasis on the word *guerrilla*.

"Right," said Suhonen, and he hung up the phone.

* * *

Suhonen stepped back into the conference room and waited till all eyes were on him.

"Well?" said Takamäki.

"A horse named Champion's gonna win at the races tonight," he said with a smile.

Takamäki looked impatient.

"So my informant tells me there's a lot of street talk about getting back at Lehtonen. Even more about her than the best places to steal Christmas presents for the kiddos."

The others were not humored.

"But," Suhonen continued, "of course there's another angle. If someone really wanted to get back at her, why would they be advertising it? Might just be a cover."

Kulta looked skeptical. "Right, a twelve-year-old girl is being stalked, but it's just a cover."

"My point exactly," said Suhonen. "If someone actually wanted revenge, they wouldn't fuck around. They'd just do it—girl in the trunk, a bullet in the brain, and the body in the drink. And mom goes too.

Right now, it's all talk, threats and games. Intimidation."

Takamäki nodded while the others just stared. "At any rate, the only charge we can work with right now is intimidating a witness. The maximum penalty is three years in prison, which means we can't use phone taps."

"And we have no suspects," said Kulta.

"Really?" said Suhonen. "It's obvious that this is connected to Korpi's trial, and Jere Siikala is one of Korpi's lieutenants. If Guerrilla's not the perpetrator, he's at least the instigator."

"Based on what evidence?" said Kulta.

Takamäki cut in. "The threshold for reasonable suspicion isn't terribly high. I won't open an investigation in Siikala's name yet, but obviously we'll have to start looking into his activities. The prosecutor never charged him in the murder investigation, so we can't use that as a pretense for surveillance."

"What about the mom and the kid?" asked Kannas.

"We'll have to consult with Joutsamo about that."

"Just thinking that a round-the-clock operation like this takes four guys per day, at the least. That's a lot of manpower..."

Kulta interjected. "Ever heard of that German prosecutor who lives in a fenced-in bunker with his family? The kids get carted off to school in an armored Mercedes?"

"There're plenty of Finnish cops who've hung it up because of threats, too," said Kannas. "Even if the cop can deal with it, the family's another story."

"Let's think about that later," said Takamäki. "For tonight, the situation is under control."

* * *

Joutsamo was sitting in a recliner in the living room, while Mari and Laura were on the sofa. An episode of an American legal drama was playing on the television.

"I'm glad you were able to come," said Mari.

"Yeah," said Joutsamo. Lehtonen had called her in a panic after opening the letter. Initially, she'd had trouble understanding what had happened, but ultimately the extent of the threat had come to light. Takamäki had sent Joutsamo to their apartment and launched some kind of an operation. What exactly that was, Joutsamo didn't know, and she didn't want to talk details within earshot of Mari and Laura.

"Have you guys been following this series?" said Joutsamo, attempting to take their minds off the case. They had already gone over it once, and Joutsamo had assured her that, although it was unfortunate, it was rare and gave little cause for worry.

"Off and on," said Lehtonen. "So what happens now?"

"Well, the Boston lawyer is probably…"

"No, I mean with *our* case."

Joutsamo smiled. "Pretty soon you guys will go to bed. I'll be here on the sofa, and we also have an officer posted at the entrance. That's about it."

"And tomorrow?"

"We'll talk about that with Lieutenant Takamäki in the morning."

"I have an English test tomorrow," Laura chimed in.

"We'll have to see about that. It's possible you'll both get a day off."

"What's that supposed to mean?" said Mari, her arms outspread in obvious frustration.

"That Laura's not going to school and you're not going to work."

Mari stood up. "I'll get your sheets."

FRIDAY,
DECEMBER 15

CHAPTER 20
FRIDAY, 7:45 A.M.
PASILA POLICE HEADQUARTERS

Takamäki was sitting in the slightly more spacious, but equally joyless office of his direct supervisor Karila, chief of the VCU. Both men were nursing cups of coffee.

"Shitty deal," said Karila.

"It is."

"We just don't have the numbers for an operation like that. It would tie up two officers during the day, one for the girl and one for the mom. Evenings and nights we might be able to make do with one. Once you figure in all the shifts, you get six, seven cops. Or eight if mom and daughter are out separately in the evening."

Takamäki took a sip of coffee. He had come to the same calculation the previous evening. "A good ten percent of our entire unit."

"Damn right. Of course we can't just leave them to fend for themselves."

"We don't really have any official witness protection program, but maybe we could rig one," said Takamäki. "We could get her an apartment in another city and help her get a job."

"Wasn't there some working group looking into witness protection?" Karila asked between sips of coffee.

"Yeah, but they didn't come up with anything concrete. Just suggestions due to lack of funding. Nowadays that famous Kennedy quote might go more like: 'Ask not what you can do for your country, ask what you can *not* do because of the economy.'"

"Right."

"Besides, we have no idea how long this will last or how serious it'll be. For now we'll take it seriously, of course, but Lehtonen is just a random citizen that testified in court, not an informant or a biker trying to get out of a gang."

"True," nodded Karila.

"The easiest thing might be to send them to a safe house for a few days or a couple weeks. In the meantime, we'll try to resolve the threats."

Karila thought for a moment. "Do you think they can be resolved? If word's out already, then…"

"I have a few ideas," said Takamäki. "First thing we do is put Korpi in solitary, so at least he can't be doling out orders. And then there're a few other things…" he said, and listed the alternatives.

* * *

An hour later, Takamäki was ringing the doorbell of Lehtonen's apartment. Joutsamo came to the door in track pants and a white T-shirt.

"Good morning," said Takamäki with a smile.

Joutsamo looked at him dejectedly and raked her fingers through her dark hair. She invited him in and he hung his coat on the hook and went into the kitchen where Mari and Laura were eating breakfast. Takamäki greeted them both and sat down in an empty chair at the table.

"Let's cut right to the chase," he said. Initially, Takamäki had wondered whether he should talk to Mari without Laura present, but the situation affected them both, so Laura's participation was helpful.

"Fine by me," said Mari.

"The threats against you are being taken very seriously, and we've opened an investigation. Your safety is our number one priority. Number two is to stop the threats, and number three is to apprehend those responsible. We strongly suspect that this is related to your testifying against Risto Korpi."

"Well, that's pretty obvious," snorted Mari. Laura sat beside her, watching quietly.

Takamäki was unfazed by the comment. "Unfortunately, we have no proof of that. We made little progress on the investigation overnight, but we're expecting some results from the crime lab today, among other things. But these have to do with priorities two and three. Right now we should talk about number one."

"What about it?"

"How to protect you," said Takamäki. He had decided not to give her any choice in the matter. "We're going to have to move you two out of this apartment."

"Move?"

"Yes. Whoever is threatening you obviously knows your address, so it's not safe to stay here."

"So where? And for how long?"

"There's a safe house in Kirkkonummi. You'll get your own room and Laura will have a private tutor. I'll talk personally with your employer about the situation. I can't say how long it will be, probably a matter of weeks, but at least until the threat against you has been eliminated."

Lehtonen was quiet. "And what if you can't do that?"

"Then we'd have to look for a more permanent solution. We could relocate you to another city. Of course, we'd assist you in finding housing, schools and employment. But I doubt it will come to that."

Lehtonen looked to Joutsamo. "What do you think?"

"I think the safe house sounds like a good idea." Of course, Joutsamo had little choice but to say so.

Takamäki went on. "Of course, this is entirely voluntary. We can't force you to go."

Mari turned to Laura. "And what do you think?"

Laura shrugged. It was unlikely her English test had any bearing on the matter. "I guess it's okay."

"Then that's what we'll do," said Mari. "When do we leave?"

"As soon as your bags are packed. They've got washing machines and bed linens there, so you won't need any. Pack any personal hygiene items, clothes, school books and reading material."

Mari nodded.

Takamäki turned back to Joutsamo and handed her a packet of papers. "Go through these with Mari and Laura before they leave. The squad downstairs will take them, but you should go along."

* * *

Their bags were packed within half an hour.

"I really don't know about this," said Mari as she paused at the kitchen door. Joutsamo was sitting at the table with the packet of papers Takamäki had given her.

"It's what's best for you and Laura. It'll also give us a little more freedom to concentrate on the case."

"I suppose," said Mari. "What's with the papers?"

"These are instructions that I'll need to go through with you and Laura."

Mari called for Laura.

"These are just some general dos and don'ts. First off, under no circumstances should you reveal your location to anybody. That's the most important rule. Not to friends, not to anybody. And no texting," said Joutsamo, glancing at Laura, whose eyes betrayed her alarm. "Once at the safe house, you'll be known as Mari and Laura Virtanen."

"Virtanen?" said Mari.

"Yes. No need to change your first names. You may not leave the safe house without an escort. Not to the store, not to the newsstand. Nowhere alone. If you want to buy something you'll have to fill out a form at the front desk, they'll purchase the items in bulk."

Joutsamo continued down the list. "All contact with the outside must be kept to a minimum. If your location is compromised, you'll be moved right away. Let's see…then I have what looks like an American list of safety measures. Not sure if this is any use to you, but since my orders are to go through them, that's what we'll do."

Lehtonen didn't say anything.

"Says here that women tend to sit in the driver's seat for a while before they start the car. That's an opportune time for attackers to strike by opening the driver's side door. So what you should do is lock the doors and leave promptly."

"I don't have a car," said Lehtonen.

"Right," said Joutsamo, continuing down the list. "Let's see…if once you're in the car, a man somehow surprises you and demands to be driven somewhere, do not obey. You should drive straight into a wall and then escape on foot. Your seatbelt and air bag will protect you, but the attacker in the back seat will be stunned by the impact."

"What if he's in the front seat and has an air bag?"

Joutsamo ignored the comment. "Then it says that you should check the vehicle beforehand, as well as the surrounding area. If a lone man is sitting in an adjacent vehicle, you should not go near your car. If there's a van parked on the driver's side, you should enter your car through the passenger door, because an attacker might be waiting behind the sliding door of the van."

Both Lehtonens were silent.

Joutsamo kept her eyes on the paper. "No stairs, only take elevators."

"That seems a bit paranoid," said Mari.

"Better paranoid than dead," said Joutsamo.

* * *

Corrections Officer Salo rapped on Korpi's cell door with his billy club. Already the previous evening, Korpi's cellmate had filed for transfer to the protective ward, so Korpi was alone inside. Not having been placed in any programs yet, he got to lie around in his cell.

Salo had brought two additional guards along in case of any trouble. He didn't wait for Korpi to open the door, just swung it open. Korpi was lying on his bunk, apparently asleep.

"Let's go."

"Where?" said Korpi, his eyes still closed.

"Get up."

Korpi sat up on the edge of the bed. "Huh. Three of you, eh? Where we headed?"

Salo sighed and glanced at the paper in his hand.

"Based on prison ordinance eighteen, section five, paragraph one, the warden has ordered that you be placed in solitary confinement."

"I don't recall just now what the wording was in that paragraph," said Korpi. "Perhaps you could refresh my memory."

Salo read off of the paper. "Says here: 'An inmate may be kept in isolation from the rest of the prison population if such is necessary to prevent the inmate from seriously endangering another's life or well-being.'"

"So whose well-being have I seriously endangered?"

"Doesn't say here."

"Then I'm not going anywhere."

Salo glanced at his partners. "Korpi, we can do this the easy way or the hard way. The end result will be the same: you in solitary."

Korpi just lay back on his bunk without a word.

"Have it your way," said Salo, and he radioed for more backup.

"Should we put him in cuffs?" asked one of the backups.

Salo nodded. "Hands and feet."

The three guards set upon the struggling Korpi. One of them pinned Korpi's hands and upper body to the floor while the others cuffed his ankles. Then they tossed him onto his belly, wrenched his hands behind his back and slapped the cuffs around his wrists.

CHAPTER 21
FRIDAY, 1:20 P.M.
KAARELA, NORTH HELSINKI

Suhonen lay in the same ditch as he had three months earlier. Then the soil had been wet, but now it was frozen, albeit mostly devoid of snow. To stay dry, he had spread a military style rain poncho over the ground, which was now thawing from the warmth of his body.

Suhonen was wearing a parka, snowpants, boots and a thick, dark stocking cap. He also had a backpack, camera and a few birding field guides. Although it was unlikely that anyone else would be out here in the woods, the birding enthusiast disguise had come in handy on many occasions.

His camera was equipped with a telephoto lens, useful because it also functioned as a telescope. Legally, his actions could be viewed as electronic surveillance, but since he never took any pictures, there was never any proof.

Jere Siikala was in the house. When Suhonen arrived to survey the place around nine in the morning, the lights had been on. He hadn't had to wait long: by nine-thirty, he had observed Siikala moving about in the kitchen. It appeared that Guerrilla had made some coffee, after which there had been no more activity.

Nobody had left the house, nor entered it. The same Mazda that was used in Tomi Salmela's murder was parked in the driveway. In October, the police had returned the car to the executor of the estate, but apparently Siikala had reacquired it.

Suhonen thought lying around here was a bit silly, but such was necessary because the offense was too minor for the police to obtain a phone tap. Siikala had probably acquired a new phone anyway, if he even used one anymore.

Since Siikala wasn't an official suspect yet, Suhonen's only job was to keep an eye on him and follow him if he went anywhere. So far he hadn't.

Time dragged on. Suhonen spotted a chickadee on a tree branch and he aimed the camera toward it, but the bird flew off.

He had already mulled over his relationship with Raija. It had gradually deepened to the point that they were considering moving in together. He wasn't sure it was what he wanted. In a way, he did, but in another, he didn't. At any rate, the matter was not up to him alone.

Right now, their relationship was about having fun, but Suhonen suspected that after the move, more mundane issues would emerge. He guessed that the biggest risk to their relationship would be that he'd end up working too many evenings and nights. That just might grate on her in the long run, though now she claimed it wouldn't be a problem.

Or maybe Suhonen was just afraid of commitment. He wasn't entirely sure.

A movement in the kitchen window interrupted his thoughts. Suhonen raised the camera and looked through the lens. Siikala was toiling at the stove. Suhonen lowered the camera. If the guy was making lunch, he wouldn't be leaving for at least thirty minutes.

Suhonen took his phone out of his pocket and speed-dialed Takamäki's number.

"Hello," answered Takamäki.

"It's Suhonen."

"Well?"

"Nothing. He's still in the house. Making lunch right now."

"Hmm."

"Kinda hungry myself, but my sandwich ended up freezing out here." Suhonen's voice wasn't so much resentful as it was probing. "How long do you want me out here?"

"If you have a better idea, I'd like to hear it. Siikala's our only lead right now. If you ask me, we ought to keep an eye on him."

"I guess. At some point I'll need a shift change, though. Feet are starting to go numb."

"Okay. Kulta will be there around three. Let's do shifts every six hours, say at three and nine."

"Would be nice to get that phone warrant if we're gonna sink this much time into it. At least we'd have his number then. It'd help."

"I'll think about it," said Takamäki, and he hung up the phone.

Suhonen lay back down in the ditch to think about what he should think about.

* * *

Mari Lehtonen was sitting on the bed with her feet atop a coarse woolen blanket, reading a book. Laura sat in a similar position along the opposite wall of the smallish room, which resembled a hotel room in as much as it had two beds, a desk, television and a small bathroom. The décor was more barren than the average hotel room's, though timeless: it had been out of fashion for at least thirty years. On first glance, Mari had wondered if the furnishings had been bought on clearance from some thrift store.

The window opened onto a gloomy snow-starved spruce forest.

The safe house was a largish building with rooms off of a long hallway: about twenty units with a common area and a kitchen in the middle.

Joutsamo had escorted the mother and daughter to the safe house. It was still unclear to Mari what sort of place this was; it didn't seem like the police ran it. Rather, it appeared to be some sort of hideout for people who had found themselves targets of serious threats. As they were escorted inside, the only other person they encountered was a thickly muscled guard. Apparently such was needed to keep out any intruders. The guard sat in a booth next to the entrance, dressed in a track suit, and accompanied by a network of security cameras. He had greeted Mari and given her a printout of the house rules.

Mari put the book down—she couldn't concentrate. For lunch, they had had sausage soup, and it was still several hours till dinner. Nothing else was happening. Just outside the door to their room was some kind of weekly schedule. Today, it included some conversation groups, a cooking class, and art and music classes for kids, but Laura was probably too old for those.

She turned to look at her daughter, now reading on her stomach with her feet kicked up. Mari felt fairly comfortable—the place was safe, at least. And, for once she had time to read. But something still nagged at her.

She picked up her book again, but was still unable to focus. She tried to pinpoint what it was that didn't seem right, but came up empty. Her instincts told her that something was wrong. Well, damn right something's wrong when she and her daughter are holed up in the woods hiding from murderers. But everything would work out, she assured herself. Joutsamo and Takamäki—indeed the entire police force—were on their side and would do everything in their power to protect them. The bodybuilder downstairs would keep them safe here and have droves of cops on the place if necessary. Everything was okay. Look at it like a free vacation, she told herself. Read a few classics and relax. It's what you've always wanted. Kind of like a Mediterranean vacation without the swimming pools and beaches— just a hotel room and a book.

Mari wasn't so sure about her attempts at being positive.

An incoming text message announced itself. Laura gave a passing glance as Mari got up, walked to the coat hooks at the door and fetched her phone out of her coat pocket, but the girl's attention soon returned to her book.

Mari read the message—it was from her boss, Essi Saari: *Hi. I chatted with the police. Lay low as long as you need. It's paid leave. Good luck!*

Mari read the message over and over again. Of course she was happy that her employer was being supportive, even promising to pay her, but "lay low as long as you need?"

Lay low—the wording seemed about as appealing as these four oppressive walls. The rules stated that she could go out in the yard, but no further.

"Who was it from?" asked Laura.

"Work."

The girl stared at her mom for a while. "You know, this is actually kind of exciting. Kinda like a movie, you know...witnesses hiding out in a hotel room. The only person that ever knocks is room service, except for the one time that the killer comes to the door."

"Stop it," said Mari. Just then, a knock came at the door. Both of them startled.

"Don't open it," whispered Laura.

The knock came again. Mari shuddered, not that there was anything to worry about—this place definitely didn't have room service. She slipped the door chain into the slot, unlocked the door and peeked through the gap.

"Hi," said a dark-skinned woman with a smile. She looked about forty, wore an afro and had a three-inch laceration running down her cheek. The wound was old enough that the stitches were gone. She spoke with an accent. "I make some coffee. You like some?"

Mari didn't know how to react. Were they allowed to speak with others here? The rulebook forbade revealing any personal details. Not even your own name.

The woman smiled, though her scar made her expression rather gruesome. "I'm Agatha. Come, come. It's okay. I been here now two months. I know rules."

Mari nodded. Agatha, huh? Was that her real name? "Laura, honey. I'm going to have a cup of coffee. I'll be over in the common room."

Laura looked up. "You're leaving me? Can't I come?"

"Oh…of course."

Laura slipped a bookmark into her book.

Mari turned and smiled at the woman waiting at the door. "Alright. We'll be right there."

Agatha had apparently put the coffee on before knocking on their door, as it was already waiting when Mari and Laura reached the common area. The chairs and table were a newer vintage than those in the rooms.

"You have beautiful girl," said Agatha, her back turned toward them as she poured the coffees at the counter. Laura looked embarrassed.

"Yes," said Mari, not knowing what else to say.

"Does she like coffee?" asked Agatha.

Mari glanced at Laura, who rolled her eyes as if to say that 'no, isn't there any tea?' Mari shrugged. "No, she doesn't."

"What about tea?" said Agatha, turning to look at Laura.

Laura nodded with a smile. "Thanks."

Agatha returned the smile, took a tea bag from the cabinet, put it in a cup and doused it with hot water from the pot. "It is no worry, but we pay for tea and coffee together. Easier for us if each just pays five euro per week, no matter if we drink tea or coffee. These I will buy," said Agatha, and she gave Laura her tea. A bowl of sugar was on the table, and Laura added a couple of spoonfuls.

Agatha sat down at the table and gazed at Mari with her dark eyes. "So…what is your story?"

Mari hesitated. "I can't say. The police…"

Agatha laughed. "Yes, we are not supposed to

talk. But here you have to. Or you go crazy. We are all here in same boat."

Mari wasn't so eager to break the rules, however, so she turned the question around. "What's your story?"

"How long version you like?" Agatha smiled, and she continued without waiting for a response. "I tell you shorter one so your daughter not fall asleep. I am a Turkish Kurd and I come to Finland four years ago with my husband and my daughter. My husband had bad situation in Turkey, and we got residence permit. Life here was quite good. I got a job and Nabila, my daughter…"

"How old is she?" asked Mari.

"Six, now." A flicker of sadness showed in the woman's eyes. "She is not here."

"Why not?"

Agatha raised her finger and smiled. "I will get to that. A year ago Nabila was in day care, and around same time Hamid get mixed up in some crimes. They steal some things and get caught by the police. Hamid got arrested, but got out quite soon. That starts a big fight. I tell him we have to obey the law for Nabila sake, but Hamid…he is very bitter because he cannot find work. Our fight just gets worse and worse, and so I go to get divorce. It takes forever, but finally the court gives me a divorce and papers to give me custody of Nabila."

A pretty familiar story, thought Mari, but she just nodded.

"Hamid does not approve, so my friend at work told that I should get a restraining order. Well, this does not help much. Hamid just violates it, and they start deportation process because of his crimes. His hatred for me just grows. So I have to send Nabila back home to Turkey to be safe with my mother. When Hamid finds out about it, he tries to kill me. The police came in time, and Hamid goes to jail again. I was moved here because Hamid has many friends, and the police think I'm in danger."

"Where did you live?"

"Savonlinna."

Mari was cradling her coffee cup in her hands. "When did this happen?"

"Three months ago."

"And?"

"Last week a policeman came and said that there is still danger."

Laura was quietly sipping her sweetened tea, but she threw in a question, "How is Nabila doing?"

Agatha smiled. "I think she's okay. She must wait there until everything is better. That can take some time."

Mari looked at Laura, who went on, "Why don't you go to her?"

"If I go, I lose residence permit. Things will settle down. Finland is better country than Turkey. I think Hamid will be deported and so he cannot travel to EU countries anymore. And Turkey will not become EU country for many years. After that, Nabila and I can be safe together." Agatha sipped her coffee. "I have time to wait for what is best."

Mari looked at the spruces out the window. Did she too have time to wait for her life to return to normal?

Agatha's smile was laden with sorrow. "Of course I miss my daughter, but here, I am like a mother to everyone. It helps me to forget." She stroked Laura's hair. "I should tell about the laundry room. There is a list there that tells you…"

Mari had a hard time listening. Agatha seemed like a nice person, and Mari was glad that she was able to talk with somebody. Still, the woman's situation made her wonder. For how long should she be afraid? Was she afraid for her own life or for Laura's? What if she sent Laura to be with her godmother in Oulu for a few weeks or months while she stayed in Helsinki? On the other hand, she thought, how could she ever be apart from her daughter in the middle of a crisis?

* * *

Mikko Kulta yawned. It was exactly four o'clock in the afternoon, and it seemed to Takamäki that fatigue was not a good sign, even if it was Friday. They, along with Suhonen, Joutsamo and Kannas, had gathered around the large table in the conference room.

With VCU Chief Karila's help, Takamäki had managed to pass the surveillance of Siikala's house in Kaarela on to the Narcotics undercover unit, which didn't have much going on at the moment. In addition to one in the ditch, two others were posted in the parking lot of a nearby office building. More men would be called in to help if Siikala left the house. The arrangement freed up resources for homicide, but had come only on the condition that Jere Siikala was officially named a suspect in Mari Lehtonen's harassment. Takamäki had decided that the threshold for reasonable suspicion had been met, and had filed for a telephone warrant.

"Apparently nothing new on Siikala?" said Takamäki.

Suhonen shook his head. "Been there all day, and still there—I just checked."

"What about Mari and Laura?" said Takamäki, turning to Joutsamo.

"Been there all day, and still there—I just checked," said Joutsamo. "Mari didn't feel much like talking. Of course, the most important thing is that they're safe."

"Pretty down?"

"Sure seemed that way."

"Is there anything new?" said Takamäki, scanning the faces.

"I probed a bit more into Korpi's organization and got some leads from Nykänen," said Joutsamo, handing out a stack of copies. "Here are some names of known contacts with phone numbers and addresses. No guarantees on whether it's up-to-date, though."

Suhonen looked over the list. Lots of familiar names.

"Are we expanding surveillance to include these guys?"

"No," said Takamäki. "Not enough manpower. If you start running into them, we can reconsider. But let Anna know if you find more names."

Suhonen nodded.

"Good. Did you find anything in the footage from Brahe Street?"

"Nothing of any use," said Kulta. "I saw the girl a few times, but no car that fit the description."

"Did you get all the tapes?"

"Yep. I went through all the cameras that were in the database and drove the route to check for any new ones. Found a few additional cameras, but nothing on their tapes. The picture quality at nighttime is terrible."

"Okay, at least it was good to try," said Takamäki, continuing around. "What about the DNA on the envelope. Have we gotten it back?"

"Nope," said Kannas.

"And you put a rush on it?"

"They promised it this afternoon, but I haven't heard anything."

Takamäki paused. "Lots of work, little result."

"Should we take a more proactive approach?" asked Suhonen.

"Meaning?" said Takamäki.

"Well, we could spread a rumor that all of Korpi's money has been confiscated and there's a mole in his organization. In other words, send a message to stay away from him and his outfit."

Takamäki thought about it. There were pros and cons to the idea. "Okay, you can do the bit about the money, but the mole part could be dangerous. Someone might actually lose their life."

"Sure," said Suhonen. "It'd be more effective with the mole part, but I can leave it out."

"Good. Seems like we have the situation under control. No new threats. The Lehtonens are safe. Just got word from prison that Korpi is in solitary, so he's cut off from the outside. So for now we just wait for the DNA and the phone data and keep an eye on Siikala. And spread a few rumors, too. Time is on our side."

CHAPTER 22
FRIDAY, 10:20 P.M.
TAKAMÄKI'S HOME, ESPOO

Takamäki was at home sitting at the kitchen table, a towel around his waist, and his hair still damp from the sauna. A half-empty beer stood on the vinyl tablecloth.

He sifted through a pile of mail from the past week that had never been read: ads from car dealerships and bills, but nothing of any interest. He sipped his beer.

Takamäki's wife came down the stairs in a T-shirt and yoga pants. "The boys are asleep."

"Good. Kinda early isn't it?"

"I guess they had tough practices today. Games tomorrow, too," said Kaarina. Joonas was fifteen and Kalle was thirteen. The Takamäkis had been married for almost twenty years, after having met at a joint party of police officers and nurses. The parties, popular in the eighties, had paved the way for dozens of cop-nurse couples, some of them still together. In the beginning, the Takamäkis' rigorous work schedules had created problems, but Kari's promotion to lieutenant and his wife's advancement to management had helped to smooth out the wrinkles.

"How was your week?" asked Kaarina.

Takamäki shrugged. "Two life sentences, so I'd say pretty good, but…"

"But what?"

"But…well…there's been a threat related to the case."

She bristled. "Against you?"

"No," he said quickly.

Several years back, Takamäki himself had been threatened, but he had kept it from his wife to save her the worry. This had created a crisis in their marriage, which they had resolved only after months of tense discussion.

"Against someone on your team?"

"Why are you so interested?" said Takamäki, turning the questioning around. Usually she wasn't terribly interested in his work.

"I want to know. Tell me."

He sensed that she felt like chatting, so he told her the story about Mari Lehtonen's role as star witness, and how she had ended up at the safe house. He also mentioned the threat against Lehtonen's daughter, which darkened his wife's mood substantially. Takamäki finished off his beer and took another bottle from the fridge. Three remained in the six-pack.

"So what happens next," she asked. "And I'll have a beer, too."

He grabbed a second beer and handed it to his wife along with a glass. He preferred it straight from the bottle. "Well, the situation is under control for now, so we'll just wait and see if the bad guys come out of the woodwork."

Kaarina was quiet for a while. "Sad story."

"Uh-huh," Takamäki nodded.

"I mean for the lady."

"Right."

"In a way, you've ruined her chance at a normal life."

"What do you mean ruined? *We* didn't do anything."

"You made her testify."

"That's the law. Witnesses have to testify. Besides, she's the one who called us."

"Well, the law ought to be changed if this is what happens. Society can't expect people to sacrifice their everyday lives for the sake of some criminal case."

Takamäki sipped his beer. "Well, there's no telling what'll happen, if anything. It might already be over."

"For you, maybe. But this poor woman will be looking over her shoulder for the rest of her life."

"Hey, we'll protect her."

"How? By locking her up like the murderer?"

Takamäki studied his wife. "So it would be better if this Korpi were on the streets dealing drugs and having people killed?"

"Of course not. But why should this woman serve the same sentence?"

"Uh-uh. It's not the same thing. Right now, this safe house is the most sensible and secure solution. Maybe it'll be weeks, but certainly not months."

Kaarina looked him in the eyes. "That kind of an experience can really scar a person. Especially the little girl."

"So we should just forget about witnesses, right?"

"It's a possibility."

"*Im*possibility is more like it. It's out of the question! Witnesses are far too important. The police need the support of the community that we protect."

"But you have to consider the witness and their family *before* you make them testify," she went on. "You've got phone taps, surveillance, hidden cameras, undercover agents, GPS tracking and who knows what else. Certainly with all that you should be able to build a case well enough to leave innocent citizens alone."

"Better yet if the criminals would leave us all alone," said Takamäki, his annoyance beginning to show.

"That's not much of an argument."

"What I'm saying is that testifying is a civic duty. The police can't go it alone—we aren't some kind of island apart from the rest of society."

Kaarina was about to say something when Takamäki's phone rang. He dug it out of his jacket pocket in the entryway and looked at the screen: Joutsamo.

"Yeah," he said, lingering in the entryway.

"Hi. Sorry to bother you," said Joutsamo. "The night shift guys called to say that Siikala's phone records are in. We can get the real-time data on the computer. You want me to go in and check it out?"

"You at home?"

"Yeah."

Takamäki considered it briefly. "Uhh...probably alright if we wait till morning. But check with Narcotics to make sure the guy is still at the house."

"Well, they promised to let me know if he goes anywhere. I haven't heard anything."

"Alright. Let's talk tomorrow."

"Bye," said Joutsamo, and she hung up the phone.

Takamäki came back to the table. His wife looked at him inquiringly.

"We've got the suspect under surveillance and now we have the call data. We'll look at it tomorrow."

"So you're going to work tomorrow?"

"Looks that way. Someone's gotta look after these witnesses."

SATURDAY,
DECEMBER 16

CHAPTER 23
SATURDAY, 1:40 P.M.
PASILA POLICE HEADQUARTERS

Joutsamo set the handset back on the base. No answer. Nothing. The call had gone directly to voicemail. She was sitting at her desk when Takamäki came in.

"Anything?" he asked.

Hope rarely had a place in the VCU's line of work, but Takamäki was hoping for a yes. Joutsamo shook her head gravely.

"Damnit."

Mari and Laura Lehtonen had disappeared. Joutsamo had found out about an hour earlier after she tried to call Mari's cell phone and it went straight to voicemail. Apparently, the phone was off. Joutsamo had Laura's number too, but the result was the same.

Joutsamo had then tried the front desk at the Kirkkonummi safe house, and what she heard from the guard nearly made her drop the phone. According to the log, Mari and Laura had left the safe house at 10:45 A.M. No reason was indicated. The guards had changed at noon, so the current one couldn't tell her anything about what had happened.

Joutsamo had wondered why the police hadn't been notified. According to the guard, they had no such protocol. The safe house was not a prison, so the guards couldn't stop them from leaving. Joutsamo had acquired the morning watchman's cellphone number, and after calling him, she had learned that Laura and Mari had simply walked out. Just the two of them. The guard hadn't seen a car, taxi or any other vehicle on the cameras. Mari had been carrying a bag.

The watchman had noted that they appeared to be heading for downtown Kirkkonummi, just over two miles away. And the weather was good for a walk: sunny and just a few degrees below freezing. That's where the trail ended, at least for now. If yesterday the case had seemed to have cooled down, now it was blazing hot again.

Tracking down Mari and Laura was now their first priority, but as such, the situation could certainly be worse. By all appearances, their departure had been voluntary, so they hadn't been abducted. Takamäki and Joutsamo were most worried about the fact that neither of the Lehtonens had their cell phone on. Of course, it was possible that both batteries were dead, but that was unlikely.

Kulta had been sent to Kirkkonummi to try to determine their route and track down any leads. Where were they headed? To the store? The train station or further? Back to Helsinki?

Takamäki had analyzed the situation, and issuing a nationwide APB didn't seem prudent. Instead, he had notified the Espoo PD, since Kirkkonummi was their jurisdiction. If the pair was spotted, the Helsinki VCU was to be notified.

Mari and Laura's disappearance was not the only active front in the case. Joutsamo had already called Takamäki at around ten to fill him in on Jere

Siikala's call data. Two days prior, the phone number that the police had on file for him had been in contact with an unidentified prepaid phone. Takamäki had already obtained a warrant from the district court for the new number.

He had also obtained warrants for the cell towers in the vicinity of the Kaarela house, which had turned up three other prepaid SIM cards. There were also other active cell phones in the area that might belong to Guerrilla. Joutsamo had already looked into these other phone owners' backgrounds, suspecting that Guerrilla, aware of police interest in prepaid numbers, might have registered a phone with a false name. According to Suhonen, mobiles registered to phony names were a hot commodity in many bars. The phone companies had promised fresh data by late afternoon.

"Anything new on Guerrilla?" asked Takamäki.

"Apparently still in the house. He was observed in the kitchen. Making toast," said Joutsamo.

Takamäki laughed. "Suhonen must've found a pretty good spot if they can see into the kitchen. At least we're getting regular updates."

"Narcotics was asking how long they should keep it up if the guy's not doing anything."

"Hell. I'd say indefinitely...at least with the current situation."

* * *

Mikko Kulta was driving along a dirt road leading away from the safe house. The road was familiar to him because he had just driven it in the other direction five minutes earlier. At the building, he had checked Mari and Laura's room. Empty: the deserters

217

had taken all of their belongings. He had also interviewed a Kurdish woman, who hadn't known anything about the pair's whereabouts.

Kulta had updated Joutsamo on his findings. The empty room changed his search tactics: no need to check ice cream parlors or coffee shops. The pair had jumped ship entirely, opting to tread water on their own. Joutsamo had sent a patrol to their home address and started hunting for close relatives. As the police didn't know much about Lehtonens' friends, they began searching for them, starting with Mari's co-workers.

Kulta came upon a couple of houses on the side of the road, but decided to skip them. It was possible that neighbors had seen a woman and a girl, but more than likely the pair had continued on. Maybe somebody had given them a ride to Kirkkonummi. His first stops would be the Kirkkonummi train station and bus depot, and if the pair wasn't there, then he'd search the cab stands. Of course, it was also possible that someone had been waiting to pick them up somewhere in town, but if that were the case, how in the hell would he ever know.

The drive to the train station took about five minutes. Kulta was playing a CD he been burned with some favorite hits. Blue Oyster Cult was playing now: "...*don't fear the reaper*." Advice Kulta wasn't inclined to take. The case had already had its share of ominous overtones, and this latest stunt was not a positive development.

Kulta pulled his little Nissan into an angled spot at the Kirkkonummi train station.

He stepped out of the car, lit a cigarette and headed straight for the train schedule next to the main wooden building. Someone had spit on the glass in front of the departures display, but Kulta could still make out the text. He knew from his car's odometer that the trip from the safe house to the station had been 2.1 miles. The Lehtonens had left the safe house at 10:45, and it would have taken them at least half an hour to walk there, more likely forty-five minutes. Thirty minutes seemed like a good number to Kulta.

All trains to Helsinki left on the hour and half hour, so the first possible train had left at 11:30 and the next at noon. Another train had left at 11:00, but the pair would have never made that without a ride. Even Kulta had spent almost ten minutes getting from the safe house to the platform.

For westbound trains, there had been an express to Turku at 10:35—impossible timewise—and next in line was a local at 12:03, followed by another express at 12:35.

Kulta was almost certain that if the Lehtonens had come to the station, they would have boarded a train to Helsinki. It seemed logical, especially since Kulta didn't think they were going into hiding. They would have been safer at the safe house. Something else was behind this.

Kulta jotted down the departures, since Joutsamo would ask for them anyway. He walked through the crisp, clear air toward the main building, scanning for surveillance cameras. He found three, all appearing to be trained on the station frontage and the platform.

He reached the entrance to the station and pulled the handle. It didn't budge. He pulled again before noticing a small sign that read, *Closed Sat.*

Can't give up now, he thought. Especially since he'd have to explain everything to Joutsamo. She wouldn't tolerate disappointments stemming from lack of effort. There was no hiding it—she could smell indolence from a mile away.

Kulta considered his options. It'd be worth a call to ask about surveillance footage—maybe mentioning "Helsinki Homicide" would carry some weight. But who to call? The Espoo PD? They had jurisdiction here. Or the state railways? The whole case was beginning to irritate him. The surveillance videos were unquestionably the most promising idea. He dialed directory assistance, which connected him with the state-owned railway company. A recording informed him that offices were closed until Monday. For train schedules, he could call the premium-rate number. A call to the security company responsible for the train station ended in a voicemail box.

Just as Kulta hung up, his phone rang. "Yeah," he answered.

"It's Joutsamo," said an irate voice on the other end. "What's the status?"

"Uhh…" Kulta cleared his throat, knowing he'd already lost. Everything from this point forward would just end up sounding like an excuse, but he explained the events at the safe house and the problems at the station.

"Well, shit," Joutsamo barked. "Get the footage, then."

"And how do you suggest I do that?" he barked back. "I don't even know who the station manager is."

Joutsamo was quiet for a moment. "Come on Kulta… I'm in Helsinki, for god's sake. You're in Kirkkonummi. Gee, I wonder where the station manager might be? Quit fucking around and do your job."

"Fine," said Kulta.

He hung up the phone and cursed, drew his Glock and searched the door for a pane of glass with a break sensor on it. Once he located it, he smacked the glass with the butt of his gun and it shattered. Inside, the alarm began to sound. Damn right, that's more like it. Security guards, a cruiser and some stiffs from the railway would be crawling all over the place in no time. Kulta stepped back with a smile and slipped out a pack of cigarettes.

* * *

Joutsamo came into Takamäki's office with a stack of papers.

"What did you hear from Kulta?" said Takamäki. "He find anything?"

"He's at the Kirkkonummi train station complaining that it's closed and he can't get any footage."

"You're shitting me."

Joutsamo smiled. "That's what I said. I'm sure he'll figure it out."

"Let's hope so. We need that footage ASAP. The million-euro question is whether they're travelling alone or if someone has abducted them... Still nothing from their phones?"

"Nope, still off. But I did get Jere Siikala's call data. I found a prepaid extension that made and received a few calls in the Kaarela area after the verdict. And a couple texts too."

"So it might be Guerrilla's new phone."

"Possible, but we don't know for sure. The phone has definitely been in the area the whole time."

"Where's it been calling?"

Joutsamo paused. "Other prepaid numbers in the metro area: Pakila, Töölö, Kallio, Lauttasaari, Itäkeskus…"

"So a fair amount of traffic."

"But we got nothing on the content or the recipients. Is he still holed up in that house?" asked Joutsamo.

"Yep."

"Must have quite the food stash in there—he never has to go for groceries? It also occurred to me that the house had a broadband connection when we raided it back in September. We don't have access to that, so he might be communicating over the internet."

"I know," said Takamäki, and he thought for a while. "With our only charge being threatening a witness, we'll have a hard time getting a warrant for a full phone tap, much less emails."

"Yeah. Same old story. What's the plan, by the way, if we actually find the Lehtonens?"

"You have any suggestions?" he said, looking helpless.

Joutsamo shook her head. "Give them an earful? Scare the shit out of them?"

Takamäki didn't reply.

* * *

A small white security vehicle swerved up to the curb in front of the train station and a large broad-shouldered man in a gray uniform stepped out. Both the car and the uniform looked ridiculously small in comparison to the man. He walked up to the door where Kulta was waiting and promptly noticed the shattered windowpane.

"What's this?" he barked, one thumb hooked on his utility belt, where a canister of tear gas was at the ready. "What happened?"

Kulta had already taken out his badge and he held it up. "Mikko Kulta, Helsinki VCU. Sorry, little accident here. I yanked on the door a bit too hard and the glass busted."

"Really. Let's see that badge."

Kulta handed him the badge, and the man stood there examining it without so much as an upward glance. Bad idea, thought Kulta. The guard should have taken a few steps back. If Kulta had had any bad intentions, he could have easily surprised the big man.

"Okay, I guess this looks legit. I'll just call the glass company."

"Listen," said Kulta. "You wouldn't happen to have the key would you?"

"Sure. Why?"

"Well, actually I'm working on a pretty serious case, and I need to see the CCTV footage. That's why I'm here."

"Oh, yeah?"

"Yes," said Kulta in a serious tone of voice. The guard seemed a bit slow on the uptake, but Kulta was glad the guy hadn't asked about the case. Few rent-a-cops could resist prying about anything related to real police work.

The lout nodded and took out his key ring. "CCTV footage, huh?"

"Yeah, you know where the monitoring station is?"

"Sure...follow me," said the guard, and he opened the door.

Kulta fell in behind him with a smug smile.

* * *

Rauli Salo, prison guard, was sitting alone at a table in Parnell's Pub drinking beer from a mug. His navy blue parka was draped over the back of the chair. The Pub, in Kallio, was furnished in the traditional British style—dominated by dark-toned woods. Salo glanced at his watch: a quarter after two. Fifteen minutes late already.

A blond-haired man came in and Salo followed him with his eyes. He wasn't sure what sort of man he was here to meet. This one stopped just inside the entrance and scanned the bar. He looked about fifty and wore a black Burberry overcoat, which he left on as he made his way for Salo's table. The man's face was tanned.

"You waiting for somebody?" the man asked from six feet off.

The prison guard nodded, and the man sat down at the table. "Hello," he said. "I had to find a parking spot."

Salo guessed the man had parked a Mercedes, or at least he seemed to have expensive tastes. The guy would fit in better at some trendy bistro downtown than this poor man's pub in Kallio. Salo had expected something between a straggly-bearded junkie and a tough-looking torpedo, but you never knew with these criminals. This was actually better—at least he'd get paid. Salo slowly sipped his beer.

"Well?" Martin said impatiently. The lawyer didn't feel quite at home, and he didn't care much for this sort of impromptu meeting. On the phone, the man had said he had a message from a certain inmate. Of course that meant Korpi. But who was this guy across the table? Martin didn't know and didn't really want to, either. He didn't look like someone on parole, anyhow. More like a prison staffer.

"Your inmate had a message."

"You already told me that."

"Money first. He said five hundred."

Martin gave the man a hard stare. "Five hundred?" He couldn't possibly know how much Korpi had actually said, and wondered to what extent this guy was padding his own pockets. Martin dug out his wallet and slipped five green bills into the man's hand. "So?"

"He says tighten the screw."

"Tighten the screw?"

"That's right," said Salo.

"I see," said Martin, and he got up to leave.

After he left, Salo stayed to finish his beer. He thought about what the message meant. Five hundred for that was easy money. Tighten the screw...must have something to do with Korpi's debts. Whatever it was, he knew he shouldn't be conveying messages from a prisoner in solitary, but what harm could it do? Especially when it was so vague, and not really even a threat.

Salo was actually glad that Korpi owed him one now. In the long run, it would make his life easier. There was one major difference between the work of police and prison guards: the former encountered criminals in fleeting moments of danger, but the latter had to live with them for years. It called for a different kind of touch that involved cooperation. And easy money.

* * *

As Joutsamo stepped into his office, Takamäki could tell from the faint smile on her face that she had good news.

"What is it?" he asked.

"Something, which is a good thing. First off, Kulta got footage of the Lehtonens at the Kirkkonummi train station. They boarded an 11:30 train toward Helsinki, scheduled to arrive at 12:08. The video showed that they were clearly alone on the platform."

Takamäki glanced at the clock. "So we're about two and a half hours behind them."

"Right, but of course they could've gotten off at an earlier stop. No sign of them at the apartment."

"I'm sure Kulta will check the footage at the Helsinki end next?"

"That's what he said," said Joutsamo.

"Well, at least we're on the trail."

That the Lehtonens were travelling alone was a relief. If someone had snatched them, they wouldn't be using public transit. More than likely they would've been tossed into a trunk. Or a trash bag.

"One other thing," said Joutsamo. "Guerrilla got another phone call. Came from a cell tower in Kallio."

"A prepaid phone?"

Joutsamo nodded. "That's the third call from the same number, but all from different towers. I think it makes sense to file for a warrant at this point."

"I think so too," said Takamäki. Given the calls had come from three separate cell towers, it made sense to dig deeper—it would be easier to limit the number of phones falling within their range. The data could also reveal the caller's other phone numbers, which might be registered to a real person. "I'll take care of the red tape ASAP."

Joutsamo looked exasperated. "I'm sick and tired of messing with all this cell tower bullshit... No question in my mind we should be able to listen to these calls. Right now we have no idea who's calling and what's being said. With a tap we'd be two steps ahead of the game."

"You're preaching to the choir. Talk to the parliament and interior ministry," said Takamäki with an edge in his voice. "Maybe you could stage a protest."

Joutsamo was quiet for a while. "Stage?" She thought for a while. Laura's theater project was over, but hadn't Mari mentioned something about a show they were planning on attending? A musical, she recalled. Wasn't it around this time? A Saturday, to be sure.

"You know what," said Joutsamo. "I think they've got tickets to a musical today."

"A musical?"

"At the City Theater, if I remember right. I wouldn't think there'd be too many musicals running at the same time."

Takamäki grabbed a copy of the *Helsingin Sanomat* and opened it to the entertainment section. "Two shows there today. A matinee at four and an evening show at seven-thirty."

Joutsamo looked at the clock. "Still a good hour before the matinee starts. Maybe we ought to have a look."

"I'll come too. If they don't show, let's stop by their apartment and take a stroll around the neighborhood."

* * *

Mari and Laura Lehtonen were sitting at a table for four on the second floor of the Hakaniemi McDonald's. There were few other customers. Mari was sitting with her back to the wall, with a clear view of anyone who came up the stairs. Laura was facing her.

The window provided a view of the empty Hakaniemi outdoor market. It had closed at two, the vendors having packed up their carts and left.

Mari and Laura ate their hamburgers in silence. The decision to run had been discussed thoroughly back in Kirkkonummi. Laura had complied with her mother's wishes.

Mari saw him the moment his face came into view on the stairs. He spotted her and cut straight for their table.

Mari set what was left of her hamburger on the table and followed his approach with her eyes. Anton Teittinen stopped and stood at the end of the table. Mari had called him an hour earlier to ask for a favor and they had arranged to meet here.

Laura's eyes went from the man to her mother with a mystified expression.

Teittinen kept his gaze on Laura. "You sure have grown."

Laura was confused. And who is this supposed to be, her eyes seemed to say.

"Laura, this is your father," said Mari.

Laura stood and threw her arms around his sturdy body. At first, he was taken off guard, but soon he wrapped his strong arms around her and held on. He couldn't speak, nor could he keep the tears from welling up in his eyes. After about half a minute, the girl let go and so did Anton.

"Sit, sit," said Mari, glancing around at the other customers. Nobody had taken any interest in them.

Anton Teittinen tried discreetly to dab away his tears, but he wasn't fooling either of them. "Been quite some time," he said. "Time you can't get back. I...uhh...I've been pretty stupid."

Mari nodded. This was probably the closest to an apology Anton was capable of. "There's no going back to the way it was," she said.

"That's not what I meant. But maybe we could meet here...or someplace else, say, a few times a year?"

"I'd like that," said Laura.

Mari nodded. "I'd be okay with it."

"Or what if dad came to see my play?"

"If he wants to," said Mari.

"I don't see why not, but..." he gathered his thoughts for a moment. "...about the current situation."

"Right," said Mari. She looked at Laura, "I've told her everything."

"Okay, then I'll just be blunt. There's a lotta rumors going around about you. Hard saying what's true and what's not, but there could be some truth to them."

"We know, but who?" asked Mari.

"Korpi, of course."

"Why?"

"That I don't know. Probably fu... Umm... Annoyed about his sentencing," he said, smiling sheepishly at his daughter.

Mari thought for a moment. "What do you think we should do?"

"I dunno. You can't show fear, but Korpi has some crazy guys in his corner. I really don't know."

Laura cut in. "Are you a criminal?"

Anton chuckled. "Uhh, how to put it... I never been much for the straight and narrow, but I'm not a bad man. At least not that bad," he said, trying to keep a gentle face.

"Listen," said Mari. "We should go. Did you bring it?"

Teittinen took a bag out from beneath the table. "I got some Christmas presents for the two of you. This bigger one is for your mom and this other is for you. I didn't have time to wrap them. This all came up kinda sudden."

He handed the smaller package to the girl. "Here. Merry Christmas. It's one of these MP3 players with a bunch of music already on there."

Laura smiled in surprise. "Thank you!"

Mari didn't want to ruin the moment by asking how and where he had managed to purchase a player with preloaded songs.

"And Mari...maybe we should duck into the restroom to open this one."

Mari nodded and stood up. "Watch our stuff," she said to Laura.

The restrooms were on the second floor, small but private. Mari chose the women's room. Anton followed and locked the door behind him. The room felt a bit cramped for Mari's tastes—she didn't care to be so close to her ex-husband.

"I haven't changed my mind about your testifying against Korpi. But let's not talk about that right now. You're both in trouble, so I'll help you because of the girl."

He opened the box to reveal a small revolver with a roundish profile. The handle was made of dark wood, and mated with chrome-plated steel. The barrel seemed remarkably short.

"It's the best I could get on short notice. A short-barrel Smith & Wesson .44. It'll fit in your purse and it's fucking easy to use."

He cocked it, pulled the trigger, and the hammer snapped shut. "The bullets are in here." He held up a small Zip-loc bag with six rounds in it, then took out a small rag and set about wiping his fingerprints off the weapon. "This is what the gun dealers always do."

"Where's it from?"

He shrugged. "Off the shelf of some gun shop in Turku for all I know."

"You stole it?"

"No, but you're not supposed to ask. It's hot, at any rate, so don't show it to your cop buddies."

"Okay," said Mari. Teittinen handed her the weapon. It felt quite solid, though it didn't weigh much more than two pounds. At least it brought a semblance of security. Now the target could shoot back if circumstances called for it.

"It'll stop the crackheads, too. Got a good kick, but as you can see by how short the barrel is, you're not gonna hit anything past fifteen feet."

Lehtonen studied her ex. "Have you ever shot at anyone?"

"Nah. Guns are more about the fear factor. But remember, you point this at somebody, you better be ready to pull the trigger. And if someone's threatening Laura, you aim for the head. They'll be picking brains off the pavement for a good while."

"How much do I owe you?" asked Mari as she packed the revolver back into the box, and the box into the plastic bag.

Teittinen smiled. "I already told you it's a Christmas present."

Mari slipped the bag and the bullets into her blue handbag.

CHAPTER 24
SATURDAY, 3:40 P.M.
HELSINKI CITY THEATER

Joutsamo and Takamäki were standing in the atrium of the Helsinki City Theater. Takamäki took in the ambience of the forty-year-old building. Back in the sixties, it had been considered modern, but now it seemed cold and clinical. The detectives had chosen a spot next to the coat check where they could see the guests filing in through the main entrance. With their coats off, they did their best to act like theater-goers waiting for friends to arrive.

The two had arrived at a quarter after three. By now, there was little to chat about. They'd already gone through the details of the case, and chitchat wouldn't move it along. Circumstances remained grim from their standpoint. If the Lehtonens didn't turn up at the theater, the police were just as lost as they were that morning. Kulta had spotted Mari and Laura on tape at the Helsinki Central Train Station, but the footage ended at the doors leading to the Railway Square.

Takamäki glanced at his watch. "If they don't come for this showing, the next is at seven."

"Yeah," said Joutsamo as she scanned the new arrivals. She noticed a familiar TV reporter: Sanna Römpötti. Shit, she thought. The reporter came in with a short-haired boy of about ten and recognized the detectives immediately.

"Just what we needed," muttered Takamäki through a smile.

Römpötti slipped out of her coat and came over to greet them. "A little culture to go with your crime, huh? What's up?"

Her question was intentionally open, as Römpötti was surprised to see the two of them at the theater together.

Takamäki smiled. "The VCU theater club donated some tickets. Apparently hard to come by."

"Yeah," answered Römpötti, and she gestured toward her young companion. "This is my godson, Tommi. Tommi, say hi to these nice police officers."

The boy smiled shyly and said hi.

"Hi," said Takamäki and Joutsamo.

The reporter's back was toward the door, but the detectives still had a view of the entrance. "I got my tickets way back in August. You know who's singing the lead in this show?" said Römpötti.

Neither detective even had a notion of what the choices might be. "I don't, actually. The programs are up there," said Joutsamo. "We're just waiting for a couple of our colleagues and Takamäki's wife."

"It'd be nice to meet her sometime," said Römpötti.

Joutsamo spotted Mari and Laura outside the glass entrance doors. They had to get rid of Römpötti fast. The reporter would quickly notice their interest in Mari. Römpötti had been at the trial, after all, and would surely recognize her.

"Are your seats on the main floor or the balcony?" asked Joutsamo.

"Main floor. Row seven on the right."

"Hm. We're in the balcony. That must be the difference between detectives and reporters," said Joutsamo with a smile.

Little Tommi tugged on Römpötti's sleeve. "That Sprite, remember?"

Römpötti grinned. "Well, we'd better go. See you."

"Sure," said Takamäki. He too had noticed the Lehtonens at the entrance. The sight of them was a huge relief, but Römpötti was still only a few feet off, so their original plan of immediately intercepting them wasn't going to work. Römpötti would presumably take a final backward glance on the stairs en route to the lounge.

Mari and Laura came into the atrium and began shedding their coats. Mari was lugging a large shoulder bag, so apparently they hadn't stopped at home after leaving the safe house. The detectives turned their backs as the Lehtonens filed into the coat check line. Römpötti was already on the stairs with the boy when she turned back and waved. Joutsamo gave a nod, which earned a questioning look from Takamäki. "Römpötti's on the stairs," she explained.

Within a minute, Mari was at the front of the line handing her jacket and shoulder bag to the coat check attendant, but she kept her blue handbag with her. Laura handed over her parka and took the ticket.

"Where to?" said Joutsamo.

"Let's go in a little further," said Takamäki. "We can't talk to them here in the middle of the crowd."

The atrium was beginning to fill up already. People were drinking coffee, wine and beer, and eating overpriced pastries. The whole situation seemed rather absurd to Takamäki. At the heart of it all was a woman and a girl, the targets of a hardened criminal, and the police were trying to figure out how to approach them.

"Let's take them back into the corner," said Takamäki, and he let Joutsamo go ahead.

Joutsamo weaved swiftly through the crowd and approached the Lehtonens from behind. "Hi," she said in a soft voice. "Everything alright?"

Mari turned around first, then Laura. Takamäki came up alongside Joutsamo.

"Yeah, fine," said Mari as she pushed onward.

"Listen," said Joutsamo, still gently, but a bit firmer this time. "Can we talk?"

"What about?"

Takamäki cut in. "Why don't you take a guess…you think this is some kind of game?"

Mari was about to say something feisty, but she bit her tongue. Not with so many ears around. She thought for a moment before responding, "Sure, let's talk. We've got a few minutes."

Joutsamo and Takamäki led Mari to a quieter section of the atrium. Laura hung back by the coat racks, about thirty feet away.

"What's going on?" said Joutsamo. "Why aren't your phones on?"

"The batteries are dead," she snapped.

They were all quiet for a while. "Let me get this straight," said Takamäki. "We work our asses off on your behalf and you scrap it all just like that?"

"And just what exactly have you done, if I might ask?"

"Really," he groaned. "Are you out of your mind? While we're trying to find out who's behind the threats, it's vital that we know you're safe. It allows us to concentrate on the investigation."

"Oh, so this is about your investigation."

"No," said Takamäki. "It's about…"

Joutsamo interrupted her boss. His tack was clearly headed in the wrong direction, and she didn't want Mari to be at odds with them. "Mari, tell me what's going on…"

"Why should I ruin my life because of some criminal?"

Takamäki was stunned. Ruin her life? Soon she'd lose it. But he bit his tongue.

Mari went on. "Seems to me this 'safe house' is just a place where you can tuck us away. Sweep us under the rug. We can't cause any problems there. While the criminal gets to do whatever he wants."

"Mari," said Joutsamo. "The criminal is in prison. You were sent there for your own good. So you'd be safe."

"For weeks or for months? I mean, the place was like a prison. Stuck in a room all day. I have a life. My daughter has a life. We have work, school, family, friends, interests. And tickets to the theater. What right do you have to lock us up?"

Takamäki was about to say something, but Joutsamo shut him up. "We're looking out for your safety. You've been threatened. This is a perfectly normal course of action."

"It might to be normal to you, but not to us. And what if the threats keep coming? What do you recommend then? That we move to Lapland or Sweden? Cut all ties to our old lives? Geez, if you can't come up with something better, then I'll take the risk."

"For Laura, too?"

"Yeah, we've talked it through. We want our lives back. If I start being afraid all the time, I'll never get my life back. I can't give up. I can't be afraid."

Joutsamo paused for a while. Takamäki had decided to keep quiet. "Let me ask you a question: Do you remember how you felt when Laura got that envelope?"

Mari swallowed hard. "Yes, I'll never forget. But I was weak then. I thought the experts could help us. But once we were at the safe house, it dawned on me. You don't care about our lives. You just don't want problems. That's why you had to get us out of the picture."

"Well, what do you want us to do?" said Takamäki, struggling to conceal his disgust.

"Do what you want, but we'll be going on with our lives."

The first chime sounded, signifying that the show would begin soon. "Right now, we're going to watch the play. Afterwards, maybe we'll have some tea and then head home. I don't really give a rip what you cops do."

"Fair enough," said Takamäki in resignation. "Enjoy the show. Good night. Afternoon, that is."

He gestured to Joutsamo, and they took their leave.

"We can't just leave them to Korpi you know," said Joutsamo as she pulled on her coat. "The wolf will get his sheep in short order."

"She said herself she doesn't care what the police do," he snorted.

"But…"

"Stop and think, Anna," he said as he held the entry door for her. The temperature had dipped well below freezing. "We're not gonna abandon the case, we'll just have to do without their cooperation. Basically, that means you get to stay here and wait till the show is over. Then you just politely ask if they'd like a ride in an unmarked squad. If they turn it down, follow them and make sure nothing happens."

"Isn't that…"

"She said herself she doesn't give a rip what the cops do. At least for now, that's the way we'll have to do it. Like you said, we can't just leave them to Korpi. To hell with the cost," he said. "I'll leave you the squad and catch a bus back to the station."

"I can drop you off," said Joutsamo. "The show will probably take a couple hours, and I didn't see any suspicious characters around."

"Except for Römpötti. Alright, let's do that."

* * *

It was nearing six o'clock and already dark outside. Suhonen was sitting in a car in the Haukilahti district of Espoo, staking out a house that belonged to Attorney Mats Martin. Suhonen had parked the car with a clear view of the façade. There was no doubt that there were people inside—the place was actually hopping. Presumably the lawyer was hosting some kind of party.

Only a few hours before, Suhonen had been spending his day off with the intention of going for pizza and a few beers with his wife candidate Raija when Takamäki called. Of course, he could have said no, but that wasn't his style.

Besides, the situation seemed pretty juicy. Based on information gleaned from phone taps, they had reason to believe that Martin had called Jere Siikala three times on a prepaid card in recent days. The lawyer was the only one whose own phone had been within range of the same cell towers as the prepaid phone that was used to call Guerrilla. It couldn't be a coincidence. And if it was, it called for a formal explanation in a police interrogation room. Martin had also gone to visit Korpi in Helsinki Prison on the Thursday prior to Korpi's transfer to solitary.

Takamäki, Suhonen, Joutsamo and Karila had held a meeting at the VCU conference room to discuss the situation brought about by the Lehtonens' desertion. Once Martin's and Siikala's phone records were added to the equation, it became clear that there was no reason to wait. Particularly with Siikala continuing to call anonymous numbers. The police had to be proactive. Anybody who could be linked to the case would be taken in and held for as long as legally possible, and potentially remanded into custody if the interviews and searches produced any evidence.

As for Guerrilla, his arrest was left up to Narcotics agents, who were overjoyed to be done with their mind-numbing surveillance detail. Suhonen, for his part, had tracked down Martin. Because the two men were connected, there was good reason to make their arrests at more or less the same time. A tentative time of six o'clock was agreed upon, just before the conclusion of the play at the Helsinki City Theater.

Suhonen considered the various ways that he could arrest Martin. If the house was packed with lawyers, sending in the SWAT team would likely be ill-advised, though quite educational. Karila and Takamäki had emphasized the importance of the lowest possible profile and minimal publicity. The goal was to turn the situation back in the Lehtonens' favor.

In terms of a low profile, Martin's party was clearly a terrible starting point. No matter how they got him out of the house, there would be an uproar amongst the guests. Suhonen couldn't wait until the party was over, because timing was important. But the bosses had only urged the lowest *possible* profile. Needless to say, they would have to search the house, so the party had to end. But how to do that without revealing the reason for Martin's arrest to his guests?

Suhonen had looked into Martin's background. The man was married with two teenage children, but more interesting was what he found in the firearms registry: a shotgun and two handguns registered in his name.

His two-story red brick house was situated just across the street from the ocean front, not far from Mellsten's beach.

Suhonen took out his phone and called the on-duty lieutenant at the Espoo police department. Takamäki had already arranged for back-up to be available. After that, Suhonen called Takamäki, who had no objections to his straightforward plan.

Within ten minutes, the cruisers from Espoo had pulled up to the agreed-upon meeting spot in the parking lot of the Toppelund school. Suhonen briefed the uniformed officers on his strategy and showed them a photo of Martin he'd gotten from a directory of lawyers.

The squad cars pulled up to the house in single file with their roof lights off. Suhonen parked his vehicle behind them and he, along with four other cops, weaved through the cars parked in the driveway. One of the uniformed officers rounded the house to cover the back door.

Suhonen reached the front door and was about to ring the bell when it opened. He recognized Martin immediately. The man had a glass of Cognac in his hand. He reeked of alcohol, and his pupils were dilated. Latin music and the smell of cigar smoke wafted outside.

"What's this?" he said. "Are the neighbors complaining? We'll turn it down."

"No need. I'll take care of it," said Suhonen.

"What? You can't just…"

"Shut up," said Suhonen, and one of the Espoo cops twisted Martin's arms behind his back. The glass of Cognac fell to the floor and shattered.

"What the hell…" Martin managed to say before the burly officer slapped on the cuffs, took hold of his suit coat and started hauling him toward the cruiser. Martin wasn't wearing any shoes, but the cop didn't care.

"What is this!" shouted Martin, struggling against the cuffs.

"I'll explain in a bit," said Suhonen, and he went inside. The furnishings looked expensive. Suhonen took a quick glance into the two downstairs bedrooms, the bathroom and entertainment room. Empty. He continued on upstairs with two Espoo officers in tow.

"What's going on down there?" shouted a woman's voice from the top of the stairs. The music shut off.

Suhonen waited until he reached the top before answering. The two beat cops stayed just behind him.

Once on the second floor, he pulled out his badge, "Helsinki Police."

Three women and four men were sitting around a large living room decorated entirely in white furnishings. Their posh clothing harmonized with the expensive decor.

"What's this all about?" said one of the women as she rose. She was slender, with long blond hair and a black knee-length dress. "Where's my husband?"

"Take it easy," said Suhonen. "Mats Martin is under arrest."

One of the men shot a quick glance toward a corner at the back of the room where a couple of chairs and a chess table were arranged. Suhonen caught the glance and walked over to the table.

Martin's wife was babbling something, and as he neared the table, Suhonen heard one of the men cursing. A couple lines of white powder lay on the marble chess board with a straw to the side. "I see," said Suhonen with a smile. The drugs would make a convenient excuse for the raid.

"You're all under arrest on suspicion of drug possession."

"I haven't done anything!" one of the men protested as he got to his feet.

The Espoo cops took a step toward him and he fell silent again. Martin's wife was in hysterics now.

"You can't just barge into someone's house like that!"

"But here we are in the middle of your coke party. Imagine that," said Suhonen. He turned to the other cops. "Take down their names and bring them to the Espoo Station. I'll call and let them know we gotta bunch of junkies on the way. I need one of you guys to come with me to Helsinki. And cuff 'em all," he hollered after them. A ride in the back of a cop car with handcuffs on and a night in jail was a more fitting punishment for these types than whatever fine they'd get for possession. Of course, if Espoo Narcotics didn't have any big cases going on, they'd search their homes and offices to find out where the drugs came from. But Suhonen was confident that that would come out in the interrogations anyway. Whatever the case, he wasn't interested in the drugs.

While the uniformed officers began shepherding the shocked guests down the stairs, Suhonen opened the door to an adjacent room and glanced inside. One look at the desk, laptop, bookshelves and stacks of paper told him it was Martin's office. A few cell phones were charging on the desk. Forensics would have fun with this place.

One of the Espoo cops came back upstairs. "We got a little problem. Couldn't fit all of them in the cruisers, so I called for another. Martin's waiting in your car, so I'll ride with him in the back seat and make sure he doesn't try anything."

"That's fine," said Suhonen.

The beat officer smiled, "Quite the coke party. Two more lawyers, one communications director and a Supreme Court clerk in the bunch."

"Ha! Looks like headline material," said Suhonen, and he called Takamäki, who informed him that Jere Siikala had been taken into custody without event.

Suhonen took another look at the man's lavish home and wondered if Espoo's Narcotics unit would dare rifle through the office of a Supreme Court clerk. Takamäki, for one, would never miss such opportunity.

SUNDAY, DECEMBER 17

CHAPTER 25
SUNDAY, 8:55 A.M.
PORVOO STREET, HELSINKI

Suhonen was sitting in the front seat of his Peugeot, parked in front of Porvoo Street 17 with a clear view of the Lehtonens' apartment building. Though it had been legally parked, a Volvo had been towed to another spot down the street so Suhonen could have the best vantage point.

Helsinki was awakening to a beautiful, sunny winter Sunday. The temperature was ten degrees below freezing and an inch of snow had fallen overnight. Suhonen occasionally had to run the engine so the windows wouldn't frost over, and he'd cracked the window to minimize the problem.

All was quiet on Porvoo Street. The Lehtonens' building was at the old terminal stop of the number 3 streetcar, once called the "five-minute stop" because of how long the streetcar waited before turning around. The stop formed a sort of plaza, decorated by about ten trees, an electrical substation building, a couple of recycling barrels and a cab stand. Seven- and eight-story buildings surrounded the plaza. The Weeruska restaurant lay on Suhonen's right behind a yellow fence.

The blue-gray building where Tomi Salmela was killed was located directly across from the

Lehtonens' apartment. On the ground floor was a convenience store with barred windows.

Aside from a few early risers out walking their dogs, nobody else was around. Three dogs went huffing past with a man in tow. Either he was deeply in love or under his wife's thumb—nobody else would spend their Sunday morning out in the cold juggling three unruly dogs.

The towing operation had been carried out at about six in the morning, and Suhonen had since downed a few cups of coffee. He'd been forced to relieve himself behind a nearby building, but it had still been dark out then.

Now that the Kaarela surveillance operation was over, Narcotics had taken the overnight shift here, which had ended at six. In Kaarela, the police had had to remain out of sight, but here it didn't matter. To the contrary, they wanted to be seen. The cruiser that had been waiting outside the building the previous day had been removed so as not to irritate Mari Lehtonen.

The Lehtonens were inside—that much they knew. Or at least the police hadn't seen them leave. After the show, Joutsamo had escorted them home. They had wanted to walk, so the sergeant had followed them in the car at a distance of no closer than thirty feet. Mari hadn't wanted to talk.

A man with a black knit hat pulled low over his eyes and his hands in his jacket pockets walked past the parked cars in front of the building. Suhonen followed him idly with his eyes. The man's step was somehow plodding, perhaps from a hangover. A couple of cars drove past. Someone scraped the windows of a Saab, then pulled out of the parking space in front of the building.

Suhonen had time to ponder again. With as much time as he spent alone with his thoughts, he could have been a famed philosopher by now. He shook off thoughts of his personal life—he didn't care to think about those now. Things were muddled enough without them. The inside of the windshield began to fog up again and Suhonen started the engine. The fan breathed cold air at first, but soon enough it began to warm up.

An old rusty Ford Escort was approaching from the oncoming lane, and Suhonen snapped to attention. That same car had driven past the building only a few minutes earlier. It was an early eighties model, with a boxy-looking body, maybe an '82, he thought. At the most—at the very most—it was worth five hundred euros.

Suhonen couldn't make out the driver, but the car slowed up and parked in the same spot the Saab had vacated a few minutes earlier. Despite the abundant space near the crosswalk, the driver had to crank the wheel a few times to get in.

A man in an army jacket got out of the car. From some fifty yards off, Suhonen put the man's age at about twenty. He wore black jeans and his hair hung down from beneath his knit hat. The man closed the car door, and with quick strides, headed back in the same direction he had come from. Clearly a speedier fellow than the hung-over bum from earlier. Something was bothering Suhonen and he lost twenty seconds figuring it out: the man hadn't locked his door. An Escort that old certainly wouldn't have remote locks. Nobody left their door unlocked in this neighborhood.

The guy was already twenty yards from the Ford and about seventy from the Peugeot when Suhonen swung swiftly out of his car. He took his key ring and reflexively locked the doors with the remote as he hurried off toward the Escort. As he drew nearer, he memorized the plate number. The car looked rough—five hundred would be asking a lot. Nearly every seam was engulfed in rust. A long crack stretched across the passenger side of the windshield.

Suhonen peered in the window. The seats looked filthy and worn. The floor was littered with garbage. He worked his way around the car and noticed a bag in the footwell of the back seat. Too many things were adding up.

Suhonen's first impulse had been to run after the driver, but the car was clearly a higher priority. He took a couple of steps back and called dispatch. Thirty seconds later, another unsettling fact was added to the list: according to the plate number, the car should have been a black BMW. Suhonen backed away from the car and ducked behind the corner of a building. He notified dispatch of a possible bomb and gave a description of the driver to be forwarded to patrol cars in the area.

Suhonen looked around. Nobody in sight. He speculated about the potential bomb's detonating device: probably on a timer, and unlikely a matter of minutes, since the driver hadn't run from the car, thought Suhonen. From further off came the wail of the first siren, and then another. For chrissakes, he thought and dialed Takamäki's number.

* * *

Within twenty minutes, several blocks surrounding the plaza on Porvoo Street were cordoned off. More than a dozen police cars were on site with roof lights flashing. An ambulance and a few fire trucks were parked on the side streets. A crowd had gathered, but the police weren't answering questions.

A bomb-sniffing dog approached the car and began barking—it had detected the scent of explosives. The fact that the temperature had dipped to twenty degrees Fahrenheit made the situation especially problematic. Most explosives became very unstable below twenty-five degrees.

Police began evacuating residents living in the cordoned area. The first to be evacuated was the nearest building: the Lehtonens'. Needless to say, the tenants were alarmed as police filed through the apartments one by one, ordering people to exit through the back door as soon as possible. They were allowed only enough time to put on warm clothes.

The evacuation was unusually extensive: there were nearly ten large apartment buildings in the area. The streetcar line had been brought to a standstill.

Mari and Laura were ushered out with the others with no special treatment, since the patrol officer didn't know who they were. Mari pressed him for a reason, but all he could say was that a police operation in front of the building required that all residents leave the area.

Now Mari and Laura were sitting in a small coffee shop on Western Brahe Street, each nursing a cup of tea and a roll. From the window, she could see the police barricade at the corner of Sture and Porvoo Streets, about a hundred and fifty feet off. All four tables at the coffee shop were full.

Mari brooded as she gazed out the window. A number of police officers were about and she noticed a TV reporter. Despite the turmoil, Mari had had the good sense to take her wallet and phone along. Her purse was on the floor, along with the "Christmas present" Anton had given her.

"What's this all about, Mom?" asked Laura.

Mari shrugged.

"Is this about us?"

"Sweetie, I don't know."

"But what if it is?"

"Just eat your roll," she snapped. She, too, felt unsettled.

The door to the coffee shop opened, and in came Sanna Römpötti. The owner of the coffee shop was an older woman with her hair in a bun, and she recognized the reporter. "Hello," she said from behind the counter.

"Hi," said Römpötti as she scanned the patrons at the tables. She recognized Mari Lehtonen.

"So what's going on out there?" asked the shop owner. A hush came over the room.

Römpötti turned back to the counter and answered loudly enough that everyone could hear. "We're still not sure, but apparently some kind of bomb threat. For now that's all we know." She turned back toward the tables. "Are there any evacuees in here? I'm looking for somebody to interview."

Römpötti's gaze fell on Mari, who gave a nod of consent and Römpötti came over to the table.

"Have a seat," said Mari, and the reporter sat down and unzipped her coat.

"We've met before," said Römpötti. "Not formally, but I was there in court when you testified. I'm Sanna Römpötti, crime reporter for Channel 3 news."

"Yes, I know," said Mari. She was sizing up the situation.

"So were you two evacuated?" asked Römpötti, glancing occasionally at Laura as she ate her roll. The reporter's approach was simple. Her job was to get potential interview subjects to talk, and that was all. An ordinary person's account would make the bomb threat seem real to viewers. The facts she could get from the police.

"Yes, we were."

"At what time?"

"Let's see...it would've been about a quarter after nine. We were just having breakfast when a policeman rang the bell."

"And what did he say?" This was good material, thought Römpötti. Maybe she could even talk Lehtonen into going on camera.

"He just mentioned some kind of police operation in front of the building. Did you say there was a bomb?"

"That's what I've heard from my own sources, but it hasn't been officially confirmed. And we don't know whether it's an actual bomb or just a threat. They're not letting anyone on the scene yet. So this was in front of your building?"

"Yeah," Mari nodded.

"What building number?"

Lehtonen told her. The reporter took out her phone and passed the information on to a roaming cameraman outside. With this information, he could look for a chink in the crowd at the police barricade where he could get footage of the car. Römpötti had considered renting a helicopter, but decided against it. The massive police operation was certainly unusual, but bomb threats weren't all that rare.

Römpötti was just wrapping up her phone call with the cameraman when Mari's phone rang. The caller was unidentified, but she answered anyway. It was Joutsamo.

"How you doing?" asked the sergeant.

"Alright," said Mari. "What's going on?"

Joutsamo paused briefly before responding. "Someone parked a car in front of your building this morning with a backpack containing an explosive. We don't yet know what kind, but we'll find out. The bomb squad is dismantling it for transfer at the moment. Where are you?"

"Not far away."

"And where might that be."

"Why do you ask?" said Mari.

"I think it's best if you two return to Kirkkonummi. I know it is."

Mari thought for a moment. "And what if we don't? We still haven't done anything wrong, you know."

Römpötti was listening intently, a puzzled expression on her face.

"Of course you haven't done anything wrong, but it's the safest option. The only option."

Lehtonen took a sidelong glance at Römpötti as she spoke into the receiver. "I don't want to hide anymore."

Joutsamo was quiet. "Well, let's talk face to face at least. Can I pick you guys up? Where are you?"

"I don't see why we should meet," said Mari. "I mean…what's the point if you can't help me. I think I'm just gonna have to change my game plan."

Lehtonen looked at Römpötti and hung up the phone.

Römpötti didn't say anything. The woman would have to take the initiative, and Römpötti was all ears.

"It was a real bomb. In a car, in front of our building," said Mari in a low voice.

"Maybe it has something to do with you?" said Römpötti. Lehtonen nodded. The story was shaping up into headline news: Car Bomb Planted at Murder Witness's Doorstep.

"So do you want to hear my story?"

She did, and Mari told her everything.

CHAPTER 26
SUNDAY, 12:00 P.M.
PASILA POLICE HEADQUARTERS

Fifteen or so grim-faced police officers had assembled in the VCU conference room. In addition to Takamäki's core group of detectives, a few other VCU investigators, VCU Chief Karila, Kannas from Forensics, Nykänen from the NBI and Syväoja from the Finnish Security Intelligence Service were present. The FSIS was in charge of national security and took an interest in the bomb since Finland was the current president of the European Union. Because Finland's term expired at the end of the year and no important conferences remained, Syväoja was the lone FSIS representative needed at the meeting.

The time was two minutes to twelve when Deputy Chief Skoog walked into the room and greeted everyone with a tight-lipped nod.

Takamäki took a final glance at the clock and commenced the meeting with a briefing on the background of the case, including Mari Lehtonen's testimony and the subsequent threats, after which he went into the events of the day.

"At nine o'clock this morning we found the most serious threat so far," said Takamäki. "A car parked in front of Lehtonen's apartment building with an explosive in the back seat footwell. This resulted in an extensive precautionary evacuation of all residents in the area. The full story hasn't yet been revealed to the residents or the public, but we'll go through the media process later. Let's start with Lehtonen. Joutsamo, what's the latest?"

Joutsamo shrugged. "I chatted with Mari. She doesn't want to cooperate with us. Thinks we're trying to solve her problems by locking her up in some kind of quasi-prison, which she's opposed to because she doesn't feel she's done anything wrong."

"What? Is she nuts?" said Deputy Chief Skoog.

"Not nuts," said Joutsamo. "More like a woman of principle. Once she's made up her mind, she doesn't change it."

"Sounds nuts to me," said Skoog. "Have you explained the gravity of the situation to her?"

Joutsamo ignored the comment and went on, "At this point we don't know exactly where she is. Apparently still in the city somewhere, but she hasn't returned home. The blockade was lifted as soon as the explosives were removed. We posted a squad car in front of the apartment building, but there's been no sight of her, nor her daughter. In a way, that's a positive sign, since if *we* don't know where they are, then it's unlikely Korpi's henchmen do either."

Takamäki interrupted. "An even better sign would be getting them back into the safe house."

"I don't think it's possible... We can't force them."

Skoog looked pensive. "Can't force them... Well, if *we* can't, maybe a psychologist can. We could have her committed, and the girl could go into foster care."

Joutsamo scowled in Takamäki's direction. "Hmm..."

Skoog was unfazed. "That's my recommendation at this point. We can't let a woman targeted by these kinds of threats prance around town while we sit around and wait for the next bomb threat. That's a good way to get innocent bystanders killed."

"So Lehtonen's not an innocent bystander?" said Joutsamo.

Skoog glared at the sergeant. "She's the target—that's what she is. No question about it. The centerpiece of this case."

"We'll talk tactics later," said Takamäki. "We haven't even gone through the incident yet. Kannas, what about the explosive? What do we know about it?"

Kannas stood up. "We've received the preliminary results from the NBI lab. The backpack was filled with a plastic explosive by the name of hexogen, also known as RDX, developed during the Second World War. Chemically, it's a nitroamine organic compound, which is basically military grade, so the same stuff the pros use. As far as its composition, more precise tests are still underway, and I'm sure we'll hear more soon. Provided they don't blow up their lab in the process," said Kannas with a campy baritone and a smile.

The others weren't amused. Takamäki was about to guide him back on topic, but for once, Kannas checked himself, "I won't go into the technical details; we can talk about that later as needed. The origin of the explosive is still unknown..." said Kannas, looking straight at Syväoja, who would take an interest in this aspect, since it was the same explosive used by the Chechen rebels in Russia. "...But we did find one fingerprint on the bomb's detonator, which, by the way, wasn't set properly.

The bomb could never have exploded because one of the safeties was still engaged. No telling if that was accidental or intentional. At any rate, based on the timer, the bomb was set to go off at 10:28. The scariest part was the fact that cold weather makes the explosive very unstable. We had to warm up the car before moving..."

"Kannas. The fingerprint," said Takamäki.

"Right. The print belongs to a man from Korpi's gang by the name of Matti Ahola, at least presumably he's still with Korpi. Twenty-six years old with a history of drugs and debt collection."

"One of Korpi's lieutenants, according to the information we have," said Takamäki. "He is—or at least was—a former drug addict himself, but Korpi's been using him mainly as a torpedo. A warrant for his arrest has already been issued. Based on Suhonen's description, it's possible the driver of the Escort was Ahola, but that's still unconfirmed."

"The car is at our lab for further analysis, but I haven't received any results yet," said Kannas.

"Photos of Ahola have been posted at all border checkpoints," said Takamäki.

Joutsamo had made copies of Ahola's photo for everybody. His nose, broken at some point in his life, was raked sharply to the left. "Ahola is one of three lieutenants responsible for his own branch in Korpi's organization. We don't really have a complete picture of everyone involved, but here's a diagram with some of Ahola's potential connections," said Joutsamo as she handed out copies. "Moving down from Korpi we have three main offshoots: Ahola, Siikala and Nyberg, and then a bunch more subordinates as you go down the line."

The names, telephone numbers and other contact information were written beneath the photos. "We matched the fingerprint to Ahola twenty-five minutes ago, so he's got about a two-and-a-half-hour head start."

"Does he have any connections to foreign operatives?" asked Syväoja, his eyes scanning the handout.

"Some Russians and Estonians, but no links to known terrorist groups."

Syväoja seemed satisfied.

Kulta spoke up, "Any link between Ahola and the envelope the Lehtonen girl got?"

"Nope," said Joutsamo. "We don't have his DNA on file, and so far we've found no matches to the DNA on the envelope."

"Kulta, how are the interrogations going with Jere Siikala and the attorney?" asked Takamäki.

"Neither's talking," said Kulta. "They're denying all involvement and demanding to be released."

"Well," said Takamäki. "Both will be remanded into custody tonight. Suhonen, what's the status with Korpi and Nyberg?"

Suhonen raked his hands through his hair. "Both in solitary. No contact with the outside. No newspapers, no TV, no visitors. The only person they see is the guard who brings in the food. Or at least that's what they tell me."

"Okay," said Takamäki. "Clearly Matti Ahola is our prime suspect in the bomb investigation and yet another connection to Korpi. The bomb was undoubtedly a retaliation against Mari Lehtonen, probably planned in advance, since Korpi shouldn't be having any contact with the outside, at least not after his transfer to solitary and Martin's arrest. We don't know what's coming next, but we have to assume that something will." He let his eyes roam the room. "They're upping the ante."

He went on. "The good news about the bomb is that now we're looking at attempted murder, which means the court will grant us warrants for phone taps. The bad news is we can't ensure the victim's safety when Mari Lehtonen is so comfortable being a sitting duck. At any rate, it's clear that the matter should be kept from the media. This morning's operation will be referred to as a bomb threat."

"So lie to the media?" wondered Karila.

"Well, not exactly. We'll just tell them our version of the truth. The bomb never exploded, so technically it was just a threat, right?" Takamäki scanned the officers in the room. "If anyone has a better word to describe the incident, they can suggest it to me later, but as far as I'm concerned, the presence of an actual bomb should be kept secret here."

"That's fine with me, as a tactical decision," said Deputy Chief Skoog. "But what about getting this woman committed? It's a smart move if you ask me. She can't be sane behaving like that. At least we could get her off the streets that way."

"Uh-huh…" Takamäki managed to say before his cell phone cut him short. He checked the caller: Römpötti. His first thought was to ignore the call, but the possibility that he could get some leads based on what the media knew or wanted to know made him change his mind. "Just a sec," he said to the others.

"Hello?"

"Hi, it's Römpötti. Bad time?"

Takamäki felt like smiling, but his voice was serious. Kannas was whispering about something with Syväoja, but the others tuned in to Takamäki's call. "Well, we're in a little meeting here."

"Why don't I call back later."

"No. What's up?"

"Well, about this incident on Porvoo Street."

"What about it?"

"I hear it's your case."

"You heard right."

The reporter tried to use silence to coax more out of him. A few seconds passed before she broke the silence. "Well, tell me about it."

"We'll release a statement within the hour."

Römpötti didn't let on that she had any new information, so Takamäki decided to test the waters a bit. "It's really nothing all that unusual. We're just trying to figure out who might be behind it."

"I see...nothing all that unusual."

Takamäki didn't care for the tone of her voice. "That's right."

"Listen, I've always thought you're a pretty fair cop and that's why I'm still on the line. We've gotten along pretty well, but don't you dare lie to me. I know for a fact that a bomb was placed in front of Mari Lehtonen's building. I also know the backstory on the threats and all."

Shit, thought Takamäki, and his eyes darted about the room in search of the mole. Who in the hell had gone and sung to Römpötti? His dumbstruck expression had gotten even Kannas and Syväoja to quiet down.

"How in the hell..." he began, but Römpötti interrupted him.

"Don't bother looking for a mole."

"Goddamn it! It can't be..."

"But it is. Mari Lehtonen told the whole story on camera."

Takamäki felt the need to sit down, but there were no chairs within reach. "You're not planning on airing it, are you?" he said in a last ditch effort.

"Why wouldn't I?"

"Because it's a death sentence. Once it's public, Lehtonen will be fair game for every criminal in the country."

"No, she won't, because she's not an informant. She's an ordinary citizen who you guys couldn't protect, so you tried to ditch her in some safe house. You had your opportunity, now let's see if a little publicity can protect her."

"And if it doesn't?"

"Well, it couldn't be any worse than under your watch."

"So you're saying Lehtonen's face is going to be on TV," said Takamäki as the others looked on in open-mouthed astonishment.

"Don't be stupid. Although that's what she wanted...to show her face, but I decided to scramble it. The thing is, her story has raised quite a few pointed questions about police performance. If you don't want to answer them, then hand me over to Skoog. I'm guessing he's there at your little meeting. And if he doesn't want to comment, I'll just keep going up the chain of command. We'll see if anyone wants to comment."

Takamäki paused. He didn't like this kind of arm-twisting, but they had to change their game plan, and there was no point in further irritating Römpötti. "I'll call you back within the hour," he replied coldly.

"Okay. And no more lies. Your wife wouldn't like that either," she said, and hung up the phone.

The others were waiting to be filled in, but Takamäki took ten seconds to gather his thoughts.

"Well, I'm sure you overheard. The game has changed. The threats against Lehtonen will be aired on the evening news tonight. Lehtonen gave an interview to Sanna Römpötti."

"Oh, no," said Joutsamo.

"What did she say?" asked Skoog.

Takamäki ran a hand over his closely-cropped hair. "We didn't get into details, but let's just say Lehtonen has been rather critical of our performance."

"We'll have to think about how this will affect the case," said Joutsamo.

"That's right, we'll cover the PR issues later," said Takamäki. "The situation has changed. Our first priority is figuring out how to keep her alive."

"Can't we stop the broadcast somehow?" said Skoog.

"Not unless you want to violate the constitution."

"Hell," said Skoog. "Then the constitution needs to be amended. The media meddles with our cases with their stories, cartoons, who knows what else. The system needs some discipline."

"Well, I doubt we'll have time for constitutional amendments. Right now, we have to find Ahola and track down the remainder of Korpi's henchman. Let's meet at five and see where we're at. Get to work."

Kulta stood up first. "Hell, if this doesn't work out we're bound for a scolding as bad as the one I got from the newly-married lingerie model at the bar last Saturday night."

Takamäki didn't laugh. "Lehtonen has given us a pretty bad scolding already."

* * *

Sanna Römpötti was sitting at her desk in the newsroom with copious amounts of paper arranged all around her in neat piles.

She didn't have a private office, just a cube in the same cube farm she shared with most of her colleagues. Back in the corner was the most hallowed ground in the newsroom, the desk from which the anchor read the evening news.

Sundays were always quiet in the newsroom. That didn't bother Römpötti. She stared at the computer screen, headphones on, watching her interview with Mari Lehtonen. The tape had been transferred to the newsroom servers.

Römpötti was humored by Takamäki's antics. Clearly, if that was the lieutenant's reaction, the police were dealing with an extremely serious threat. First he downplays its importance, then can't string together a single sentence about it. But the most striking thing to Römpötti was that the lieutenant was downplaying it by saying that there was nothing serious about the case. Perhaps therein lay the root of Mari Lehtonen's problems.

The outline of the story was taking shape in Römpötti's mind. She had already begun editing some of Mari Lehtonen's interview on the computer "So I decided to stop being afraid... This Korpi's the criminal, not me... I'm just an ordinary citizen doing my civic duty... If I fulfill my civic duty and testify, it shouldn't mean that my daughter and I become pariahs to be hidden away indefinitely... I'm very disappointed in how the police have handled the situation. It seems that to the police we're part of the problem, and they solve it by sweeping us under the rug... If society expects citizens to testify in court, then it needs to able to protect them."

Scathing commentary, thought Römpötti.

During the interview at the coffee shop, Römpötti had thought Mari to be somewhat crazy for spurning the security of the safe house, but once she explained the prospect of being trapped there for weeks and months, Römpötti had begun to understand. Her predicament applied specifically to the ordinary citizen. Certainly a criminal striving to break free of a gang could adapt to life in a safe house, but Mari Lehtonen had done nothing wrong. To the contrary, she had done everything right. And if that resulted in unbearable circumstances for her, something was seriously wrong with the system.

After the interview, Römpötti had asked Lehtonen if she needed any help, but she hadn't. She and her daughter had decided to see a movie and then go home. "Make it good," she had said to the reporter.

Römpötti had managed to find some additional material from foreign sources, including a sobering interview with Danielle Cable, her voice altered and her face scrambled. Cable gave an account of hiding from a criminal organization for seven years because she had testified against the man who murdered her husband. A second witness from the same trial, a father of three, had been murdered after a year of constant threats. The material wouldn't fit into this evening's news, but perhaps in a few days, once the story had really broken.

Römpötti had also researched anonymous testimonies, where the witnesses' identities were hidden. This was an unattractive alternative, since witnesses, police officers or courts weren't infallible. The defense needed the right to cross-examine witnesses as to the reliability of their testimony, as Martin had done with Lehtonen.

Römpötti's thoughts returned to the news story. She wondered what clips she would use. She had managed to get some footage of the blockade on Porvoo Street, and later in the afternoon, toward dusk, she planned to take her cameraman to Lehtonen's building, and to the spot where Laura was accosted.

She'd need some commentary from the police. If neither Takamäki nor Skoog would comment, she'd send a regional reporter to interview the minister of the interior, now attending an Emergency Services Christmas party in the Joensuu area. The minister, who had almost certainly been briefed on the case, would undoubtedly comment on camera, at least on a general level. Römpötti would instruct her colleague to word the question, "How important is witness protection?" She could already hear the response in her head, something in the vein of, "More robust witness protection is a crucial part of the landmark Internal Security Program passed by the legislature two years ago. It is our top priority to safeguard anyone involved in the investigation of serious crimes."

With the minister's comment as an intro, she would then move on to the account of an actual witness. The contrast would be stark. Then on the following day she'd run a follow-up story on what the Internal Security Program had accomplished: not much of anything.

* * *

Takamäki, Joutsamo, Karila, and Skoog were crowded into Takamäki's already cramped office. "Just let me say something. I think we should go public with the case, maybe even issue an apology," said Karila, the head of VCU.

Deputy Chief Skoog shook his head. "We can't do that… The best course of action is to do nothing and let the storm blow over. It's not the kind of story other media outlets will pick up anyway."

"Really?" said Karila. "I'd say it's exactly the kind of sensationalism the media loves—easy to understand and emotionally charged."

Takamäki sat behind his desk and wondered briefly if he should mention his wife's reaction from a couple of days earlier, then decided against it. He sided with Karila. "I think we should answer Römpötti's questions. I can do it. I'll just say it's a difficult problem, but as always, we do everything we can."

"If you admit publicly that we have a problem, where are you gonna get witnesses for these kinds of cases going forward?" said Skoog.

"Well, if we sit on our hands while Lehtonen and Römpötti have their say, we won't be getting any witnesses anyway," said Joutsamo.

"My point is that you can't take an isolated case as an indication of systemic flaws," said Skoog. "Sometimes it's a good idea to talk to the media and try to sway public opinion in our favor, but in this instance we have no choice but to keep quiet. The witness chose not to take advantage of the safe house that we provided, and instead went solo with a tell-all to the media on a sensitive case. I still think she belongs in a mental institution, but that's off the table now that the media is involved. Like I said, we'll put out a statement like this, 'Police were called to Porvoo Street this morning on reports of a bomb threat. For reasons pertaining to the investigation, no further information will be provided. The police are doing everything possible to hold the person or persons behind the threat accountable, and are asking for any information that might be connected to the case.' And that's all we say. I'll take responsibility for all communications with the media."

Takamäki sat behind his desk, arms folded, trying to keep a straight face. "So you'll take media responsibility. Maybe you'd like to lead the investigation as well?"

"Don't fuck with me. If this blows up in my face, I'll have Internal Affairs look into your role in this mess," said Skoog, and he stormed out.

Takamäki, Joutsamo and Karila sat and watched as he left. Once the door had closed, Takamäki spoke up, "Well, looks like I'm still in charge of the case. Any ideas on how to proceed?"

"You already said it," said Joutsamo after a long silence. "Let's find Ahola."

* * *

The SWAT officer stood behind the door, his face masked, a helmet on his head, and in his hand, a three-foot iron ram at the ready. Three other SWAT officers were lined up behind him on the stairs, the first clutching a heavy ballistic shield, the second a shotgun, and the third an MP5 submachine gun. Suhonen stood further back in his leather jacket. He too wore a mask to protect his identity.

Suhonen nodded and the lead man slammed the ram into the lock, reducing the surrounding wood to splinters. The door sprang open, and the shield man swung into the lead, followed by the officer with the shotgun. They moved more hurriedly than at the

Kaarela house—the apartment had to be secured as quickly as possible.

"Police! Nobody move!"

Next came the submachine gun man, then the ram wielder, who had ditched the ram in favor of a pistol. Suhonen came in last.

The apartment was a two-room flat in one of the high rises on Kallvik Street. The address had come from Joutsamo's list of residences associated with Ahola and his accomplices. They had no indication that Ahola would actually be here, but there was only one way to find out. They'd already searched three other apartments, and six remained on Suhonen's list. Kulta had his own list and another SWAT unit. Both teams were scrambling.

Suhonen stepped into the entryway, which was littered with shoes, clothing and garbage. One of the SWAT officers was standing in the doorway on the left. "Empty bedroom," he said as Suhonen came up.

The entry hall ended at the bathroom door, with the living room on the left. A rotten smell permeated the apartment. Suhonen entered the living room, which had every mark of a typical gang hideout. A couple of mattresses on the floor with a blanket and a worn-out sofa on the opposite wall. On the floor in the corner was a small television playing some crime drama.

One of the SWAT officers stood at the end of the sofa with his weapon at the ready while the other pressed the barrel of his shotgun against the head of a man lying there. The aggressive approach had been agreed upon in advance.

"Harri Nieminen?" said Suhonen as he came abreast of the officer holding the shotgun.

The man on the sofa didn't respond. He had the brawny build and square jaw of a boxer. His hair was closely cropped and he wore a gray, hooded sweatshirt with the GYM logo.

Suhonen tapped the officer with the shotgun on the shoulder and he withdrew the barrel some four inches.

"Where's Matti Ahola?"

"Matti?" the man rasped.

"You heard me."

"I dunno. Haven't seen him for days."

"Where'd you see him last?"

Nieminen thought for a second. "Some bar over on the east side. Had a couple beers with him."

"I need an address."

"What'd he do?"

"Something bad."

Nieminen was still lying on the sofa, his eyes darting from one masked cop to the next, then to the guns trained on his face. "That bad, huh?"

Suhonen nodded. "He's been working for Korpi. Korpi's causing trouble, and we're looking for his associates. Do you work for him?"

"Uhh…no."

Suhonen just waited. Nieminen squirmed on the sofa for a while before speaking up, "Anything else?"

"The address."

"Fuck if I remember. Shit. I don't know…at some point he had an apartment over in Kannelmäki. In those old buildings by the Maxi store, or what used to be the Maxi. Just across from it on the other side of the turnabout."

Suhonen nodded. He knew the spot: Kanteletar Street 4.

"He had some broad there who rented the place. First stairwell looking from the street, maybe fourth floor. Yeah, that's it."

Suhonen wrote down the address and tapped the officer with the shotgun, who began pulling back out of the room, the barrel fixed on Nieminen until he had ducked behind the wall. The other gunman still had a submachine gun aimed at the man's forehead.

"Alright. If you see or hear from Ahola, give me a call," said Suhonen, and he put a scrap of paper with his number on the arm of the sofa. "That way you won't have any problems. And steer clear of Korpi. Lots of heat on him."

Nieminen nodded. "I can see that. Shouldn't be hard to do with him in prison."

Suhonen wasn't exactly reassured, but it wouldn't take long before word of these shakedowns got out. "Good bye," said Suhonen, and he turned to leave.

"What about that door? Who's gonna pay for that?" shouted Nieminen from the sofa, a submachine gun still staring him down from the doorway.

"Call customer service at the Helsinki police department. Hours are eight to four-fifteen," said Suhonen. Then he left.

Two of the SWAT cops were already in the stairwell when Suhonen came out with the last. "Next stop Vartiokylä," said Suhonen. "Another apartment building on Arho Street. Over there by the parking lot at the end of the road."

* * *

Takamäki and Joutsamo were in the VCU break room when the theme song for the Channel 3 nightly news struck up on the television. "I can hardly wait," droned Takamäki. He had a bad feeling about this.

An image of a police barricade came up on the screen as the headline announced that a bomb had been found in front of a murder witness's home. The next headline mentioned a bombing in Turkey, but the detectives weren't interested.

Now the anchor appeared on screen. "A car bomb was discovered today on Porvoo Street in Alppila. According to our latest reports, the incident was a retaliation against Mari Lehtonen, a witness at a recent murder trial. Last Wednesday, Lehtonen testified against gang boss Risto Korpi, leading to a murder conviction and life sentence. At the trial, Lehtonen linked Korpi to the scene of the murder."

The picture cut to the minister of the interior as he was addressing an audience. Römpötti's voiceover mentioned the minister's recent emphasis on witness protection. "Witness protection is a key component of solving serious crimes," the minister thundered.

The picture cut back to the police barricade on Porvoo Street, and Römpötti's narration continued. "So says the minister. But what about in real life? After Helsinki resident Mari Lehtonen testified last Wednesday in a murder trial resulting in a life sentence for gang boss Risto Korpi, a car bomb was discovered in front of her apartment building this morning. The threats began a couple of days earlier when Lehtonen's daughter received a note threatening to abduct her."

Lehtonen's scrambled face appeared on screen. "I'm very disappointed in how the police have handled the situation. It seems that to the police we're part of the problem, and they solve it by sweeping us under the rug."

Römpötti went on, "Lehtonen was disappointed when the only option presented to her by the police was that she and her daughter go into hiding. The Helsinki VCU provided her with a safe house, which she was prohibited from leaving."

Lehtonen came back on, "If I fulfill my civic duty and testify, it shouldn't mean that my daughter and I become pariahs to be hidden away indefinitely by the police machinery."

Römpötti asked her, "Wouldn't that make more sense in this situation?"

Lehtonen answered, "I decided to stop being afraid. This Korpi's the criminal, not me. I'm just an ordinary citizen trying to do my civic duty. If society expects citizens to testify in court, then it needs to be able to protect them. Maybe this safe house might work for some criminal, but not for an ordinary citizen. I'm very disappointed in the police's performance."

Römpötti's face appeared on screen. "At high profile speeches, the interior minister trumpets the role of witnesses, but in practice the authorities are powerless. Mari Lehtonen helped the criminal justice system convict a murderer, only to be offered her own sentence in return. According to our exclusive sources, the police have even considered having Lehtonen committed to a mental hospital for refusing to comply with their wishes. So first a witness, then a mental patient. Nobody from the Helsinki PD agreed to appear on camera to answer our questions."

The screen cut back to the news anchor, who encouraged viewers to follow the discussion on the morning talk show.

Joutsamo shot Takamäki an inquiring look across the coffee table.

"Not good."

"Mm-hm. Somebody from here should have answered their questions."

"Apparently Skoog didn't feel up to it."

"I guess not. But with that minister priming the pump, the shit's really gonna hit the fan," said Takamäki.

"You think Römpötti did it on purpose?"

"Absolutely. Without an answer from us, she just kept going up the ladder. The minister doesn't know anything about the case," said Takamäki. "If I were a betting man I'd say the boss' phones are ringing off the hook right now. First the police commissioner will get a call, then he'll call the commander and on and on all the way to Deputy Chief Skoog, and from there the shit will pour right down the back of Lieutenant Takamäki's collar."

"But Skoog was supposed to be in charge of media."

"I'm not really worried about the media or getting yelled at. I'm more worried about how Korpi's goons are gonna react. Might be pouring fuel on the fire."

"Or not," said Joutsamo.

"How not? Don't tell me you buy this bit about publicity protecting her?"

"No, but the bad guys like it when the cops get smeared on TV."

"I dunno... I'd say she's lucky they scrambled her face... But, I have been thinking about it a little. It *is* true that we don't have any tools other than the safe house. Having the SWAT team running tactical raids and arresting everyone we can think of can't be standard procedure every time we face this situation."

Joutsamo could see where Takamäki was going. "In other words we need to think twice before using witnesses."

"Maybe... I don't know. We can't isolate ourselves, but at the same time we have to preserve the public's trust. Anyway, I'd better have another cup of coffee. Won't be long before my phone starts ringing."

Before he made it to the coffeemaker, his phone rang. At least it was easy to pass the reporters on to Skoog, who had "volunteered" as the media contact. After a while, there was a lull in the calls and Joutsamo brought him a cup of coffee.

The fourth call was from a very enraged Skoog.

"What the hell," he blustered. "How is this possible?"

"Free press?" suggested Takamäki with a smirk. Joutsamo, the only other person in the break room, was sitting across the table.

"Don't fuck with me. This is a major crisis. That reporter made a laughing stock of the minister and that's bad news for all of us."

Takamäki didn't respond—he was waiting for Skoog's threat to transfer him to some rural district to process gun permits.

The silence made Skoog hesitate. He didn't want to hesitate. He'd been lambasted, and now he wanted to lambast someone else. "Answer me! How is this possible?"

"Didn't you watch the broadcast? Lehtonen talked to a reporter. What more do they need?"

"So where'd Römpötti hear about having Lehtonen committed? She didn't know about that part."

"How should I know?"

A foreboding silence prevailed. "There's a mole on your team. Find out who it is!"

"You know..." said Takamäki, the irritation audible in his voice now. "I think we've got enough to do around here without launching an internal investigation."

"Well... I want a full report for the minister by nine A.M. outlining everything that's happened and when."

"Fine."

"This won't be good for your career."

"So where'll it be... Lapland or someplace else?" said Takamäki in a weary voice.

"Huh?"

"Don't you always threaten to transfer us to the backwoods whenever something goes wrong? I'd just kind of like to know what district you think is at the bottom of the bucket."

"You really don't get it, do you?"

"Actually, I do. But I have some real work to do here. We have a witness who wants...uhh...*needs* protection."

Takamäki was getting tired of the conversation, and his coffee was getting cold.

"You're in deep shit."

"Is there anything else? I got work to do."

"No," said Skoog, and he hung up the phone.

Takamäki tasted his coffee. Still warm enough. "Y-eaah..."

"Well?" said Joutsamo.

"Nothing," he smiled. No point in burdening Joutsamo with the details. She'd already heard enough. "The chiefs are taking out their rage on everyone else, meaning all of us here in the field. No point worrying about it."

"No?"

"Not if your conscience is clean," he said. "In any case, Skoog wants a report on the case to give to the minister. Would you have time to do it?"

Joutsamo nodded. "Sure, I'll be burning the midnight oil anyway."

"Don't make it too long. Two, three pages max. The attention spans at the ministry can't handle anything longer. So no unnecessary details or confidential material. No addresses, for example, since it'll be passed around the ministry and political circles. Who knows where it could end up."

"Got it," said Joutsamo.

"Oh yeah, and one more thing," said Takamäki. "Let's put another patrol car in front of the Lehtonens' building tonight."

"Just in case the publicity stirs up any nutcases, huh?"

He nodded. "Damn, we're like a medical team trying to treat somebody who's asking us to pull the plug."

* * *

Mari Lehtonen was at home, sitting on the sofa in front of the TV with her legs folded beneath her and a glass of red wine on the coffee table beside her. She had just watched the news, and Laura, tired from the long day, was already asleep. It felt good to be home.

Mari got up and looked out the window onto the street below where a blue and white cruiser was parked. Despite her hard feelings, it still felt comforting. She thought about the news story, which had been rather critical. Joutsamo and the others were doing their best, of course, and maybe her words were too harsh. In the actual interview, Lehtonen had made it clear that her grievances weren't against any particular officer, but against the system in general. Römpötti had edited that part out. For a moment, Lehtonen considered calling Joutsamo, but decided against it.

Mari returned to the sofa, took a sip of wine and thought about the coming Monday. Most likely she would go to work as usual, and Laura to school. She would have to schedule her day so she could bring the girl to school and get off early to pick her up. That would be best, no doubt.

Her attempts to analyze her own feelings fell short. Home felt good, if a little scary. Her eyes went to the handbag on the coffee table.

She didn't feel tired yet, and was flipping through the channels when the phone rang. It was her ex-husband, Anton Teittinen. After a brief deliberation she answered.

"Hello."

"Hey, it's Anton. Sorry to bother you." Mari could hear what sounded like the din of a bar on the other end.

"No worries."

"Listen, you were great on TV, even if I couldn't see your pretty face."

She couldn't decide whether to be warm or cold, so she settled on neutral. He had, after all, helped them out earlier. "Yeah, well…"

"I'm serious," he went on. "You really put those pigs in their places. Fucking right on, you know."

Lehtonen didn't respond.

"But listen. There's something I wanna talk to you about," he said. "I got a call from a couple buddies who wanna help out. You know, be kinda like bodyguards for you two since the cops flopped so bad. These guys are definitely not Korpi fans…very much the opposite."

"I'm not so sure," said Mari. Anton's buddies sounded shady, and she didn't really want bodyguards, just a normal life. What she definitely didn't want was to end up in the crossfire between two gangs.

"Come on," he urged her. "Yes, they have criminal records, but that could make a good story: Ex-cons protect a witness when cops fail."

"Well, I'm not so sure…"

"Seriously. Give it a chance," he persisted. "Might take some of the heat off you on the streets if people hear these guys got your back. Don't ya think?"

Mari didn't want to say yes, but she did anyway. "Alright. That's fine with me, but tell them to stay on the street—nobody comes inside my place. If we come outside, they can walk in front or behind, but nobody follows Laura into school or me into work."

"Of course not. Trust me…it'll be great. Just like an American president with the Secret Service and all," he said and hung up the phone.

Mari took a sip of red wine as the same feeling of defeat that she had known so well during their marriage descended. Anton had always known how to twist her arm to get his way. After a divorce, several moves, and a restraining order, she had finally managed to break free of him, and now he was shouldering his way back in because Mari was too tired to argue.

MONDAY, DECEMBER 18

CHAPTER 27
MONDAY, 8:00 A.M.
MARI LEHTONEN'S APARTMENT

Just inside the door of the convenience store across the street from the Lehtonens' building was a newspaper stand boasting the word *hero* in one of its headlines. Just beside the headline was a scrambled screenshot from Mari's TV interview; the subhead read *Murder Witness Marked for Death*.

Mari Lehtonen hadn't seen the paper, nor the headline. She was at the breakfast table, drinking tea with her daughter and discussing their plans for the coming day. Some danger was unavoidable, but they couldn't let it bother them. Mari had also instructed Laura on what say to her friends at school, the main message being that life was to go on as normally as possible. Mari would answer the inevitable questions at work in the same way.

* * *

Kulta and Kohonen were staked out in a car in front of the building—the same Peugeot 206 that Suhonen had used a day earlier. With such an ideal spot, the car had never been moved. Another police car, this one a cruiser, was posted just in front of the entrance.

Kohonen yawned. She'd been arranging phone taps at the station till midnight, hurried to bed, then risen again at six. She and Kulta had climbed into the stakeout vehicle at seven. Division of labor between the two was clear cut: Kohonen had the girl, Kulta the mom. Neither were allowed to get any further than thirty feet. The previous evening, Takamäki had worked out the details with Laura's teacher and Mari's employer. The police were not to enter any classrooms nor Mari's cubicle area, but were to wait outside in the hallway and reception area. Mari hadn't responded to Takamäki's calls.

Kulta fixed his eyes on a car pulling into a parking space in front of the building. A man wielding a camera got out of the driver's side door and a youthful, dark-haired woman stepped out the passenger side. Reporters, thought Kulta. The media circus had begun. By 8:30, three cameramen and three reporters had gathered in front of the building, with one of the patrol officers tending the crowd. Kulta had asked Takamäki for advice, but had received none.

The clock in the Peugeot showed 8:36 when yet another vehicle pulled up to the curb: a matte black American muscle car. Kulta knew the model, a 1974 Chevy Nova.

The car was parked about a hundred and fifty feet from the Peugeot with its front bumper concealed so Kulta couldn't make out the plates. The two men inside gave no indication of getting out. Kohonen had noticed the car too.

"Should we go have a look?" she said, already out the door. Kulta brought up the rear.

Both officers made sure their coats were open and checked their guns in their shoulder holsters. Despite freezing temperatures, neither felt particularly cold with their bulletproof vests on.

The Chevy was parked about a hundred feet past the entrance to the Lehtonens' building, and the detectives breezed past to the whir of camera shutters. Kohonen signaled one of the patrol officers to come too, and the entourage of cameramen tailed along.

At fifty feet, Kulta began to make out the men's faces. The guy in the passenger seat had sunken cheeks and bad skin. His hair was long, and he had a small mustache. Kulta felt a glimmer of recognition, but couldn't quite place the man's face.

Then it came to him.

"Careful," he said. The one in the passenger seat was Butch Willer, previously Pekka Viljamaa. The details of the name change were unimportant at the moment. What *was* important was the fact that Willer was a member of the Skulls, a hard-core organized crime ring fronting as a motorcycle gang.

"They're Skulls," said Kulta as he drew his pistol. "I got the passenger side, you take the driver."

Kohonen and the other officer drew their weapons and sidestepped to the other side of the car.

The officer who'd been posted in front of the building came running up to shoo off the cameras. "Move away! Now!"

The herd took a few steps back, but the shutters kept clicking.

"Out of the car!" bellowed Kulta loud enough for the gangsters to hear. "Get out! Slowly!"

Inside, the two men glanced at each other and nodded. They opened the doors and stepped out slowly. Both had on gang vests over long-sleeved black T-shirts.

"Show me your hands!" Kulta ordered.

"What is this?" protested Willer in his shrill voice as he got out. Kulta didn't respond, just kept his gun trained on Willer. The patrol officer came up from the side, and with one swift movement, threw the man to the ground, wrenched his arms behind his back and clapped the cuffs on. Kulta turned to the second gangster on the other side of the car—he was already in cuffs as well.

"What the hell," said Willer from the sidewalk, his voice loud enough that the reporters could hear. "We didn't do anything. All we're doing is protecting Lehtonen cuz the cops can't do it. We're no criminals."

"Shut up!" shouted Kulta. He swapped his gun for a phone and called for a patrol car to take these goons away—the one already on site was for security detail only.

One of the reporters took a couple wary steps toward Willer. "Did I hear you say you guys are Lehtonen's bodyguards?"

"That's right. The police can't do it, so someone has to."

The patrol officer glanced over at Kulta, who was still talking on the phone. He decided to break it up himself, "Okay, that's enough. Press conference is over."

"Can I ask who's paying you?" said the reporter, the cameras whirring all around.

"Mari Lehtonen, of course," said Willer. "She doesn't trust the police."

"That's enough!" shouted the officer.

Kulta hung up the phone and came to his aid.

"Media, move back," he ordered, but nobody listened. The thought of pulling out his gun crossed his mind, but he suppressed it quickly.

"Are the police so incapable of protecting Lehtonen that she has to pay gangsters to do the job?" stammered one reporter.

Kulta was getting very annoyed, but he managed to stay calm.

"Can you tell us what the reason is for this arrest?"

"Now *there's* a good question," said Willer from the sidewalk. "I'd like to know, too!"

Kulta tuned out the racket. His eyes scanned the surrounding area for more thugs. The Skulls weren't exactly known for their bodyguards. Body counts was more like it. These two may well have been sent here on a hit.

Kulta's eyes were drawn to the entrance of the apartment building, where two figures were exiting— Mari and Laura—apparently going somewhere. The two peered over at the ruckus before veering off in the opposite direction.

Shit, thought Kulta. If he started chasing them now, he'd drag the reporters and cameras along, but if he stayed here the Lehtonens would be sitting ducks, which was out of the question.

"Uhh," Kulta hesitated. "I have to make a call here. Officer, uh..." he glanced at the name tag on the beat officer's shirt pocket. "...Räsänen can field your questions."

Räsänen looked at Kulta with desperation in his eyes. Kulta gave a quick nod as he motioned for Kohonen to follow him.

"So why are we being arrested?" Willer bellowed from the sidewalk. "We haven't done anything wrong!"

"Yes, can you tell us the reason for this arrest?" the reporter yelled after the detectives as they hurried off.

Räsänen peered after Kulta and Kohonen. "Uhhh, well…it's a question of public safety and keeping the peace," he stammered.

The other beat cop led the second Skull out of the road and set him down next to Willer.

"That's right, public safety and keeping the peace," he repeated.

By then, Kulta and Kohonen were about twenty yards behind the Lehtonens. Once around the corner, they picked up the pace. Wailing sirens were drawing near. Backup for Räsänen was on the way. The situation there was under control.

Kulta turned to Kohonen, "Laura's probably on the way to school," he said. They picked up the pace once more and finally caught up.

"Morning," said Kulta. "We're from the Helsinki Police. We'll be helping you out today."

"We don't need any help," said Mari coldly. Laura wore a red knit hat, jacket, and had a book bag slung over her shoulder. She stayed close to her mother.

"In any case, we'll be looking after you. I'm Mikko Kulta and this here's Kirsi Kohonen."

"Fine," said Lehtonen. "Same rules as before then. Stay at least thirty feet away at all times."

"As you wish."

"So what was that all about back there?" asked Mari.

Kulta smiled. "Well, in order to establish a monopoly on your protection we have to squeeze out the gangsters."

"Gangsters, huh?" said Mari.

"That's right. On your payroll, apparently."

"I'm not paying anybody. My ex-husband called yesterday and said a few of his friends wanted to look after me. I told him it makes no difference to me."

Her impudence was beginning to grate on Kohonen. "Don't you think you could have at least let us know?"

Lehtonen glared at the redheaded policewoman. "I didn't ask you to come. It really makes no difference to me. Thirty feet, please."

"Are we headed for the school?" said Kulta.

Mari nodded curtly, annoyed by the fact that her day wasn't shaping up to be so normal after all.

Kulta hurried ahead, and Kohonen dropped back to a distance of thirty feet.

* * *

Takamäki was in the VCU break room reading the news on teletext, a text-based news service on TV. The headline read, *Conditions Reach Boiling Point for Threatened Witness.*

The lieutenant read the article: *An incident occurred this morning on Porvoo Street near the residence of the same murder witness targeted in yesterday's attempted bomb strike. Police arrested two gang members in front of the building, one of whom told reporters on the scene that the threatened witness had paid them as bodyguards because the police weren't fit for the job. The Helsinki VCU has not commented on the incident.*

Further down were two headlines in different colored fonts. *Interior Minister: "We're looking into the matter." Minister of Justice: "Improvements are forthcoming."* Takamäki couldn't bring himself to care.

VCU Chief Karila came into the room and poured himself a cup of coffee. "Have you looked at *Ilta-Sanomat's* site yet? They posted the pics already. Kulta pointing a gun at the gangsters."

"I haven't looked," said Takamäki, not that he had any desire.

"What about these two Skulls?"

"In jail. Both claim they were paid to protect Lehtonen. We didn't find any weapons in the vehicle. According to Kulta, Lehtonen says her ex set it up."

"What about our bomber? Ahola."

"We searched all night. Suhonen and Kulta probably raided upwards of twenty apartments with no result. Of course, it sent a message that working with Ahola right now isn't too smart."

Karila sipped his coffee. "This is turning into quite the farce."

"It already is. I think Kulta said it best on the phone: 'It's all a downhill slide from here.'"

"What's the situation with the Lehtonens?"

"Kohonen's covering Laura at school. Kulta's waiting in the lobby at Mari's work."

Karila paused for a while. "Skoog called."

"Sounds ominous."

Karila shrugged. "I don't know. He got this idea from some psychologist that we should bring Mari into prison to meet Korpi. That way he could see that the target of his hate is just an ordinary woman. It's called cognitive behavioral therapy, the idea being that Korpi would learn to monitor himself by managing his emotions."

"You're telling me a psychologist recommended this? Have you read Korpi's psychological assessment? It says right there the man is incapable of empathy. I think by definition that rules out any sort of mediation."

"I don't know. Might be something to it," said Karila. Obviously, he had made his decision. All he wanted now was to get Takamäki on board. "Skoog says we're moving more toward mediations, where face-to-face meetings with victims can prevent repeat offenses. According to this psychologist, human interaction is the best way to resolve any crisis. The idea is for Korpi to learn to control his own violent behavior and take responsibility for it."

"I see. And you buy into this?"

"They'll meet in a controlled environment. Maybe Korpi will see that it was nothing personal, she was just doing her civic duty—just part of the system. That's what he needs to understand."

"I'm lucky if I understand it. Well, I suppose you'll be joining them."

Karila smiled. "Sorry. Budget meetings. Unless you have any better suggestions, it's gonna have to be you. I'm dealing with reams of political bullshit right now. The Interior Ministry is fielding hundreds of calls and emails demanding the minister's resignation. I hear that parliament has started three separate inquiries into the minister's performance. And all this will trickle down to us."

Takamäki was still looking at the headlines on TV. "Well, I guess it's worth a try. Things couldn't get much worse anyway. But we'll have to arrange to get Lehtonen into the prison."

"I already took care of it. You take Joutsamo, pick Lehtonen up from work and drive in the side gate. They'll take you straight to the visitation room. There'll be a couple guards for extra security."

Rauli Salo was on his way to Korpi's dreary cell on the northern block with his 10:30 lunch. The guards on the block didn't mind at all that Salo had volunteered to take the gang boss his meals. A small note on the cell door read: "No contacts."

The northern cell block, sometimes referred to as the "hazardous waste ward," was among the most poorly maintained in the complex. All prisoners on the block were either in isolation or under protection, so the cells were under constant lock-down. To make matters worse, the cells had no running water or toilets. Buckets served as bed pans, which had infused the wing with a distinctly revolting stench.

The routine was rigid: breakfast at 7:00, lunch at 10:30, and dinner at 3:10 P.M. At some point during the day, prisoners were permitted one hour outside. That was it.

The green cell walls were dirty and dilapidated, and the cramped windows served only to complement the oppressive atmosphere.

Salo opened the cell door. Korpi sat up on his cot with a grin. "Look who's here, room service. What's it gonna be today?"

"Sausage soup," said Salo, before lowering his voice to a whisper, just in case Korpi's cell was wired. An isolation cell was probably not worth the trouble, but you could never be too careful "The number you gave me doesn't answer anymore."

"Really?"

Salo shook his head. "There's news all over the TV and papers about a bomb threat against Lehtonen. You know…the witness from your trial. She bitched out the cops pretty good on TV."

"That's good," said Korpi. The man behind the bombing was no mystery to Korpi– few besides Ahola had access to such explosives. The man had a stash of them at a cabin out in the country. Korpi tried to reason out what had happened. If Martin had stopped answering his phone, he was probably in jail. That was to be expected. And the cops would certainly have launched a major operation after the bomb threat. But if Martin was in jail, then Guerrilla probably was too, since he had been Martin's contact.

"Did they catch the bomber?"

"As of this morning they were still looking."

Korpi smiled as he nodded. "You got some paper? I got another number."

"I...I can't," whispered Salo. "This whole thing... It's getting kinda heavy."

Korpi narrowed his eyes at the guard. "You think you have a choice?"

Salo didn't respond.

But Korpi knew when to let out the reins and when to pull them in. Now it was time to let them out. "Alright. This'll be the last time. I'll give you this number...all you have to do is say 'game over.'"

"Game over." he repeated. "What's that supposed to..."

"You don't need to know. But I'll tell you anyway. We're gonna leave her alone. You do this, and I won't ask you for anything more. Once everything cools down, you'll get a grand."

"A grand. And no more jobs after this."

"That's right," whispered Korpi, and he recited the telephone number.

His face was serious, but behind it was a barely suppressed laugh. Did the guard really think he could get off this easy? But he'd taken the bait, and swallowed the hook. And the story Korpi had given him about the message was just that: a story.

Korpi spooned himself some soup, and Salo closed the cell door behind him. He felt unsettled about the message. Korpi was clearly behind the threats on Lehtonen's life, so calling the phone number would be construed as aiding and abetting a convicted criminal. Of course, he had already been guilty of that when he met that suit in the restaurant, but then he hadn't known what a serious crime it would lead to.

Salo considered his options. Maybe he could just deliver the message, collect the money and hope nobody found out. And if the message brought an end to the threats, it would actually be a good deed.

As he strode down the hallway of the isolation wing, he struggled to come up with any other alternatives. He could contact the police and tell them about this latest message, but then they would grill him about any previous messages. Nobody would believe that this was the first, because it was too farfetched. It would end with a conviction for aiding and abetting, and then he would be fired.

Shit. It was just one call. And for that, a grand. With the five hundred from before, that made fifteen hundred—a nice trip to Thailand for a couple of weeks, where he could relax and forget the whole thing.

The sooner he did it, the less it would bother him, he decided. But he wouldn't use his own phone. He'd use the phone in the break room at the prison.

Game over. That wasn't so bad.

CHAPTER 28
MONDAY, 1:00 P.M.
KALLVIK STREET, EAST HELSINKI

Matti Ahola was lying on the sofa, staring at the sweeping patterns in the plastered ceiling. To him it was much like a starry sky—it let the mind roam free. Ahola imagined a swan, but the image transmuted into a dragon and he was forced to close his eyes.

He felt tired, not having had any decent sleep in twenty-four hours. Always on the move. That the cops were after him for the car bomb was obvious, but all he wanted was to sleep. The car wasn't a good place for that. He'd awake to a masked SWAT cop busting in the window and jamming an MP5 against his temple. It would be just his luck for someone to call the police about a guy sleeping in his car.

Harri Nieminen's apartment had been Ahola's only hope. Nieminen was an old boxing buddy with whom he had traded plenty of blows in the ring. When Ahola arrived, Nieminen had told him that the cops had busted in his door last night. The broken lock hadn't gone unnoticed. Now a padlock dangled from a hasp on the inner jamb, and Nieminen simply swapped it to another hasp on the outside when he left the apartment.

Nieminen had at first resisted when Ahola showed up, but the business end of a Nagant Russian revolver had settled the matter in Ahola's favor.

Ahola heard Nieminen rustling on the mattress, where he'd been told to stay. Ahola sat up halfway, the revolver resting on his stomach.

"Gotta take a piss," said Nieminen.

"Alright. Go on."

Once he heard the unmistakable sound coming from the bathroom, Ahola assessed his situation: Korpi's go-ahead for game over had finally come, so Lehtonen's time was up. Earlier on, Guerrilla had given him information on where she lived, where she worked, and her daughter's movements. The kidnapping threat was easy, but the bomb had called for more careful planning. His orders then were only to scare her, so he had left one of the safeties on. When Korpi turned the screw, it was usually a full turn.

Now it was time to kill. Ahola was dreaming of the ways to do it when Nieminen came back from the bathroom. He waved the gun toward the mattress, and Nieminen sat down.

"How long you planning on staying? I need to take care of some things."

Ahola laughed. "I'll stay as long as I want, so lie down and make yourself comfortable. Don't worry though…won't be long."

"I heard Korpi's out of money. That the cops found his stash."

"That's not true, just rumors…" said Ahola. "By the way, how's your little bro?"

"Kaappo?"

"Yeah."

"Doing a four-year stint for dope. Haven't heard from him in about a week."

"Hmm." Ahola thought for a moment. "Korpi's got money, that much I know. Spread the word."

Nieminen shook his head and lay down on the mattress. Under as much pressure as Ahola seemed to be, it was probably best not to aggravate him.

Ahola's thoughts turned back to killing the woman. How should he do it? Ring the doorbell and blow her brains all over the front entry? First the mom, then the girl? Lehtonen didn't own a car, so planting a car bomb was out, and the cops were bound to be on high alert anyway. Maybe he could run her over if he found the right time and place, but that left too much room for error. Complicated schemes were too difficult—there had to be a simpler way. A drive-by shooting? Not bad. The getaway would be fast, anyhow.

Ahola sat up. His head hurt from thinking. But what to do about Nieminen? If the cops had raided the place, Nieminen would surely rat him out at the first turn. Like the time Ahola lifted all the wallets from the locker room at the boxing gym. He'd always figured Nieminen had squealed. The others had proceeded to give Ahola a severe beating, for which the most visible mark was a broken nose. The prison doc, however, had once mentioned something about brain damage. Payback time had come.

Ahola stood up to stretch. He held a pillow in his left hand, which concealed the revolver in his right. Nieminen watched him from the mattress on the floor.

In an instant, Ahola was upon him, smothering his face with the pillow. He plunged the barrel into the soft batting and pulled the trigger, but it didn't muffle the shot like he had hoped. His eardrums slammed shut. The pillow muffled the sound waves from the tip of the barrel, but the gap between the barrel and cylinder had allowed air and sound to escape.

Fuck! That wasn't supposed to happen, he thought, and stepped off of the limp body. It had worked on TV! Shit!

* * *

Takamäki was driving and Joutsamo was sitting with Mari in the back seat. The car was stopped at a red light on Aleksis Kivi Street.

"You're serious?" said Lehtonen, which was the same thing she had said when the detectives had arrived fifteen minutes earlier to pick her up from work. After a little coaxing, Lehtonen had fetched her coat and purse, and followed them out.

"We wouldn't be doing this otherwise," said Joutsamo. "The psychologist says it could help. I don't know if that's true, but it can't hurt."

"And who is this psychologist," said Lehtonen.

Only then did Takamäki realize that he didn't know either. "I don't know."

"So how can you buy into this if you don't even know who it is?"

"Well, Deputy Chief Skoog did speak with him."

"And you believe what your superiors tell you?"

Takamäki smiled. "We have to. The boss has more brass. We're just cogs in the police machinery, right?"

"Right…" said Lehtonen. "…I was a little upset… During the interview and all…"

"Well, don't worry about it," said Takamäki. "I must admit, it actually raised some important questions about our witness protection. It has made me think… Now if only we can resolve the question of your safety."

Takamäki's phone rang and Joutsamo picked up where he left off. "At least we're making an attempt at something other than just hiding you away."

Takamäki answered and Karila informed him of a car chase on the East Highway. The suspect, believed to be Matti Ahola, was bound for downtown Helsinki. Takamäki checked his mirrors.

* * *

Ahola stepped on the gas. The speedometer in the old Fiat showed 95 mph, all the engine was capable of. Ahola jerked the wheel, veering in and out of traffic. Someone leaned on their horn, and Ahola felt like sending a salute with his Nagant. The whine of sirens approached from behind.

Goddamnit, he thought to himself as he changed lanes again.

Why the fuck did he have to believe what he saw on TV. That shot echoed through the whole damn building, and some guy was already on the stairs with a phone to his ear as he was leaving. So the cops had gotten the news immediately, even if Ahola had interrupted the call with a gun butt through the man's teeth.

Ahola knew they'd spotted his Fiat because a cruiser in the oncoming lane with its sirens on had pulled a U-turn just after it passed him. Ahola floored it, and the car zoomed ahead.

He glanced in the rear-view mirror. At least two squads were on his tail and a third was coming down the ramp from the Kulosaari bridge. One of the cruisers came abreast of him on the right, and he fired off a shot. The bullet shattered his passenger-side window, but had no other effect except that the cruiser dropped further back.

The Fiat hurtled over the East Highway bridge toward downtown Helsinki. Up ahead was a crossroads: straight onto Juna Street which would quickly turn into Teollisuus Street, or right up the ramp and then down to the waterfront road. The choice to the right looked too congested. The lights at the top of the ramp could turn red at any second. Going straight, he could make it to the streets of Kallio, maybe even lose the cruisers with a few quick turns, ditch the car and disappear down the alleys and backstreets.

The brake lights on a Volvo station wagon popped on in front of him, and the Fiat bounded ahead with a quick swerve to the right.

Just off the Häme Street bridge, at the point where Juna turned into Teollisuus, he could cut into oncoming traffic through the bus lanes, and from there to the streets of Kallio.

The East Highway curved gently to the right and then again to the left. Up ahead, more flashing lights were visible, and as he reached the bus stop, he caught a movement to his left and heard two loud bangs. Officers on the shoulder had pulled a spike strip, puncturing all four tires. The car began to track wildly, but Ahola stepped on the gas. Just before the next intersection were four cruisers lined up in a barricade. This one he wouldn't be breaking through with the Fiat. Maybe with a Range Rover, but not the Fiat.

Ahola jerked up the emergency brake and swung the wheel sharply to the left in an attempt to swing the tail around. If he could make it back a few hundred yards, he could take the ramp the wrong way down to the waterfront road.

With tires, the one-eighty may have stood a chance. But without them, the bare rims bit into the asphalt and the Fiat flipped, spun along the pavement on its roof, and flopped over onto its side.

Ahola struck his head and shards of broken glass lacerated his face. His chest hit the wheel, knocking the wind out of him. His knee was hurting too, but still, he remained conscious.

He snatched up his pistol and began bashing out the windshield. Shouts came from all sides: "Police! Don't move! Drop your weapon!" But he wasn't listening. The subway tunnel was just on the other side of the fence. If he could make it there, they'd never find him.

He stood up in front of the car, and his peripheral vision caught a dark movement bounding up from the side. K-9. He fired off a shot and the dog fell yelping to the ground at his feet. He fired again and the yelping stopped. The cylinder held seven rounds, so three remained.

The shouts came again. Ahola looked around. There were at least twenty cops. Shit, he thought. He wasn't going back to prison, but there were few alternatives. The subway tunnel was too far. He lowered his weapon to think. Maybe he could take a few cops with him. Then he'd be a legend.

Ahola raised his gun and managed to fire off a couple rounds toward the nearest cruiser. Then he felt two thuds in his chest just before he heard the shots. An immense pain took hold of his body for a moment, and then there was nothing. He never even felt the third bullet. Matti Ahola was dead before his head hit the pavement.

An orange subway train made a hissing sound as it disappeared into the tunnel.

* * *

The visitation room at Helsinki prison had about ten glass-partitioned tables, each with four to five chairs bolted to the floor. The room had been updated during the remodel, and the ambiance was quite modern. A tall window near the ceiling let in plenty of bluish winter light.

Joutsamo and Lehtonen were talking at one of the tables. Along with them was police psychologist Maija Saarni, sent by Deputy Chief Skoog. The forty-five-year-old woman was an instructor at the police academy. She was slender, and had a radiant face that seemed always to be smiling.

In addition to them, there were also two armed prison guards, both bald and well over six feet tall. Firearms and tasers hung from their belts.

Takamäki had driven in through the side gate, where the assistant warden was waiting to take them to the visitation room. They had bypassed the security checkpoint, so none of them had to relinquish their phones. Joutsamo and Takamäki had left their weapons in the glovebox of the car, as it was a bad idea to bring them into prison.

Takamäki was lingering near the door of the visitation room, talking on his cell phone.

"That's too bad," he said. Karila had just explained the turn of events on Juna Street. All of Ahola's bullets had either hit squad cars or missed, but three of the police's had found their target—all in the chest.

Takamäki listened for a while. "Yeah, clearly justifiable force, but naturally the state prosecutor will have to conduct an investigation. What's the status on the shooting at the apartment?"

"I put Kafka's team on it since you got your hands full with Lehtonen," said Karila. "It's pretty obvious Ahola shot Nieminen, even if the details are still a little murky. Considering they're both dead, that's the way it'll probably stay. But Nieminen's apartment was one of the ones Suhonen and Kulta shook down last night."

"Okay. Set up a meeting between Kafka and me for around five and we'll all meet at five-thirty for a full briefing."

"Got it," said Karila. "Sounds good."

Takamäki slipped his phone into his coat pocket and strode back to the table. Just as he was about to ask if everything was alright, he stopped himself. Saarni was explaining the objective of mediation. "...the goal is to reach a point where everybody has something to gain. A win-win situation."

Lehtonen eyed the psychologist. "So what would a win situation look like for me?"

"Well, for the threats to stop," said Saarni with a smile.

"Okay, so my life goes back to where it was before this whole thing started. But what would the win-situation be for Korpi, then?"

"That he see the bigger picture and comprehend it. And stop the threats."

Lehtonen was stupefied. She looked from Joutsamo to Takamäki. "You can't be serious. Geez. How can you talk about a win-win situation when nobody's winning anything. I'm going home."

"Hold on, Mari," said Takamäki. "Right now, it's lose-lose. You're right. But if we can use this to rally back to even-lose, where you're back at zero and Korpi's the loser, then isn't it worth a try? I'm not saying it'll work, but since we're already here I think we should see it through, don't you? The only other option we can offer you is the safe house."

Lehtonen looked at Takamäki. Her blue purse rested in her lap. "Well, since we're already here."

Saarni had little to add. "A positive attitude is important. The goal is simply to communicate and understand," she managed.

Mari was about to snap at her again, but Takamäki set his hand on her shoulder and she checked herself.

A prison guard opened the door and glanced inside without a word. A couple of seconds later Korpi walked in followed by another guard, Salo.

Salo escorted Korpi, who was dressed in brown prison coveralls, to the opposite side of the table. Mari Lehtonen sat between Joutsamo and Saarni. Takamäki remained standing behind them. The burly guards stood further off.

Korpi's bald head drew even more attention to his piercing eyes, which wandered from one person to the next. He began with Lehtonen. "Three of hearts. Phh."

He went on to Saarni. "Two of diamonds."

Joutsamo was ten of diamonds, and Takamäki, jack of clubs.

Saarni played along. "And what would you be?"

"What do you mean?"

"Well, it would nice to know so we can start the game."

Takamäki was certain he'd drop the ace of spades, the toughest card in the deck, but he blindsided them.

"A joker. I'm whatever I want. A couple days ago I was a two of hearts. Couldn't even stand up to that three over there," he stared at Lehtonen. "But I'm wild... Right now I could be anything."

The guy's not dumb, thought Takamäki.

Korpi sat calmly with his hands folded on the table. Nobody said a word for at least ten seconds until Korpi spoke up again. "So I understand that you all wanted to meet. I know Lehtonen, Joutsamo and Takamäki, but who are you?" he asked the two of diamonds.

"Maija Saarni. I'm a psychologist."

Korpi sniffed. "A police psychologist."

"Correct."

"Well, just as I figured. The cops would never trust any shrink but their own. What do you want?" he said with a smug look. "I got plenty of time."

Takamäki gazed at the gang boss in his prison duds. What a smug bastard. Korpi wasn't stupid. He just wanted to play games and flaunt his so-called intelligence. The thought of abruptly calling off the meeting occurred to Takamäki. Saarni clearly didn't have any experience with hardened criminals if she was playing along with Korpi's games and letting a criminal set the tone. On the other hand, she *had* gotten him to talk. A few months ago, the gang boss had been impenetrable in police interrogations.

"We'd just like to talk," said Saarni. "About our situation."

"What situation?"

She took a firmer approach. "Don't play dumb with me. You're not fooling anybody. You know exactly what I'm talking about."

Korpi didn't like her tone of voice, especially coming from someone he'd ranked as a two of diamonds. Nobody of that rank got the better of him. "I do? Well, let's see. I'm an innocent man doing life in prison. The last few days I've spent in the hole because apparently I pose some kind of risk. So I hope you don't mind if I don't know much of anything right now."

Takamäki felt like saying that in that case all was well, but it wouldn't be constructive. A positive attitude was important, and the only way he could think of to be positive was to keep his mouth shut.

"What we do know is that you've been convicted. I can't really comment on the rest. I'm a psychologist, not a lawyer."

Takamäki and Joutsamo looked on with their mouths agape. Whoa, what was this woman trying to pull? Was she throwing the verdict into question or baiting him? Mari Lehtonen's face was expressionless. She just stared straight ahead at Korpi.

"Allow *me* to comment, then," said Korpi. "The only thing I'm guilty of was being in the car with that idiot Nyberg when he went and shot Salmela without telling me. I had no idea what he was planning. If I had, I'd have gotten him another driver."

"So Nyberg screwed up?" said Saarni.

"Nyberg screwed up because he *is* a screwup. That's why I'm serving a sixteen-year sentence."

This last comment earned a smile from Takamäki. Sixteen years was hardly enough for Korpi.

"What is your relationship to Nyberg?"

Korpi stiffened. "What's that supposed to mean?" he said, his eyes narrowing to slits. "What…is this an interrogation? You pigs record everything. You probably wanna use this against me in appeals….son of a bitch!"

Takamäki's eyes shifted to the three guards. The two armed guards were still standing off a ways, and Salo stood to the right.

"This has nothing to do with your appeal. I'm looking for the object of your hatred," said Saarni. "What is it?"

Korpi looked at her with a baffled expression. "All of you...don't you see? The whole fucking system. Every one of you put me in a cage for life," he said. His finger swept from Takamäki to Joutsamo. "These dirty pigs were prejudiced from the very beginning. Everything against me they took into account, and everything in my favor was ignored. I already said it in court, but you still don't get it. How can you think I'd be dumb enough to drive on a stupid hit job like that? Just think about it. To collect a few thousand euros, okay, I'll drive. But a hit job? Hell no. I got enough fucking money to..."

Takamäki wanted to ask where the money was now. In court, Korpi had mentioned a 400-euro TV which had now ballooned into a three-thousand-euro debt. Yet another mark of his lies.

Saarni's game was beginning to dawn on Takamäki. She was going through the objects of Korpi's hatred. As much as he seemed to hate himself, he'd never admit it. So his hate always needed a surrogate, and this time it was Mari Lehtonen.

"You remember Mari Lehtonen from the trial, right?" said Saarni.

"That's right," said Korpi, turning toward Lehtonen. "Pretty damn good memory you've got for a three of hearts. Pretty convincing show you put on, too, when Martin put you on the spot."

"Let's try to stick to the subject," said Saarni. "What did Mari do wrong?"

Korpi looked at Saarni, confused. "Wrong? Nothing. Absolutely nothing."

Now even Takamäki was dumbfounded. "Nothing?"

Korpi was outright laughing now. "Absolutely nothing. Mari Lehtonen did exactly what she was supposed to. She called the police and testified in court like a good little girl. There is nothing wrong with that."

Saarni was at a loss for words. "Well… I don't understand. Why retaliate against her, then? Why put glue in her lock? Why threaten to kidnap her daughter? Why plant a bomb at her doorstep? I don't understand."

Korpi folded his arms on the table and gazed down at them for a while. Then he raised his eyes and surveyed his audience with an almost theatrical flair. His gaze went from Saarni, to Joutsamo, then Takamäki, and finally came to rest on Lehtonen.

"You're right. You don't understand," he said. "Sorry about all this, Mari. But obviously I'm angry that you testified against me. If not for your memory, I'd be a free man."

He scanned the faces again. It gratified him to see their confusion. "To me it makes no difference if you pin those threats on me. Appeals won't change the murder verdict, so what do I care? This has nothing to do with her. It has to do with every other mari lehtonen in Finland," he said with a laugh. "It's a question of principle. Let's see once and for all who the public dares side with. I can prepare for anything but some mari lehtonen seeing me in the wrong place at the wrong time. I can eliminate every fucking bug and tap, and flush every rat out of the system. Money can be moved abroad. But the only thing I can't anticipate is some fucking mari lehtonen. So that's the last variable I have to control."

Takamäki was beginning to understand what Korpi was thinking, and it frightened him.

"This isn't about me. It's a question of principle. It's a war between cops and criminals. Innocent bystanders don't have to have any part in it. But if they decide to get involved, then they're part of the game."

Korpi stared directly at Mari.

"So when you called the cops you chose your side. Before that call you were neutral, but now you're part of the system. An enemy."

Mari glowered across the table at Korpi. "Listen, asshole," she said. The psychologist tried to tug on her sleeve, but to no avail, "Neither I nor any other citizen is neutral. Shit... As if we should stand by and watch as someone gets raped in the park. We *are* the system, but you, Risto Korpi, are a stinking sack of shit. The worst kind, and I'm damn glad that I helped put you away for life. I'm happy to be your enemy."

Korpi looked at the woman. "Sure, I got the life sentence. But you're already dead. Maybe not today, maybe not tomorrow, but soon."

"That doesn't scare me. We all die sometime."

Takamäki cut in, "You're powerless now, Korpi. Ahola's dead. Nieminen's dead. Nobody will take orders from you anymore. Nyberg, Siikala, Martin...they're all in jail."

Korpi smiled. "So Ahola and Nieminen are dead. So what. Temporary setback. Fresh troops are always on hand. But I'm interested in what you, Mari Lehtonen, are afraid of. If not for yourself, then what about for your daughter? There're a lotta guys in here that would take a piece of her for free, to say nothing of getting paid for it."

Takamäki tapped Joutsamo on the shoulder, signaling that this had gone too far. No amount of mediation would get them out of this. Saarni sat frozen in her chair with a vacant expression.

"If you touch her, I will pay to have you killed."

"Doesn't bother me. Why would I care about the life I have here? For me it's a question of principle, but you care about the girl."

Mari Lehtonen gave a sigh of resignation, then stood as if to leave. She stepped to the side, pulled the short-barreled .44 out of her bag, and leveled it at Korpi. "Are you afraid now?"

Korpi didn't say anything, but his eyes went first to Takamäki, then to Joutsamo.

"I think you're lying when you say you're not afraid," she said, her voice tense. She circled to the other side of the table where neither Takamäki nor Joutsamo could surprise her from behind.

"Mari, don't," said Joutsamo. "This won't solve anything."

Saarni gave it a go, "Let go of your hatred. Don't let it control you."

Lehtonen smiled and waved the gun in the air. "Right. Use the force."

Takamäki shoved the psychologist under the table where she'd be out of the way. "Mari," he said. "If you fire that gun, your daughter's future will be destroyed."

Mari Lehtonen grinned as she peered down the barrel at Korpi, "But if it's really a question of principle, then let's settle it, good versus bad. Who's got more guts?"

She had two hands on the revolver now, and it seemed to Takamäki they were trembling. She took another step toward Korpi. Too close, thought Takamäki. She was no more than five feet away.

The armed guards had taken a couple of steps closer, but neither dared draw his weapon.

Salo had circled out of the line of fire.

"Are you afraid?" Mari asked. "Will you be afraid if I pull the trigger? It makes no difference to me. I'm dead already. I'll gladly go to prison if that's what I need to do to save my daughter."

She inched a little closer.

"Watch it!" said Takamäki as Korpi's right hand lashed out and wrenched the gun from hers. He spun her around, clamped his arm around her neck, and pressed the barrel of the gun against her temple, her body shielding his.

The psychologist shrieked from the floor.

"Shut up bitch!" shouted Korpi, and she fell silent.

One of the armed guards had drawn his weapon, but the other hesitated. At some point in his training he had learned not to provoke a gunman in this kind of situation. Salo jerked the man's gun out of its holster and aimed it at Korpi and Lehtonen. Takamäki and Joutsamo stood helpless, having left their firearms in the car. Saarni was still huddled on the floor.

"Give it up, Korpi," said Takamäki. "There's no way out."

Korpi smiled and cocked the hammer.

"Really? You listen to me, pig. With this bitch on my arm we could waltz out the front gate. I'll get a helicopter...an airplane...I'll go anywhere in the world."

"If you can get outta this room," said Salo, taking another step closer.

"Well, well. A real prison guard...fantastic room service. Gets friendly with the inmates and enjoys it, don't you, punk."

Korpi turned his gaze back to Takamäki. "But what if I don't want to go anywhere? What if all I want is to blow this bitch's brains all over these walls? Might suit my purpose just as well. Imagine the field day the media would have over what happens to your witnesses. Heheh."

Takamäki's eyes were fixed on the trigger of the gun. Only a sliver of light was visible behind it now. One little squeeze and Mari's head would fly apart. The stout little gun would make quite a mess. Takamäki kept imagining Korpi's hand squeezing the trigger.

"Don't do it," he said. "Let her go. Take me instead."

Korpi laughed. "A hero cop, huh? You really think I'd switch?"

"Think about it. If you do, you'll get your helicopter."

"And you'd be a legend," said Korpi. He wrested Lehtonen's head to the side and pressed a kiss onto her cheek.

"What soft skin you have. I'm sure the girl's is even softer."

"Eat shit," said Mari. "Joker my ass. You're a four of clubs. Nothing more, nothing less. A four of clubs. Pathetic."

Korpi's eyes flared. "You wanna die?"

"Go ahead," she said with a wooden expression. "I'm already dead. Just do it!"

"Fuck you!"

312

Takamäki looked on helplessly as Korpi's trigger finger began to close. The lieutenant had managed to inch a little closer—maybe he could make a lunge for the gun. But that wouldn't work, the distance was too great. Korpi squeezed his finger and Takamäki's mind pictured the hammer as it flew home, but a shot from the left rang out at the same time. Takamäki's ears went deaf from the blast. Risto Korpi sank to the floor with Mari in his arms.

One shot or two? Takamäki wasn't sure. He looked to the left and saw that Salo had fired. Joutsamo scrambled to the other side of the table and pulled the bloodied Mari away from Korpi's body. Takamäki looked at the inmate. The bullet had shattered his skull. He was dead.

"Is she okay?" asked Takamäki. Joutsamo was holding Lehtonen in her arms some fifteen feet away.

"She's alright. She's not hit."

The second armed guard reclaimed his Glock from Salo's trembling hand. Takamäki couldn't understand why Mari wasn't dead. He felt certain he had seen Korpi pull the trigger before Salo.

He found the revolver on the floor and picked it up. The hammer was closed, so Korpi had definitely pulled the trigger. He snapped open the cylinder. Empty: the weapon hadn't been loaded.

Takamäki realized that Mari was watching him. Their eyes met for what seemed like a minute. Had she planned this all in advance? he wondered. Her eyes offered no clues, but that gaze was intense.

"It's all over," he said calmly. "Put your safeties back on. Nobody talks to anybody till the interrogations are done."

CHAPTER 29
MONDAY, 6:00 P.M.
PASILA POLICE HEADQUARTERS

The lobby of the police station was nearly full. What used to be the press briefing room had been remodeled into a monitoring room for traffic enforcement cameras, so press conferences had to be held in the lobby now. A couple of tables had been set up in front of a glass wall near the elevators, and about twenty chairs had been assembled for the reporters.

Half a dozen TV cameras and upwards of a dozen newspaper photographers were lined up in the front row. The first few reporters to arrive on time had had the good sense to take the outermost seats in the front row, the only ones with sightlines not obstructed by the photographers' backs. Other reporters stood to the sides.

Sanna Römpötti was standing about thirty feet from the tables when Deputy Chief Skoog arrived. The cameraman gave the signal and the live broadcast cut from the news desk to the police station.

"I'm here at Pasila Police Headquarters where a press conference on today's dramatic turn of events is about to begin. Let's listen in," said Römpötti, and the picture cut to a second camera trained on Skoog.

Deputy Chief Skoog sat behind a table bristling with microphones and recorders. Alongside him sat the equally grave-looking state prosecutor, Roosa Kemppinen. Skoog began, "Hello. I'm Mika Skoog, Deputy Chief of the Helsinki Police Department, and here with me I have State Prosecutor Roosa Kemppinen. To begin with, I'll read a statement that will be available in printed form after the conference."

Skoog cleared his throat and began reading, "In recent days, the Helsinki Violent Crimes Unit has been investigating a series of threats toward a witness who testified in a recent murder trial. Among the threats was a car bomb that was found in front of the witness's home. After a relentless search, police were able to locate the bombing suspect, but this afternoon the investigation ended in an unfortunate incident on Juna Street, in which the suspect fired shots at police officers. The shots missed, but officers at the scene were forced to return fire and the suspect was killed. The same individual is also suspected of a homicide in Vuosaari earlier in the day."

Skoog looked up. "We ask that anyone with information on this incident contact the Helsinki VCU," and he listed a phone number.

The reporters were silent.

Skoog returned to his paper. "In a related incident at the Helsinki Prison today, a corrections officer shot and killed an inmate who was threatening the life of another individual. This same inmate was suspected of being behind the threats against the aforementioned witness."

He went on, "Because police officers were involved in the shooting on Juna Street, State Prosecutor Roosa Kemppinen will be leading that investigation. Both the shooting in Vuosaari and at the prison will be investigated by the National Bureau of Investigation, as it would not be prudent for the Helsinki VCU to investigate the matter themselves. At this time, State Prosecutor Kemppinen will make a statement."

"Yes. I don't have anything to add at the moment," said Kemppinen dryly, "Except that the state prosecutor's office will conduct a thorough investigation."

She turned back to Skoog.

"I think we can open it up for a few questions at this time. Go ahead."

"Was Risto Korpi the inmate who was killed?" asked one of the newspaper reporters.

"Yes, he was."

"Can you tell us what happened?"

Skoog paused for a while. "That's still under investigation. Unfortunately the lead investigator is still at the scene and was unable to attend this press conference. At this point I don't have any more information."

Römpötti blurted out her question without being called upon, since that would never happen after last night's news story, "This whole case seems to revolve around threats against a witness who testified in court. Now both suspects behind the threats have died at the hands of the authorities. Was this an intentional message to criminal organizations that they shouldn't tamper with witnesses?"

Skoog stared coldly at Römpötti, but then looked directly at one of the TV cameras. "Of course not. We don't work that way here in Finland."

But something in his expression or perhaps the tone of his voice left a shadow of doubt in viewers' minds, just as Skoog had intended.

"What about Mari Lehtonen?" asked Römpötti.

"She's fine," he said, and followed up quickly with, "Thank you. The next press conference is tomorrow morning at ten. Hopefully we'll be able to tell you more then."

Römpötti took up her position in front of the camera and reiterated the day's events and what little they had learned from the press conference.

* * *

The live broadcast at the police station came to a close and Mari Lehtonen turned off her television. Laura was sitting on the sofa reading a book.

"So what now?" asked Laura.

Mari shrugged. "I guess our lives will return to normal. There's nothing to worry about anymore. That's what the police said. I might get a fine for an unlicensed firearm and for threatening with a deadly weapon, but Joutsamo said the prosecutor might not even press charges given the circumstances."

Next to the television was a handsomely decorated Christmas tree, a traditional gift from the officers at a military base near the safe house.

"So when do we get to go back home?"

"I don't know, but after all these shootings I think it's best if we stay here for a while."

"So they can solve the cases?"

"Shouldn't be much to it, but they'll find the rest of Korpi's gang and locate his money. There shouldn't be much else after that. Joutsamo said they were checking into a warehouse of Korpi's somewhere around Hämeenlinna."

Laura looked at her mother, who was smiling faintly.

"How long?"

"I don't know. A week or two, that's what Joutsamo said. We'll be just fine," said Mari.

A grave expression came over Laura's face.

"What is it?" said Mari.

"Well…about what happened at the prison…"

"Yes?"

Mari had decided to tell her about the incident immediately, so she wouldn't be left wondering. Laura had gotten the same story as the NBI investigators who had questioned Mari as a suspect immediately following the incident. She had become overwhelmed with rage, she had told them, and that was why she had pulled the gun. Mari had learned during the trial that witnesses and plaintiffs had to tell the truth, but suspects did not. As a mother, she also had the right to bend the truth with her child.

"When you pointed the gun at him, did you know it wasn't loaded?"

Mari smiled. "Listen to me, Laura. Do you remember when we were at McDonald's and your father brought you that MP3 player? Well, he brought that gun at the same time. I thought it might come in handy if we ever got into trouble. But your dad said if I ever point it at someone, I better be ready to pull the trigger. That's why I never loaded it. I could never kill anybody."

And she spoke the truth. Somebody had to kill Korpi for her, and in such a way that they wouldn't be convicted. But that was something she would never reveal to anybody.

Laura nodded.

A cheerful voice rang out from the kitchen. "Come in here, you two!" Agatha called. "I need some help with these tarts!"

Mari looked at Laura.

"I suppose we should go," said Laura, and she set her book down on the sofa.

* * *

Salmela was sitting at the corner table at the Corner Pub. The Christmas tree languishing near the door seemed to cough on the cigarette smoke. Suhonen was weaving through the crowd with two steaming mugs of glögi, a suitable treat for a snowy yuletide evening. He reached the table, took a seat and slid one of the mugs over to Salmela.

"Thanks," he said.

The men sat and sipped the hot, spiced wine. Apparently the bartender hadn't spared any vodka. Or maybe some rookie had messed up the recipe. Both men coughed at the same time.

"Well, poetic justice, they might call it," said Salmela.

Suhonen shrugged.

"Aren't you gonna tell me what happened? Word on the street is that Korpi and Ahola were executed for bucking the system."

Suhonen couldn't help but smile. "Some reporter asked the chief the same thing on TV. His answer was no."

"Bullshit. I saw his expression. Said execution all over it."

"I actually wasn't there, but my boss Takamäki was. When I left the station tonight he was still there writing up reports. I got a look at the draft and I gotta say, everything went according to the finest letter of the law." Suhonen smiled broadly and stroked his beard. "Those sections on self defense are pretty broad."

Salmela sipped his glögi. "I don't suppose you guys would mind a little rumor circulating that you're taking extreme measures to protect witnesses?"

"Should we?"

"No, the balance of terror needs to be maintained, just like in Soviet times."

"Well, go ahead and spread it then."

Salmela nodded. "Alright... I hear Korpi's outfit is teetering on the brink. And that psycho Nyberg doesn't have what it takes to run it either, especially not from the slammer. People fear him, but they don't respect him. But what about Guerrilla Siikala. What's gonna happen to him?"

"Tough to say yet, but we'll throw the book at him. Gotta maintain that balance of terror. I bet he'll get accessory to attempted murder for the car bomb, and maybe something else for the drugs. All this publicity has made the case a top priority, so we'll be going full tilt to the end. Martin will get to see the inside of a prison too, that's for sure."

"He was involved, huh?"

"Korpi's lawyer."

"Right, I know," said Salmela. "I hear some of Korpi's guys have already split away to some gang from Vantaa. They'll probably take the rest with them, too."

"Yeah."

Usually, Suhonen would be interested in hearing about new players in the game, but today he'd talked enough about work, and so he let it be. The vacuum would fill quickly—when one gang was busted up, another would soon take its place.

The men sat quietly for a minute, sipping their drinks.

"Listen," said Salmela. "I got this diamond ring that'd be a perfect Christmas present for that lady of yours, Raija. Five hundred and it's yours. She'd love it!"

Suhonen laughed.

"I'm serious. Tell you what. I'll throw in a Christmas tree and a ham on the house."

Also from Ice Cold Crime LLC

Helsinki Homicide: Against the Wall
Jarkko Sipila (2009, 291 pages)
Winner of 2009 Best Finnish Crime Novel

An abandoned house in Northern Helsinki, a dead body in the garage. Detective Lieutenant Kari Takamäki's homicide team gets a case that looks like a professional hit but they are perplexed by the crime scene. Takamäki's trusted man Suhonen goes undercover as Suikkanen, a gangster full of action. In pursuit of the murderer, he must operate within the grey area of the law. But, will the end justify the means?

Helsinki Homicide: Vengeance
Jarkko Sipila (2010, 335 pages)

Tapani Larsson, a Finnish crime boss, walks out of prison with one thought on his mind: Vengeance. Wanting to reclaim his gang's honor and avenge those who have wronged him, Larsson targets Suhonen, the undercover detective who put him in prison. Meanwhile, Suhonen's best friend, an ex-con himself, wants to wash his hands of crime, but in the process, is driven deeper into it. With the help of his boss, Lieutenant Takamäki, and the National Bureau of Investigation, Suhonen hunts for the loose thread that could unravel the entire gang. But with every string he pulls, he flirts with death itself.

Raid and the Blackest Sheep
Harri Nykanen (2010, 242 pages)

Hard-nosed hit man Raid is driving toward the Arctic Circle with Nygren, a career criminal in the twilight of his life. As they journey northward, Nygren puts his affairs in order, wreaking vengeance on those who have wronged him and paying penance to those he has wronged. Their first stop is at a church, where a sham preacher is fleecing his congregation for money. Soon, both cops and crooks are on the trail of the mysterious pair. Detective Lieutenant Jansson and his colleagues are interested in any potential jobs the notorious criminals might be planning. A couple of accomplices from Nygren's past believe he has a hidden stash of cash, and want a share for themselves. In the end, the pilgrimage leaves a trail of wounded and dead in its wake.